Matthew Heald Co[illegible] born in 1952 and is now a Senior Clerk in th[illegible] Commons. His previous books are *The G*[illegible]*5: Its Political and Military Failure*[illegible]*man Struggle against Soviet* [illegible]*an Air Force 1933–4*[illegible]ten two novels: W[illegible]*ger.*

By the same author

Fiction

To Ride a Tiger

Non-fiction

The German Army 1933–45: Its Political and Military Failure
Phantom War: The German Struggle against Soviet Partisans 1941–45
The German Air Force 1933–45: An Anatomy of Failure

MATTHEW HEALD COOPER

When Fish Begin to Smell

PANTHER
Granada Publishing

Panther Books
Granada Publishing Ltd
8 Grafton Street, London W1X 3LA

Published by Panther Books 1985

First published in Great Britain by
Victor Gollancz Ltd 1983

ISBN 0-586-06326-9

Printed and bound in Great Britain by
Collins, Glasgow

Set in Sabon

To Allyson

Author's note

An American, Franklin Adams, wrote: 'The best part of the fiction in many novels is the notice that the characters are all purely imaginary.' In this book the reader lacks even that. The majority of those who appear once lived, just as most of the events are a matter of history. All that has been done is to weave them together to produce fiction – in part.

When fish begin to smell, they start at the head.
– Russian proverb

Prologue

Twenty kilometres from Smolensk in western Russia is Kozlinaya Gora, 'The Hill of Goats'. It lies in the district of Katyn, covered by primeval forest, among whose pine trees in the spring of 1943 an L-shaped grave was found containing the bodies of three thousand men, shot through the head. Further mass burials were uncovered nearby, and the fate of fifteen thousand Poles became known to the world.

Eight years later, in 1951, at the height of tension between East and West, those graves were to play their part in a conspiracy at the heart of the Cold War. . . .

Principal Characters

THE BRITISH

Sir Stewart Menzies, Chief, Secret Intelligence Service

Sir William Strang, Permanent Under-Secretary, Foreign Office

Valentine Vivien, Deptuy Chief, Secret Intelligence Service

Nicholas Pelham, Assistant Private Secretary to Sir William Strang

Harold 'Kim' Philby – 'Stanley', SIS Liaison Officer, Washington

Donald Maclean – 'Harold', Head of American Section, Foreign Office

Guy Burgess – 'Hicks', Foreign Office official, sacked

THE AMERICANS

Walter Bedell Smith, Director, Central Intelligence Agency

Allen Dulles, Deputy Director of Plans, CIA

John Anderson, Head of Soviet-Bloc Intelligence, CIA

THE RUSSIANS

Joseph Stalin, Secretary-General, Soviet Communist Party

Lavrenti Beria, Member of Politbureau, responsible for security

Viktor Abakhumov, Minister of State Security

Georgi Malenkov, Member of Politbureau, in charge of Party apparatus

Georgi Zaroubin, Ambassador in London

Alexei Manjoulo, Head of Intelligence, London Station

Gregor Orlov, General in Military Intelligence

THE POLE

Michael Lubienski, Secretary of Committee for Free Poland

Chapter One

The end of love is nearly always bitter. In the case of Nicholas Pelham it was dangerous too. He fell out of love with his country, and she with him.

1951 in London, early spring. Smog. And across St James's Park, Whitehall rose, the world of 'them', a block of grey shadow changing by degrees to a dirty yellow ochre. A small man, dressed neatly in overcoat and bowler, coughed into his handkerchief, stopped to listen for the low rumble of hidden traffic, then crossed Horse Guards Approach. His movements were brisk. Taking Clive Steps two at a time, past the statue of the great empire-builder, pigeon-white, he turned left towards the classical façade of the Foreign Office and disappeared. An attendant saluted. The Permanent Under-Secretary of State had arrived.

'Good morning, good morning,' he said as he bustled into his office, prompt as always at nine-thirty, eyes averted from a weak-chested secretary who inclined her head, mumbled and blinked. Too timid even for talk of the weather, she suited her master that way.

'I need Pelham, Miss Edwards.' In a short rasp of a cough the Permanent Under-Secretary expelled the last of the smog from his lungs. 'At once if you please', and without removing his coat and barely glancing at the paper neatly arrayed on his desk, he moved over to the window. In silence he stood, slowly rocking on his heels, hands thrust deep in his pockets, staring out over the few trees that emerged from the gloom. His face, grizzled, eager as a foxhound and made hard by the small brush of a moustache, bore a set expression. Sir William Strang was worried.

Noiselessly the secretary left, running in search of Nicholas Pelham, though she found him easily enough as she always could at that time of morning, sitting in his office with feet up, sipping tea, gathering strength for the day. Handsome if it wasn't for a nose too large and a mouth too wide, he was conventionally dressed in pin-stripes and old school tie, shirt-cuffs showing half an inch. Yet there was something incongruous about the man – his shock of jet-black hair sticking up at all angles as if perpetually struggling to be free.

Nick turned when the secretary entered and removed his legs from the desk, the smile in his eyes moving to the corners of his mouth as she urged him to hurry. He declined, and finished his cup to the dregs, but he burned his tongue nevertheless. Rising and stretching, he ran his fingers through his hair as he swept it back off his forehead, then, with a wink, he chucked the flustered woman on the cheek and left. In the corridor he imagined her twitters of disapproval, and laughed. There was the devil in Nick Pelham, she thought.

The devil perhaps, but there was more than that.

At his chief's door Nick knocked and entered, then stood like all Assistant Private Secretaries before him, half to attention, always available, inevitably there, civil – and despising himself for it. He peered into the gloom. The office was cavernous, with a slight chill as if overlaid by the smog, its heavy Victorian furnishings and illustrious portraits declaiming against the Twentieth Century. A moment's pause, and the Permanent Under-Secretary turned, a black dwarf against the window opaque with hazy light, yellow from the street lamps. He was authority at its most impersonal.

'Ah, Pelham. Good morning. Yes . . .' Sir William squeezed the crow's feet around his eyes. He paused again, putting his hands behind his back. 'Yes. Damned nuisance and all that, but I have to go out at short notice.' His delivery was staccato, harsh blocks of sound. 'Be so good as to cancel everything for this morning, and be particularly apologetic to the Belgian Ambassador. Insist on speaking to him personally, will you?'

Nick nodded. 'Where will you be, Sir William?' It was his job to know.

The desk lamp caught the whites of Sir William's eyes as they flickered. 'Oh, just five minutes from here, Pelham. Not far.' He turned away, back to the window. 'That will be all.'

Smog swirled round and engulfed the diminutive Permanent Under-Secretary, but his pace was quick for a man of fifty-eight, and he made short work of the lonely walk across the south-east corner of St James's Park and over Birdcage Walk. At Queen Anne's Gate he turned left and stopped at a red brick Georgian House, No 21, whose brass plate read 'Soldiers', Sailors' and Airmens' Families Association'. He rang the bell, the door was opened, and he went in, to be confronted by a uniformed attendant. Brief formalities were entered upon: identity proven, a telephone call, and a form completed, giving time, date and destination. Then he was taken by a cage lift to the third floor and escorted along glossy-white passages to Room 300. He had arrived in No 54 Broadway, known to passers-by as the 'Government Communications' Bureau'. In an ante-room a grey-haired secretary sat guarding a door, over which a green light flickered uncertainly, its bulb almost spent. She rose, and without a word and with barely a glance ushered Sir William through.

The office was small, oak panelled, with an attractively moulded low ceiling, made cosy by indirect lighting, and now seemingly detached from the world, encased by the smog at its windows. Bookcases lined the walls, on which hung several pictures: a Millais, a Samuel Palmer and two Claudes. An antique oak desk occupied one end, armchairs and a coffee table the other. In the grate a coal fire glowed. It was a warm, comfortable room, and only the red and green lights outside and the three telephones on the desk indicated that its occupant was anything other than the senior partner of a well-established law practice. But instead it was the head of SIS – the Chief, Secret Intelligence Service as he was called by those few who knew him officially, or 'C' to his subordinates, the only man in the Firm allowed to use green ink – who every day since 1939 had sat there in quiet deliberation over the affairs of the world.

Major-General Sir Stewart Menzies rose and smiled, though not with his eyes. Sir William bared his teeth in friendly fashion. 'Morning, Stewart.'

'Good morning, William. Kind of you to come at such short notice.' Menzies's voice sounded tired, as it always did, but now its tone was hollow: the affected boredom had gone. He avoided shaking hands and instead motioned to an armchair with a flourish, then moved over to join his guest. 'Make yourself comfortable, old boy.' Eton and the Guards. It all showed: superficially at ease, but underneath remote, unconnected.

The head of British Intelligence was a tall, willowy man, immaculately dressed in a charcoal-grey double-breasted suit from which a white handkerchief billowed. But his elegance was on the wane. The years of cabal in his country's service had left him with a slight stoop, almost an emaciated look, so that his face was pale, his silvery-blond hair thin, and the bags below his eyes deep. That morning they were also tinged with purple. Perhaps, too, his cheekbones were more prominent than usual, but Sir William wasn't sure.

Sir Stewart turned to the man perched on the edge of his desk. 'Vivien, take a pew.' Again a gesture with his hands, fine hands the colour of ivory, etched pale blue.

Lieutenant-Colonel Valentine Vivien, Deputy Chief, SIS – with the sole right to red ink – straightened his back, smoothed his crinkly grey hair and adjusted the monocle which hid a watery eye, inclining his head by way of greeting to Sir William. He was small, lean, smart rather than elegant, and vain. His colleagues thought him superficial too, but they were mistaken. Not for a moment did he take his eyes off the newcomer as he declined the invitation to leave his perch.

They sat down, Vivien remaining on the desk. The pleasantries were brief, unusually so where the head of SIS was concerned, and they got down to business.

'This might interest you, William.' Sir Stewart leaned forward and handed the Permanent Under-Secretary a sheet of paper, unheaded and unsigned. On it were twelve names, handwritten.

Sir William put on his glasses, a thin, horn-rimmed pair, and squinted at the paper as though offended. There was silence in the room as the others watched for the least sign of reaction: Menzies languidly, as if hardly caring, Vivien eagerly, intently. Only the angry sound of a taxi-horn from down below in Broadway cut the stillness.

The head of the Foreign Service read and re-read, agitated his moustache, then looked up and frowned. 'An odd assortment.' He took off his glasses. 'Some sort of Russian hit list?' He laughed nervously.

'Nearly there, William.' Sir Stewart might have sounded relaxed, but the flesh around his lips was tight-drawn. 'The Russians do have an interest in those men. You see, they pay them.'

'They're traitors,' added Vivien, needlessly. He liked things cut and dried.

Sir William jerked upright. 'Traitors?' he snapped. 'These?' He felt sick.

'Yes. These.'

Dismemberment of a country by treaty was one thing;

betrayal by associates quite another. The Permanent Under-Secretary had no training for that, and made little effort to hide his horror. His jaw dropped. He pressed his right hand to his forehead. 'Are you sure? Quite sure?' He sank in his chair, deflated.

'Afraid so, old man.' Sir Stewart smiled sympathetically. 'Like a drink?' That was his recipe for most shocks, and the past twenty-four hours had been no exception. But the head of the Foreign Service seemed not to hear.

'And there's absolutely no room for doubt?' he asked again.

'Not much. Well, none at all actually.'

'But why?' Sir William picked up the list and read the names again. 'Why these men?'

'Like the peace of God, my dear William, it passes all understanding.' Sir Stewart's self-assurance seldom left him, nor his blandness. 'A Scotch?'

'Who else knows?'

'No one. Just us three – which is how it should remain.'

The Permanent Under-Secretary understood; that much he had been trained for. In Whitehall secrecy was endemic, its need unquestioned, however trivial. 'But how on earth did you discover this?' he asked.

Sir Stewart hadn't the energy. He looked over to his desk. 'Tell him, Viv. You like stories,' and he got up to busy himself with the whisky.

Vivien told the tale well. He went back to 1948, to Austria still occupied by the Allies, where, in Salzburg, a Jewish Intelligence network was active, gathering information in the fight for a Jewish homeland and the search for the Nazi murderers of six million of their race. Early in 1948 they made contact with a Russian official newly arrived in the Soviet Repatriation Commission. The man, later identified as Colonel Gregor Khopliakin of Soviet Military Intelligence, happened to be a homosexual and a half-Jew. Either one of these 'defects' was rare in Soviet officialdom, the combination unique.

Khopliakin's cover was soon broken. His real job was to infiltrate the new government services being set up in post-war Austria, and the Jews arranged several meetings under the pretence of establishing links valuable to both sides. On the first two, business was discussed. On the third, after a substantial amount of alcohol, a young man was produced whose charms Khopliakin was unable to resist. On the fourth the Soviet colonel was shown a series of photographs of himself and his male lover entwined, naked. An old trick; it had to come one day, and with little protest Khopliakin accepted his fate. He had not enjoyed the love-making and had shown himself impotent, but the consequences were what they were and he would make the best of them. As requested, he supplied the Jews with details of former Nazis. Several were killed, others exposed and their careers ruined. Occasionally, too, he would supply information about Soviet Intelligence.

For four months Khopliakin maintained regular contact with his blackmailers. Then, one day in May, he failed to keep a scheduled meeting, and was never seen again.

According to Khopliakin's story he had served as a special assistant to the head of the *Glavnoye Razedyvtalnoye Upravleniye* (GRU) – the Intelligence Directorate of the Red Army – during the Second World War. The GRU was one of two Soviet intelligence organizations, the other being civilian, incorporated within the secret police apparatus, and called in those days the *Narodyni Kommissariat Gosudarstvennoi Bezopasnost* (NKGB) – the People's Commissariat for State Security. Rivalry was strong, but the demands of a war in which the Soviet Union was struggling for its survival blurred division and forced collaboration. One of the more sensitive pieces which State Security gave Military Intelligence was a list of twelve NKGB-controlled officials in British Government service as of May 1944, together with the type of information each was supplying. The NKGB had been careful to keep the list general, providing neither real names nor jobs, but Khopliakin had recognized its importance. Matched with other information, it could prove decisive. He made a copy. This he handed to the Jews in late spring 1948, which they in turn passed to SIS in early 1951, when it suited them, for a favour. Weeks later, an Egyptian spy network in Israel was broken.

On its own, 'Khopliakin's List' amounted to little. Certainly, no identification of the individuals concerned could be made. There was, too, the possibility that it was false, leaked by the Russians to spread doubt in Britain and the Western Alliance and produce an atmosphere in which co-operation broke down. No one could ever be certain that secrets known to the British were not being handed straight to Moscow. The list, then, might have aroused more suspicion than interest in No 54 Broadway. But it was one word, 'Homer', that made the SIS chief recognize its value.

Since the middle of the Second World War information had been dribbling into SIS from both British and American code-breakers pointing to the presence of Soviet agents in British service. A number were exposed, among them prominent scientists working on the atomic bomb with the Americans – 'Alec', who turned out to be Dr Nunn May, 'Golia' – Dr Fuchs, and 'Gini' – Dr Pontecorvo. All three were 'owned' by Soviet Military Intelligence.

But there remained others, unidentified. One in particular worried the Western Allies – 'Homer', whose existence had been discovered in 1945. It was clear then he was highly placed within the British Embassy in Washington, but all efforts to trace him met with failure. Lead after lead resulted in dead end. The Americans even involved other agencies in the search, including Jewish Intelligence, with no luck. But then came Khopliakin's list.

It had taken Vivien sixteen days to unravel its secrets, matching the information with that already in SIS's files and those of Government departments. One, 'Hicks', eluded identification. But the eleven others. . . .

'And that's that. We're as riddled as a sieve at sea,' concluded Vivien with a flourish, slapping his thigh. A little dramatic, thought Sir Stewart, but he said nothing. Nor, for a moment, did the Permanent Under-Secretary, who had sat through Vivien's explanation with head bowed, unmoving except for his hands, clenching and unclenching on his lap, his whisky left untouched. When he finally looked up the pain was clear to see, scarring his face, and his reaction was that of a person betrayed, instinctively searching for an escape. The self-confidence was gone, utterly.

'What about the source of this information – Kholiky, or whatever his name was?' Sir William grasped at a straw. 'Is he reliable?'

But the straw slipped away. Vivien shrugged his shoulders. 'Khopliakin. We can't find any trace of him in our records, but the information he provided all ties in with the facts at our disposal. It can't be a false plant.' It wasn't. Vivien had checked and double-checked.

Again, Sir William looked at the list, a sadness now in his expression as he shook his head. 'It's just not what I would have expected, that's all. Not this.'

It had taken only eleven names to unnerve the head of the Foreign Service, a man who had lived through two world wars and what could be the development of a third. Eleven names. He had known there were traitors in the system: that wasn't new. Based on experience he was prepared for men destined never to get above middle rank, frustrated, desperate for recognition, if only from an enemy power. The mules of life, he called them, ambitious but without pride of ancestry or hope of posterity. There might be a prominent scientist or two – that, perhaps, was only to be expected. But this. . . . This was a different magnitude altogether. Sir William felt like a prisoner in the dock who, expecting to receive five years, had just been given life.

But there it was, on the paper before him. There was reality – three highly-placed diplomats, one of whom, it was widely predicted, would reach the top of the Foreign Office; an important nuclear physicist serving in Washington; two senior civil servants, one in the War Office and the other in the Admiralty, each with direct access to sensitive information; a respected member of the Home Office; two members of counter-intelligence, MI5, and two in SIS, all of them senior men. Britain's security, her military and foreign policies, were blown wide open. Few secrets of any worth over the past six or seven years of Cold War could have been kept from the Russians. Whitehall, as Vivien said, was riddled.

But there was no hatred, no bitterness towards the traitors shown by the three men, just sorrow they had been let down, a feeling of great hurt.

'But look at them. They're such decent chaps.' Sir William slapped the paper. 'That's what I can't understand. They're our type.' He paused, waiting for a reply. None came. Sir Stewart raised his eyes to the ceiling. Unlike his subordinate he was prepared to wait. The wind, he knew, had to blow itself out; contained, it might become a storm, impossible to control.

'Just look at my Service,' Strang continued. 'That man Gould . . . Maclean. Well, I know MI5 have suspected him for some time as "Homer", but . . .' He shook his head. 'Damn it, we've just made him head of our American Section! And Stoddart as well! It's staggering. Why? How were they recruited?'

'We've no idea. None at all.' Sir Stewart raised his right index finger to his right eye to stop an imperceptible flicker. Any sign of weakness annoyed him. 'I worked so closely with Lascelles. Our Far East section would be nothing without him. And Philby. How many of our agents are safe?'

Vivien, sitting stock still, pursed his lips as he always would, making himself look prissy. Philby was one of SIS's best; he had headed the Firm's Soviet Intelligence section, and was now liaising with the CIA in Washington. Yet there he was, on the list: Soviet State Security's 'Stanley'. It was a blow to Vivien's affections and his professionalism. He had been deceived, utterly.

'And the others!' Sir William ploughed on. 'Another damned scientist – John Calder, working on the bomb and with the Yanks, just to make things more difficult. Then there's the War Office – Alistair Lawrence, a swine but brilliant and on research and development. And the Admiralty – Gerald Holman, who, I suppose, for the past couple of years has been busily giving the Russians everything we've got on naval development.' Strang knew them all. He had trusted some as friends.

'The only one they're welcome to,' Vivien interrupted, trying to speed the process, 'is that fellow Carter in the Home Office. A nonentity. But just look at MI5 – Blunt and Jamie Gordon.'

'Hasn't Blunt retired?'

Sir Stewart smiled. 'He's Surveyor of the King's Pictures now.' Then he laughed. 'It's more suited to his temperament.'

'Damned nancy.' Sir William showed no amusement. 'But this "Hicks" you mentioned. Where does he fit in?'

Menzies drew in his breath. 'Hicks' worried him. 'Khopliakin's list describes the information he was giving in 1944 as general, and that doesn't give us enough to work on, I'm afraid. But he's somewhere out there.'

'And those traitors are all State Security men,' added Vivien. 'What about those run by GRU? Fuchs was

Military Intelligence; so was Nunn May. God knows how many more they've got.'

'What on earth do we do?' Sir William knew the answer wasn't as simple as locking them up; but what was it?

'Whatever it is, we've got to tread carefully. So no charging about getting MI5 involved.' Sir Stewart was adamant.

The others nodded. That much was obvious.

When Sir Stewart had read the word 'Homer' in the Israeli proposal over a month previously, his official duty had been clear: inform MI5. The division between Britain's two security organizations was straightforward. Espionage was the responsibility of SIS; counter-espionage of MI5. But instead he had passed Khopliakin's list to his deputy. When Vivien returned with the names, Sir Stewart's duty had been even clearer: MI5 would have to be told. That, however, was furthest from his thoughts. It was simply too absurd.

Over the years there had grown an intense rivalry between the two services, almost an enmity. The men of SIS referred to themselves as 'Friends', and to those in MI5 as 'Snoopers'. A spy was considered a cut above a spy-catcher. MI5 was made to feel the junior partner in Britain's security system, while it, in turn, regarded the amateurish 'old boy' attitude of SIS with contempt. A lifetime's experience, then, had conditioned Sir Stewart to keep Khopliakin's list to himself. SIS would unravel its own secrets.

'Our first priority must be to prevent any of this leaking out,' he continued. 'The press and the politicians will have a field day. We'll be hung, drawn and quartered.'

Sir William narrowed his eyes; the scheming had begun, born of fear. 'But why should it get out? Can't we keep this between us and the Russians? It must be just as embarrassing to them. They've been caught with their trousers down, and there's an end to it, surely?'

'But it's not, my dear William. So have we, and they will realize that. Revelation will hurt them, but by God it'll devastate us.'

Sir William nodded, rose, and in his nervousness began to pace the room. He was never still for long. Vivien got off the desk, pulled at his cuffs and stood, arms folded, leaning against a bookcase, looking down on his chief. Sir Stewart remained sitting, arms spread out across the width of his chair; only his words gave an indication of the anguish deep down, where it would stay.

'Just imagine,' he began, his eyes following Sir William. 'Just imagine how our political masters would react. This Socialist Government is organized hypocrisy at its worst, and the PM has never shown himself well-disposed towards us. Look how he cut our overseas operations. Can you imagine that in what will probably be an election year our ministers would jump to our defence? Put their political reputations on the line for us, the public-school mandarins? Oh no! We would be enquired into, overhauled and reorganized out of existence. We'd be sacrificial lambs, William. If these traitors were revealed now, in a month we would be gone. Over. Washed up.'

The Permanent Under-Secretary looked glum. He knew that one day he would have to retire with a barony and a seat in the Lords, but he wasn't yet ready for obscurity, and certainly not untitled.

Sir Stewart raised a hand to his right eye. 'But it's not only us. Can't you see what the apostles of socialism and the common man would make out of this? The Establishment bringing down everything they have a duty to protect! Just look at the background of these men. . . .' He gestured at the files on the floor around his desk. 'They're all top drawer. Three went to Westminster, one to Winchester, one to Eton, and so on. Only one didn't go to public school. They are either Cambridge or Oxford men without exception, all brilliant, and all seem mostly to have a network of relations throughout society. Maclean – son of a former Cabinet Minister and a Lord. Blunt – works at Buck House of all places. Lawrence – son of a bishop. And so it goes on . . .'

Sir William stood stock still. 'The public will become impossibly moral about this,' he said.

'But there's more, William. What about our standing in the world?' The head of SIS moved effortlessly from his class to his country. 'Who's going to trust us again, knowing that two minutes after they tell us anything it could be in the Kremlin? The Western Alliance will have a hole a mile wide blown through it. It will take years – decades – to rebuild confidence. Look what happened over Nunn May, Fuchs and the Bomb. There was hell to pay with the Yanks. But now, quite frankly, co-operation would be over. We would get nothing from them, absolutely nothing. And we can't go it alone – that's impossible.'

'It would be the most significant Russian victory of the Cold War. Nothing else comes up to it.' Sir William spoke those words mechanically, without emotion. He had regained his composure. He understood.

'Precisely, William.' Sir Stewart was relieved there was no objection. He hated argument, found it vulgar, and the man could be awkward if he chose. 'Precisely. So it's not just us we've got to fight for. It's the Western Alliance . . .'

'And liberty, conscience and Christianity, too,' Vivien intervened. Prolonged justification was an anathema to him: a cover-up was necessary whatever the reasons.

His words had their effect. Sir Stewart smiled wryly. 'Sorry, old man. Straying a bit into dramatics. But the question is, what do we do?'

'Trade with them?' suggested the Permanent Under-Secretary.

'What?'

'Their men?'

'Not a chance. Those traitors are useless to Moscow, except to destroy us.'

There was silence. Again, Sir Stewart laid a finger across his right eye and looked out at the yellow-grey smog blanketing the window. Sir William stood still, shoulders slightly bowed, and fiddled with his wedding ring. 'We must involve the politicians somehow,' he said. 'Haven't we got anything on them?' He was beginning to sound desperate. Playing with politicians was like playing with fire.

'Blackmail, you mean, William? There's the usual – buggery. Not very common with the socialists though. Womanizing? Well, yes, but rather a low standard. Nothing exciting. Those chaps are quite without style, you must know that. Backhanders are out – among the Cabinet anyway, and I shouldn't think the activities of a few councillors in the Midlands will be sufficient to trade with. There's really nothing to keep them on our side, William. Nothing.'

The spy had the edge over the diplomat. But, though recognizing the magnitude of the problem, Sir Stewart was unable to resolve it. His impotence was complete.

'Coffee?' was all he could come up with. He pressed the intercom. 'Janet, coffee for three please, and the decent biscuits. Thank you.' Sir Stewart was nothing if not courteous, even under pressure.

'But MI5? Aren't they on to it already?' Sir William sat down, keeping to the edge of his armchair. His expression was alert, eager, with nothing about him now of the deflated diplomat. 'They suspect Maclean.'

'Yes, but only Maclean. As far as we can tell, they haven't even got a whiff of the others.'

'But what about him?'

'The Snoopers will just have to carry on.'

'It will take them a couple of months at least,' Vivien intervened. 'Everything by the book, Sir William, a good policeman's motto. And if you chaps aren't over-helpful, we'll have time to play with.' The Foreign Office, he knew, found procrastination easy. It accounted for much of their success.

The Permanent Under-Secretary gave a smirk, then shifted uneasily in his chair. 'But what if they get to know about the others?'

'Then we'll just have to face the music, won't we?' Sir Stewart had no illusions as to the limits. 'Ah, Janet, that's good of you.'

A matronly figure glided across the office. She wore a confidential air. Head on one side, eyes downcast, she gave each man his coffee, placed sugar and biscuits on the desk, and left as discreetly as she had come.

'Well, where have we got to then?' Sir Stewart paused, munching a Bourbon. 'Viv . . .' He turned to his head of security. '. . . any thoughts?'

Vivien continued stirring his coffee, staring into the black liquid for inspiration. 'It seems to me,' he began slowly, 'as if we are being unnecessarily defensive. If we continue on that line, we'll get nowhere, except to an early retirement.' His spoon clattered on his saucer. 'We've got to hit the Soviets hard. Match them blow for blow.'

'With what?' Sir Stewart asked.

'You don't demand much.' Sir William was unimpressed, and showed it.

Vivien shrugged, readjusted his monocle, and said nothing. Nor, at once, did the others. There was nothing to say.

'Well, let's think about it,' Sir Stewart suggested at last. 'Why not chew it over and come together soon, when we're fresher?'

The others agreed, realizing they could go no further that day; after some more conversation of an inconsequential kind, the meeting came to a close. As they were making for the door, Sir Stewart put his hand on the Permanent Under-Secretary's shoulder.

'Don't worry, old boy. We'll manage.'

Sir William, embarrassed by the show of warmth, however restrained, smiled weakly.

'I'm sure, Stewart,' he replied, and slipped his shoulder away.

They sat under the Polish flag, four of them, old men in poor contrast to the eagle, white upon red, nailed to the wall above. The room, brown, hazy with cigarette smoke, was small and ill-lit, its only furniture four chairs and a table on which stood a vodka bottle, empty.

'So we're agreed, then?' said one, Adam Lesniowska, clutching his hands together. 'Katyn.'

The others nodded.

'That's it,' echoed a skull-faced man, Jozef Dudzinski, his spidery fingers in motion. 'We'll drown the Russians in the blood of our martyrs.'

'And we start with the letter?' asked Lesniowksa, the leader. Nods signified assent.

'So the Committee is unanimous?'

Each man raised a hand.

They sat for a moment in silence, the only members of the Committee for Free Poland. Yet they had high hopes. Like so many exiles too old to forge a new life, they lived with memories to no purpose, in a world of unreality and hate. Sure of the justness of their cause, convinced of its success, they didn't care that they were only four men, and old men, with little money and no country they could call their own. Decisive action would compensate. Katyn. And then? Poland?

Such were the dreams.

'You, Lubienski, will be responsible for the letter,' said Lesniowska, disturbing their thoughts. 'You know what to say.'

Michael Lubienski, Secretary of the Committee, looked up and blinked slowly. 'Yes, I know what to say.'

He was the academic of the four, a lawyer who had practised with some success in Lwow before the war, and was now a clerk in an East End warehouse.

'It shall be sent tomorrow. I know what to say.'

Again, they lapsed into silence, Lesniowska looking determinedly to his front, Lubienski staring at the ceiling, Dudzinski playing with his fingers, and the fourth, Wladyslaw Klimecki, staring to one side, chewing at his nails, each lost in memory. Old men, broken by Soviet power, fit only for dreaming.

Chapter Two

Thursday, 5 April. At eleven in the morning an envelope was handed to the solitary policeman guarding No 10 Downing Street. It was addressed to the Prime Minister. A secretary's mistake, and, instead of being re-routed, its contents ended up in the despatch box marked for his attention, so that by six that evening, the letter was before him: a request for a war memorial. He gave it a cursory glance and grimaced, though signs of emotion were unusual for him, and with the words 'Shuffle this one down', he passed it to his Private Secretary hovering in attendance.

The following evening, before leaving the Foreign Office for the weekend, Sir William Strang undertook his customary task of going through his absent minister's correspondence. The Permanent Under-Secretary liked to be well-prepared: no politician would take him off his guard, not if he could help it. Eternal vigilance was the price he paid for influence, and willingly.

The pile Sir William leafed through was standard stuff, easily manageable: requests from Parliamentary colleagues for special favours abroad, invitations from foreign embassies, the latest Cabinet minutes, and a selection of matters passed on from other ministers. Towards the bottom No 10's notepaper caught his eye. He read it, and the attached letter, sighing with boredom. Lubienski: he had never heard of the man, nor the Committee for Free Poland. The usual request, he supposed, to be rejected in the politest possible way.

But when he reached the word 'Katyn', his manner

changed. Memories flooded back. It had been a near run thing, Katyn . . .

Not only fifteen hundred miles separated Whitehall from that primeval forest in western Russia known as Katyn, nor the eleven years between Lubienski's letter and the events to which it referred. Rather, it was a magnitude of sensibility and experience so great as to lead an observer to wonder whether a British diplomat, safe in his elegant office that April evening of 1951, came from the same world, let alone the same period in history, as the Soviet security men who, in April 1940, stood in a clearing among the dark pine trees, shivering in the easterly wind that knifed through their thick coats, waiting.

They were ten in all, under the command of a sergeant with heavy Turkoman features. In thick Russian he cursed them, hollow-eyed and so racked with exhaustion that they kept awake only by smoking one filthy cigarette after another. Through the gloom of the forest a line of uniformed men could be seen, most wearing the distinctive Polish four-cornered peaked caps, their heads bowed, coughing, trudging, limping, spitting, white faces peering along the narrow path, anxious, half-suspecting their fate.

'Get ready,' the sergeant growled. Rifles, bayonets fixed, were taken up from resting places, pistol-holsters were undone and cigarettes thrown to the ground.

The Poles were halted at the edge of the clearing, sixty of them, cowed, fearing their end. Betraying no emotion, the guards pointed and prodded with bayonets, while others tied the victim's hands. Several prisoners protested, and rifle butts hammered them to the ground. Greatcoats were thrown over their heads and tied fast, with the rope placed around their necks and hands so that when they moved they strangled themselves.

Then the Poles were led in twos to the edge of a vast pit, dug deep into ground only recently thawed out. Those that could see looked down on to the bodies of their comrades, skulls shattered, lying spread-eagled among the blood and warm grey spatterings of brain. Some they might have recognized, but most were made formless by death and, as often as not, faceless by a bullet.

Suddenly one of the prisoners went berserk, turning violently from side to side, trying to break the grip of his captors, but in vain. He was bayoneted to the ground by the guards, stabbing and stabbing again in silence, his agony ended only by the arrival of the sergeant who, straddling the Pole, placed a pistol to the nape of his neck and fired. The body was thrown carelessly into the grave. The rest, those who accepted their fate, were shot while kneeling, some crossing themselves before jerking violently forwards and falling into the pit. Occasionally a single bullet would fail to kill, and a man's screams were only ended by a second. Others, less noisy, were left to die in their own time, or by suffocation under their comrades. In such a way Soviet State Security could dispose of sixty men in a quarter as many minutes.

These were the events which took place over a period of two months in the early spring of 1940 at Kozlinaya Gora, 'The Hill of Goats'.

Sir William had been on the Committee. He sipped, swilled and swallowed. Yes, they had selected that on his recommendation; a '29 claret. The club prided itself on its cellar. It was renowned. 'Nutty, don't you think?' he said.

It was half past midday on Saturday, 7 April, and Menzies and Vivien were seated at the Permanent Under-Secretary's favourite table in the coffee room of the Travellers', by a window, yet not too far from the fire. To mark the day they wore tweeds; stripes were strictly for weekdays.

There was a cough in the distance as a waiter advanced. Sir William half turned.

'The beef, sir?' A full plate was placed discreetly before the diplomat. Sir Stewart had steak and kidney, and Vivien the Pepper Pot – service in India had given him a predilection for the hot.

'Basic but nourishing,' commented Sir William, a little unenthusiastically. The club's kitchen was *not* renowned. 'It'll keep the fires going.'

They began to eat. The room they were in was vast, with magnificent pale blue and gold walls, life-size portraits of eminents and a fine view over Pall Mall. Only a few tables were occupied, and they were well-spaced, and when not serving the waiters kept to the corners. Sir William had been a member of the Travellers' for years, and was well known as head of British diplomacy – not that the fact was ever mentioned, but a discreet distance was always kept, part of the unwritten code, the tradition that a member didn't approach another unless asked. As a result, it was said, more secret business was conducted in clubs like the Travellers' than in all Whitehall's offices put together.

A mouthful of beef, some more claret, and Sir William was ready. He seemed confident, relaxed, but his guests knew otherwise. All that pedantic talk about the quality of wine: pretentious, and Sir William was seldom that. He was nervous. What he was about to suggest didn't come easily to a man whose career had centred around the avoidance of risk, but there was too much at stake for caution. Back to the wall, he was about to show how savage an animal a diplomat could be.

'I think I've found our solution,' he said, leaning forward. 'It's blackmail. Katyn.'

There was silence as the others digested.

'Unpleasant business that.' Sir Stewart took some wine and swilled it round his palate, sceptically.

'Yes. Embarrassing to the Russians.'

'As far as I remember, William, we weren't exactly whiter than white.'

'No alternative, my dear fellow.' The Permanent Under-Secretary had no doubt, and skewered a boiled potato.

'Perhaps. But it might be best to leave well alone.' A good recipe, and very British. 'And anyway, I don't see the link.'

Sir William was undeterred. From an inner pocket he took several sheets of paper and dropped them on the table, photo-reproductions of two letters in the Russian Cyrillic script with English translations attached. Both bore the inscription of Soviet State Security.

'This came in at the time, and more besides. We suppressed it of course, but there's no reason why we can't present it as new evidence.'

The head of SIS read, while Sir William explained. 'It's clear that Katyn didn't account for all the men lost. Those documents give a total of 4,250. The other ten thousand were shot at Dergachi, near Kharkov, or drowned in barges in the White Sea. It all seems pretty conclusive.'

'And so?' Sir Stewart, still fingering through the documents, remained sceptical.

'And so we can declare to the world we were duped by Soviet scheming – all very understandable in the circumstances, etc. etc. "Now we have new evidence, we have a duty . . ." You know the line.'

Sir Stewart did. And Vivien. They knew only too well the honeyed phrases that obscure the endless malevolence of affairs of state.

'But I still don't quite understand.' Sir Stewart toyed with a kidney; he hated confessing naïvety. 'What are fifteen thousand Poles now, in a war in which millions were exterminated?'

'Remember the stink at the time?' asked Sir William between chews.

'Yes. Somewhat tedious . . .'

Katyn had left its mark on them. Not because they felt

any particular sorrow for its victims: at a time when they were fighting for survival in a world war how could they? But because, then, those fifteen thousand dead men threatened to upset their carefully-laid plans for post-war Europe. National policy was at stake.

'But that was ten years ago,' Sir Stewart cautioned.

Sir William shrugged. 'The Poles don't see it that way, Stewart. Katyn is a major tragedy for them. Remember the mass demonstrations last year to mark the tenth anniversary? And look at the pressure building up in the States, with Congressmen pushing for an investigation.'

Sir William was eager. Food was forgotten as he leaned over the table. 'Katyn's a symbol to the Poles – a symbol of their nation, if you like. A symbol of their subjection to the Russians. And the Poles have need of that just now.'

The state of Poland was well known to the three men. Reports from the Embassy in Warsaw and the Firm's operatives coincided: the country was falling apart. Prices were rising faster than wages, consumer goods were scarce, and food shortages were growing acute. Factory conditions were severe and discipline harsh, but that hadn't dampened unrest. Dislike of the Communist regime was matched by hatred of the Soviet Union. Even Polish party members had suffered at the hands of their 'comrades' across the border in successive purges inflicted on all levels of society. Deaths were many, and at least seventy thousand Poles were in labour camps.

'So you think Katyn could be the spark which ignites all that dry tinder?' Sir Stewart spoke slowly. He was becoming convinced.

'Precisely. I don't think that Stalin would like to risk it, not for the pleasure of seeing our embarrassment over a couple of handfuls of spies. Not after Tito's defection from the Soviet camp. That hit him hard.'

'There's something you don't know, William.' Sir Stewart placed his knife and fork neatly on his plate, then rearranged them as he spoke. 'The Firm has just made contact with an underground opposition group, in Poland. It . . . it seems they might be ready to act.'

'Who?'

'Oh, the usual. The military.'

Since the war, the Communists had regarded the Army as a centre of reaction, and in late 1949 the soldiers were forced to accept a Soviet Marshal, Rokossovsky, at their head. Around fifteen thousand Soviet 'advisers' were brought in, and the officer corps subjected to almost constant purge. A number of generals disappeared. Within a short time, 'Rokossovsky' had become a term of abuse; he was a Pole, but Russified, who even had difficulty speaking his native tongue when he returned. To his countrymen he remained a turncoat, typifying Soviet domination. As Sir Stewart said, twenty-six million people wanted him dead.

'And don't tell me, Stewart, that's exactly what they'll get.' Sir William knew that SIS wasn't above giving a helping hand.

Sir Stewart smiled. 'Well, let's just say there's a handful of senior officers who are interested in co-operation. And you're right, William. This claret *is* nutty.'

There was silence as the three men thought out the implications. There, in their comfortable chairs, warm and well-fed, each imagined the turmoil that lay within their gift: Katyn, the Army, Poland . . .

'But if the country does erupt, we've lost. That's our threat gone.' It was Vivien who spoke. The red pepper had made him awkward.

'We'll just have to make sure it doesn't, not until this is all over, anyway.' Sir Stewart raised a lanquid eyebrow. 'I think we can manage that, don't you?'

'So we bargain. Poland for the spies? Silence on both? Agreed?' The Permanent Under-Secretary wanted a conclusion.

'Agreed.' SIS was committed.

'And the traitors?' asked Vivien.

'I propose we do nothing.' Sir William's knife scratched his plate. He had finished.

'Quite agree,' said Sir Stewart firmly.

'We'll have to tell their Permanent Under-Secretaries, but that's no problem. They'll be as keen to hush up the whole sorry business as we are. Then we cut off the supply of information to the, ah, traitors, and gently ease them out. Early retirements, sinecures, that sort of thing. Even a promotion or two. Everything gradual. Nothing suspicious.' And that was all. No animosity, just practicality.

'And MI5?' persisted Vivien. 'Now they're on to "Homer".'

'We'll present the Snoopers with a *fait accompli* concerning Maclean. I'll get Percy to agree,' replied Sir Stewart. 'The whole thing shows him up as an incompetent, after all.'

'I don't envy your task.' Sir William had no time for the ex-colonial policeman, Sir Percy Sillitoe, who had come to head Britain's counter-espionage. 'Extraordinarily straightforward fellow. Black's black – that sort of thing. Difficult.'

'I'll manage.' Sir Stewart was confident, and with good reason. His art of persuasion was highly developed – it was why he remained head of SIS.

'Well, that's all very satisfactory, then.' Sir William finished the last of his wine, pursed his lips, and dabbed them with a napkin. 'I suggest coffee and port in the smoking room. We can discuss details there.'

They rose. Waiters converged to clear the table. A discreet bow from the club secretary to Sir William, a signature on a cheque, and the three men left.

As they walked down the wide staircase, the head of SIS began to smile.

'What's wrong?' Sir William asked, sharply fearing Sir Stewart's condescension.

Sir Stewart paused, hands in pockets. 'Nothing really, old

chap. But after the war the Poles gave me a decoration – *Polonia Restituta* they call it, Poland Rebuilt. Just struck me as amusing.'

Sir William grimaced. His laugh, immediate yet uncertain, fell away at once, leaving no trace of humour. 'Very good, Stewart. Very good.'

Chapter Three

Two bicycles, one ridden by a girl in her twenties, dressed in blue, golden hair billowing from under her beret, the other by a man in drab coat and breeches, his face indistinct. Together they cycle through fields and across dykes. The country is flat; mist lies like smoke. They reach a town – red brick and high gables, grey in the early morning – and stop near a large house. Over the door, an eagle clutching a swastika. There are guards at the gate. The couple wait, acting like lovers. They light cigarettes, talk, and the girl laughs, a pretty, carefree laugh, tossing her curls back, her eyes on the man – large, blue eyes which are trusting. Someone appears on the steps of the house, pauses and walks off. When he has turned the corner, the cyclists follow. He is walking fast, anxious to be home. He crosses a canal. The street is deserted. The cyclists still follow. Now the girl takes the lead. She is being tested: she will do the killing. She takes out a pistol and draws level with the man. She pulls the trigger. A click echoes in the silent street. Click – she tries again. Click, click. The man is drawing his own gun now, and round the corner comes a lorry, a black cross on its front. The girl looks behind to her companion, who has come to a halt. Why doesn't he shoot? He sees the terror on her face, then the cross on the lorry. She shouts as he turns his bicycle in the opposite direction, and screams as she is shot. The sound of the lorry fills the empty street. He turns a corner, pedalling, pedalling. His face becomes clear, and Nicholas Pelham, seeing his own, wakes up.

The dream, always the same dream, unchanging for seven years since that morning in a small town in Holland . . .

* * *

Eight chimes, sing-song and ponderous, and across Whitehall Big Ben announced nine-thirty to the assembling multitude.

The door opened and Nicholas Pelham entered his office, flung his bowler at the coat-hook, missed, cursed, then went to his desk and sat down, looking askance at the paper laid out for the day. And that was the little ritual that had formed a minuscule part of Whitehall's daily life for the past two-and-a-half years, never varying, indifferent to the seasons, imperturbable.

Tea was brought by a gap-toothed clerk. The obligatory light-hearted comment centred on the disagreeableness of work, and he left. Nick looked at the cup. A pattern of roses, chipped. Mr Pelham's cup. He would see it twice more that day.

Nick pushed back his chair and put his feet up. It was almost as if he were growing into his desk, he thought. Then he picked up *The Times* and turned to the overseas news. Keep well informed 'They' had said. But for what? The Foreign Office had its own view of things, and wasn't about to be influenced by Nicholas Pelham, APS to PUSS. He took his first sip of tea, always too hot, and grimaced.

It was the mirror first thing in the morning he dreaded most, Nick decided. That reflection staring dumbly back. Thirty-four, his features strong, his eyes an intense blue, and a physique which was still good, except that his stomach was developing a mind of its own. But the signs were there: the mouth set hard, disillusioned; the creases around the eyelids, almost petulant; a certain tiredness of expression, and already the puffiness of soft living. He envied his hair, though – spiky, with a mind of its own.

And not only his hair. Nick was untidy, irregular in his habits, quite prepared to let life drift between a desk and a garden. He was a strange combination. At once all British and stiff upper-lip, doing things he didn't want to because they were expected, yet a loner, loose, restless, wanting to taste life rather than digest it, then move on. It showed in his approach to women. He was a bachelor who knew how to play the game, getting involved with many to avoid being ensnared by one. But there he was, a bureaucrat following the golden rule: avoid criticism. Do nothing; say nothing; be nothing. For seven years ago, Nick had lost confidence in himself.

The Service – that had been a mistake, following his father, Sir Anthony, once Ambassador to Madrid, now deceased. For the war had given Nick a taste for something other than the rarified pleasures of Whitehall. Fighting in the desert, a year in Special Operations – life since then had been rather like an onion, appetizing at first, but the more layers that were peeled off, the less there was to it. And in any case, there was little about him sympathetic to bureaucracy, even the genteel form it took in the Foreign Office, with its quiet diplomacy, easy hours, clubs and connections. He had the pedigree – Harrow, Cambridge, a family name – but that didn't satisfy. His colleagues managed to exist in Whitehall's desert happily enough, forming habits and revelling in their banality, even growing to look alike. But not Nick. He was a loner, an odd number who took a strange delight in unsettling the evens. Not a second eleven sort of chap, his fellow diplomats said about him, but too cynical – the type who, when he smelled flowers, looked for a coffin. All in all, they whispered, he could be a dangerous man to have in the Foreign Office.

But that morning, as on so many previously, Nick obediently read the paper and entered the complacent sleep of Whitehall. The day that had started at nine-thirty would end at six, he told himself, and then he could begin to live – it was the Savoy that evening, with Teresa. Pleasant dreams.

'Well, and who's dropped a bollock then?'

The dreams, barely begun, were shattered by a sarcastic

drawl from outside, so upper-class that Nick imagined the plumb had become displaced.

'A whopping, enormous bollock.' A head appeared around the door. 'Morning, Pelham.'

Harrison, a sickly Principal from Protocol, entered and stood lounging against the door, hands in pockets. His face, disfigured by a seraphic sneer, was the type which looked as if its owner was perpetually struggling to keep awake, with eyelids half-raised. 'A bollock such as never has been dropped before.'

'Oh?' Nick kept his feet on the desk and scanned through *The Times*, hoping to annoy. 'I appear to have both mine, thank you.'

'Don't be touchy, Nicholas. I heard it on the grapevine and thought you might appreciate a warning.' Harrison shifted his position so that his voice could be better heard in the corridor. 'Remember that *intime* dinner party you organized for PUSS and the Bolivian Ambassador last week? Well, you left off Tomlinson's CMG, and you know how much he has lusted after that little gong. Didn't take it at all well. Invitation, menus, seating plan – all affected. Makes a difference, you see, being a Commander of the Order of St Michael and St George.'

'He ate the same food, didn't he?' Nick saw no need to affect concern.

'Not the point, old boy. It's these minutiae we're paid to bother about. Look after the dots and commas, and the treaties take care of themselves – the first rule.'

Nick put down the paper and turned to Harrison, who failed to notice the expression in his eyes, and be warned.

'Must pick up on all this, Nicholas. Get on top,' the man continued. 'Must . . .'

'Strange place isn't it, Whitehall?'

Harrison looked surprised at Nick's curt interruption. He had been a bureaucrat long enough for his character to have taken on the dryness of paper, and its flimsiness.

'Have you ever thought why it is that we have a statue to Charles I, a murdered king, at one end, and another to Cromwell, his murderer, at the other?'

'Well, no, actually. And I don't see the . . .'

'Think about it then.' Nick picked up *The Times*.

'I say . . .' Harrison stuttered, 'I just thought I'd tip you the wink about Tomlinson, that's all, but it seems one can't be decent to you, Pelham. A pity.'

'The milk of human kindness soured in you a long time ago, Harrison.' Nick turned a page. 'Now trot along, there's a good fellow, and go and shuffle some papers. Cheerio.'

Harrison left. And from outside, the chatter of a type-writer began, and became incessant.

Promptly at ten that brisk April morning, the second Monday of the month, Nick presented himself to the chief, expecting trouble. The Permanent Under-Secretary was a methodical man, finickity, who felt honour bound to find error – and to a diplomat a CMG was no minor matter. But Sir William appeared not to know, and was unusually friendly.

'Pelham! Good morning!' he barked, looking for a moment as if he would even rise from his desk to greet his Assistant Private Secretary. But temptation was resisted. 'An enjoyable weekend? Good. Now, I found this in the Secretary of State's in-tray on Friday.' Sir William held up Lubienski's letter by a corner. 'And thought we should do some preparatory work before bothering his busy little head . . .'

Nick noted Sir William's condescension towards his political master, but refused to smile. He reached out and took the letter.

'I think we can do with some revision of our policy on this. Changed circumstances, Cold War and all that. You know the form. See what you can dig up. The PM will be pushing it. Could be quite important, you see. Liaise with Gould, would you?'

Nick flinched. Gould was a frightful little man, humourless too. Time spent with him was certain to be tedious.

'He worked on the matter during the war. Knows the files inside out. Tell him it's fairly urgent, top priority, that sort of thing. Possible courses of action, the lot. That's all for the moment, I think.'

Nick left, a dismissive wave escorting him to the door. Outside, he looked again at the letter. Katyn: the name rang a bell, a rather cracked one. He grunted. There wasn't much in that. A matter of history, nothing more.

Nick saw Gould later that morning, a diplomatic luminary who was all he abhorred about the public service. True, in that whiny voice of his Gould provided the information required to track down the relevant files in the Foreign Office's vast Registry, but not without fussing as to why it was needed, what sort of policy changes were under consideration, how long the whole process would take. Typical, thought Nick. The man was a pendant, and that was an end to it. But by the time he reached the Registry, ill-lit and airless in the basement, smelling of paper's slow decay, Nick's good humour had returned. He found a clerk, a shapely brunette, and watched her figure, hugged neatly by a tight-fitting dress, as she got up to consult the catalogue. All thoughts of Lubienski's letter left him as she bent down. K for Katyn was in a lower drawer. Nick's fantasies soared, and were interrupted only by their subject returning and informing him in high-pitched cockney that one of the files was classified Secret. It could not leave the Registry.

Nick sat down at a desk from where he could get a good view of the girl, and waited. After five minutes she returned with two files in their usual buff folders, one with red lines crossing at the centre.

'Sign here,' she said, chewing gum provocatively.

'Twice.' Nick put his signature in the spaces provided. 'Don't go to sleep,' she added cheekily, and walked off, hips swaying self-consciously. Nick sighed, and opened the file marked *Katyn – Secret.*

The officers were shot at point-blank range, in the area between the back of the head and the neck [ran a résumé Nick turned to first], the bullet usually coming out at the root of the nose or forehead. One shot, occasionally two, from a 7.65 mm pistol was required to kill each man, administered with such precision as to destroy the medulla.

What the hell was a medulla, Nick wondered, vaguely aware he couldn't care less. He glanced up at the brunette. It was true, he reckoned – the tighter the dress, the looser the morals. It might be fun finding her medulla.

The bullets were manufactured by the firm of Gustav Genschow and Co, Berlin, whose trademark, Geco-7.65, was stamped on the bottom of the cartridges found in the pits. They were of a type which had been supplied by Germany to Russia before the war. All the victims had been shot. Some had sawdust stuffed in their mouths . . .

Nick felt more bored than revolted by such details, and he looked up again. The girl, conscious of his interest, turned her head to present her profile. Trying to be statuesque: a good sign.

The bodies were placed in the graves, side by side, twelve deep. The stage of decay varied in accordance with their position. Mummification took place on the top and at the sides, and, because of the damp, a humid process was at work in the centre, which caused the bodies to stick together.

So the morning and a part of the afternoon passed. The brunette excited Nick by her obvious enjoyment of her own sexuality but, as time went on, he found himself increasingly absorbed by the history of the Foreign Office's approach to Katyn. At no time, the files revealed, did

Whitehall seriously consider apportioning blame to the Russians, despite detailed reports pointing to their guilt. From the beginning it was decided that others were to be accused. Nothing – no fact, no ideal of justice – was to detract from that.

On September 1939, Germany had invaded Poland from the west. On the 17th, with the Poles near defeat, the Soviet Union moved in from the east to occupy land it had long claimed. When the fighting ended five days later, the two dictators simply divided Poland between them. In their new domains the invaders took severe measures, Soviet security no less so than the SS. In the first year alone the Russians deported over a million Poles, many to undertake heavy labour in Siberian mines, from which less than half were to emerge alive. Eastern Poland was incorporated into the Union, and additional territory bought from the Germans for gold. But 'Sovietization' was interrupted when, on 22 June 1941, Hitler attacked again in the east. At the end of July, with all Poland in German hands and the Soviet borders deeply breached, Moscow and the Polish Government-in-Exile in London renewed diplomatic relations. The Poles interned in Russia were released to form a Polish Army on Russian soil. But where were its officers? Around fifteen thousand had been taken in 1939, and of these only a third could be found. No fewer than ten thousand, together with five thousand other ranks, policemen and officials, had disappeared.

Unitl March 1940, over a year before the German invasion, letters had been sent home by these men, via the Red Cross. After that day, however, not one was received. Despite repeated requests for information, Moscow gave no positive reply. Polish suspicions were strong.

Then, on 13 April 1943, Berlin announced that German troops had discovered the mass graves of Polish officers at Katyn in western Russia. Nearly three thousand bodies had been unearthed, with more to come. The Soviet secret police were accused of the killings. Two days later, Moscow placed all blame on the Nazis.

Even at the time proof was strong that the Soviets were lying. Apart from the disappearance of the Poles over a year before the German invasion, there was evidence from the graves themselves – evidence scrutinized by Poles as well as European pathologists. Although the killers had taken valuables from the dead, they had left notebooks, letters and papers, all bearing dates between August 1939 and April 1940, and none later. Moreover, the young conifers on the graves were shown by botanical analysis to have been transplanted in 1940. But most important of all was the evidence of a crust around the surface of the victims' brains which forms only in bodies buried for three years or more. The latest date by which the Poles could have been killed, therefore, was as the Germans claimed: the spring of 1940.

The Poles reacted strongly. So too did the Soviets. Moscow brought great pressure to bear on the British and United States governments, and hints were made that, should they side with the Free Poles, the wartime alliance might break down. Such threats could not have come at a worse time, at the turning-point in the fighting: the future of post-war Europe was in the balance, and the search for an acceptable division of power between East and West at its most delicate. Soviet blackmail was heeded. The Poles were ignored, the Germans were judged guilty, and the unnatural alliance between democracy and communism against Hitler survived.

But despite its public pronouncements, the Foreign Office was keenly aware of the truth. Of particular interest to Nick was a despatch in May 1943 from the Ambassador to the Polish Government in London, Owen O'Malley, which cast serious doubts on Soviet innocence. Unusually for diplomatic reports, the Ambassador concluded with a demand for honesty. To recognize reality for what it was, to accept that Britain's Soviet ally had massacred fifteen thousand Poles would, O'Malley believed, be 'a reaffirmation of our allegiance to truth and justice and compassion' – the principles, after all, for which Britain was avowedly fighting a world war. It was a powerful plea, heightened by the practical argument that immoral acts made bad politics.

Nick read the reactions to O'Malley's despatch with growing interest. Of the five senior Foreign Office officials who had made their comments, only two recommended that it be circulated in full to the King and War Cabinet as its author wished. One, Nick noted, had been Sir William, then plain Mr Strang. Of the others, two believed that only the factual paragraphs should be sent, preferring to omit the 'devious argument' of morality. In diplomacy, they believed, heads should not be governed by hearts, a cardinal principle which the Poles themselves continually broke. The then Permanent Under-Secretary, Sir Alexander Cadogan, was against the whole despatch: whilst recognizing the moral dilemma which Soviet guilt posed, he rationalized Britain's attitude by pointing out that such massacres were nothing new; that the Communist regime had murdered countless of its own citizens; and that, like it or not, it was necessary to co-operate with the Russians to defeat Hitler. Sir Alexander concluded: 'Of course, it would only be honest to circulate it. But as we know that the knowledge of this evidence cannot affect our course of action, or policy, is there any advantage in exposing more individuals than necessary to the spiritual conflict that a reading of this document excites?' By such arguments, O'Malley's despatch was filed away, and the consciences of King and War Cabinet, in this matter at least, were saved.

Nick's interest was further aroused when he read of the efforts made to ensure that the International Red Cross did not conduct an investigation. The official British line was simply that German guilt was indicated by German presence at Katyn – that, and nothing else. It had been a successful cover-up. Lies and fraud – actions which, had they been committed by a man, would have been criminal – were, for diplomats, deemed a necessity.

There was an itch in the air around Nicholas Pelham when he left the Registry that Monday afternoon, and before going home he discussed Katyn with Sir William. He was certain there had been a miscarriage of justice, and that the granting of Lubienski's request could help make amends. In the present international situation, too, with war in Korea, he argued that the Govenment's recognition of Soviet guilt could be useful. Nick chose his words carefully though, for he knew of Strang's involvement. But caution was unnecessary. Sir William listened, as he so often would, inattentively. Contemporary documents before him appeared to require greater attention than history.

'Quite so. You've got a point, Pelham. How about talking it over with Gould? Possible reactions by the UN, that sort of thing. Let me know the upshot.'

Nick left, his enthusiasm aroused. There were things that could be done with Katyn, important things – though Sir William's attitude was worrying. The Permanent Under-Secretary seemed unprepared to give the matter the attention it deserved, and Nick promised himself he would just have to make sure the man did so. APS to PUSS had the bit between his teeth – if nothing else it would be a useful way of escaping boredom.

The most inaccessible area of the Soviet Union's London Embassy is known as the 'Referentura'. Situated in what was the wine cellar, it is the centre of Soviet subversive operations in Britain. Here, in 1951, the activities of all agents were directed, whether by State Security, then the *Ministerstvo Gosudarstvennoi Bezopasnosti*, the MGB, or

Military Intelligence, the GRU. Reached by a narrow corridor, guarded by a heavy steel door, the Referentura is windowless and, to those who have to spend any length of time there, airless. No briefcases, cameras or recording equipment are allowed in. No documents can be taken out. Even its staff live in conditions of virtual house arrest, unable to leave the Embassy grounds unless in groups accompanied by armed guards. This is the 'dungeon'.

It was here, in the conference room on the night of Tuesday, 10 April 1951, that three men gathered – Georgi Nikolaevich Zaroubin, the Soviet Ambassador, Alexeï Nikolaevich Manjoulo, officially the Deputy Trade Representative but in reality the MGB *rezident*, or chief, in Britain, and Boris Yastrebov, an MGB agent posing as a Third Secretary. Zaroubin was the amateur, merely the representative of the Central Committee of the Communist Party. The other two were the professionals, the men to whom the secrets of the Referentura belonged. Zaroubin's presence, however, indicated the importance of the meeting. The past twenty-four hours had seen a number of developments that required the highest diplomatic presence.

First, there had been the report from the spy Gould which arrived late the previous day: the British were reopening Katyn. That had been of sufficient interest to be reported to Moscow, but little more. However, its combination with a second incident proved explosive: the Permanent Under-Secretary of the British Foreign Office had begun an attempt to blackmail the Soviet Union.

Early that morning Ambassador Zaroubin had arrived at Sir William's office, as requested. Strang was at his most guarded, and little of substance was discussed, so that after an hour Zaroubin, tired of the pointless sparring, rose to go.

Then came the bombshell. Sir William leaned over his

desk and pushed a document to the Ambassador, a photo-reproduction bearing the Soviet State Security letterhead, dated in 1940. Zaroubin read it, but said nothing. Sir William did not explain. Instead, he informed the Ambassador there was more evidence of a similar nature, and suggested a meeting to discuss it. Remarkable though such an approach was, Zaroubin was totally unprepared for what followed.

'Two other persons are interested in this matter,' continued Sir William. 'They go by the names of Menzies and Vivien. I think you may know of at least one of them . . .'

'C''s name might have been a closely guarded secret from the British public, but it was well known to its enemies. The Ambassador's face showed surprise, but still he said nothing.

'And, Your Excellency, they wish to meet one of your staff. He's called Manjoulo.'

Zaroubin tried bluff. 'But Manjoulo is only a Deputy Trade Representative. What use can he be?' He forced a smile, trying to be carefree, but it didn't come out that way.

Sir William countered effortlessly. 'So I believe. But that's just what we want: a trade.'

And that was the history behind the meeting in the Referentura that night.

'What can it be, Alexei?' the Ambassador asked. He looked like a man who has lost his innocence, tortured, his heavy jowls hanging limply. 'What can we tell Moscow?' He drew deeply on his cigarette, a Player's Navy Cut – the only brand he took – letting the smoke dribble out of his mouth. His eyes were bloodshot. 'What can we say?'

Manjoulo, fat, slow and sticky, sporting a bow tie, looked the old hand he was. He shook his head, knowing that any report to Moscow would have to be carefully worded. 'Whatever it is they're up to, Georgi Nikolaevich,' he replied, enjoying the familiarity that seclusion in the dungeon gave, 'it's obviously considered policy.'

Manjoulo's small black eyes turned on Yastrebov at the end of the green baize-covered table. The little man blinked nervously behind heavy glasses. Manjoulo ranked as a colonel; he was a mere lieutenant.

'Well, Yastrebov?' Manjoulo snapped.

'I was in touch with Gould again today, Comrade Colonel, as you ordered.' The rapidity of Yastrebov's speech emphasized his nervousness. 'He must submit his views on a re-evaluation of British policy on Katyn by tomorrow, with special emphasis on our likely reactions if the case is brought before the United Nations. A deputy of Strang's has been made responsible for the whole business, a man called Nicholas Pelham. Gould doesn't think that the Foreign Minister is involved – at least, his Private Secretary hasn't heard anything. I cannot add any more, Comrade Colonel.'

Yastrebov's eyes fell to the table. 'You may go,' the Colonel said from the corner of his mouth, and he waited for the Lieutenant to leave before continuing. 'We've had nothing from "Homer", Georgi Nikolaevich. That could indicate the Americans aren't involved, although they would have to be with any approach to the United Nations.'

'And what's happening on the Polish front?' Zaroubin nervously tapped the table and exhaled.

Manjoulo moved to avoid the smoke. He couldn't prevent the Ambassador from indulging in the habit, but as head of State Security in Britain, with responsibility for Zaroubin's loyalty, he had no reason to hide his dislike.

'Yesterday we put another three men on to the Polish organizations. We've also been in close touch with Polish Security here. Their man in the Embassy is sending us a list of likely targets. We'll find out if any of them is behind it.'

Manjoulo rolled up a handkerchief and wiped the grease from under his eyes.

'But why Katyn?' Zaroubin addressed the air as much as Manjoulo. 'And why SIS?'

Manjoulo had little time for the Ambassador's questioning. When dealing with men like Menzies and Strang conjecture was pointless. 'Whatever the reason, we can only find out at the meeting.'

'Quite. But I'm not bedding down with Menzies unless I'm told to do so – in triplicate, with Stalin's signature for preference.' Zaroubin dropped ash down his front.

'Quickest way to the gallows, otherwise, eh?' Manjoulo smiled, but a scar on his fat upper lip made the smile hideous.

'You too, Comrade.' The Ambassador nodded towards the MGB Colonel. 'You too.'

The joke was over. It was not funny. The knife-edge was too thin.

'We must get our request off tonight.' Manjoulo said. 'That's all we can do. Just facts – nothing that can be taken as a suggestion. Let them decide.'

Safe, and also inevitable. Moscow's grip was always there, at the throat.

That night, using the highest code, the duty radio operator in the Referentura transmitted a five-minute signal. The Government Code and Cipher School at Eastcote picked it up, but was unable to make sense of it. In the Soviet capital, however, Manjoulo's message had its impact. As a pebble tossed in a pond, its ripples began to expand ever outwards.

There are two cities in Moscow. One is the historic capital of an empire, home for eight million people, with theatres, palaces and the remnants of one thousand one hundred and one churches. The other is the half-hidden capital of Soviet Security, a network of highly intricate connections which form the most suspicious system ever designed for the protection of a ruling caste from its people.

At the centre of this web of fear governing the activities of two hundred and fifty million Soviet citizens, sits the head of State Security. In 1951, the office was held by Colonel-General Viktor Semyonovich Abakhumov, a man not of any great evil, but one who viewed men in terms of units, to be subtracted or multiplied as circumstances demanded. The organization which came under his control, the Ministry of State Security, the MGB, was the single most powerful in the Union, and composed of 1,350,000 men – the police, border guards, 'special-duty' troops and guards. But it was the 150,000 secret police who formed the most feared group of all, the men on whom power rested.

It was the Minister's habit to arrive at the MGB's headquarters in the grey-brown Lubyanka building on Dzerzhinsky Square every morning at eight o'clock. The saying 'the early bird catches the worm' had special significance for him, and he liked to see the reports which, overnight, had arrived in Moscow from all parts of the Union and the world. By such vigilance he hoped to remain ahead of his enemies, capitalist or communist. He knew other ways, too, some less peaceful, and used them. For whatever happened, Abakhumov did not intend to go the way of his predecessors. Of the five in charge of Soviet Security since 1917, four had been removed from office, and two killed in the process, shot in the same cellar within months of each other, while it was rumoured that two others had died of 'unnatural' causes.

This was the spectre that haunted Minister Abakhumov. There was no doubt he had power, perhaps greater than any of his predecessors, and an official position which allowed him to destroy any person he wanted, almost without exception. But it was those exceptions who might, at any time, destroy him.

The cold, grey morning of Wednesday, 11 April was like any other. On arriving at the Lubyanka, Abakhumov went straight to his office on the third floor, a room of a grandeur befitting his position as one of the less equal members of Soviet society. The ceiling was high, decorated with stucco mouldings, and from its middle hung an ornate gilt chandelier. At one end was a large marble fireplace below a high mirror, and in the corner was a grandfather clock, whose loud tick could be heard at the other end, where a large table stood, surrounded by chairs. The desk, a gilt-inlay affair, was arranged at an angle so as to get the best light from the windows, and, at the same time, avoid a bullet should an assassin escape the security precautions in the square below. The desk furniture, too, was ornate: inkstand, pen-holder and lamp, all gilt. A large chair, with enormous armrests, stood behind, giving the final impression of solidity and power.

But of everything in that room, the visitor was always struck by two features: the stillness, and the life-size portrait of Stalin, resplendent in Marshal's uniform, which dominated all around it. The great dictator was reflected in the mirror on the wall opposite, and, when the curtains were drawn back, in the windows. His likeness was also on a signed photograph the Minister kept in a gilt frame on his desk. The Generalissimo was everywhere.

Into this office, which overawed most who entered it, Abakhumov strode with confidence. A tall, well-built man, heavy without being fat, his features coarse and made aggressive by the backward sweep of his black hair, wearing green uniform with gold braid, he looked well enough in his surroundings. Nodding curtly to his adjutant who stood to attention holding open the highly-polished double doors, he went as always straight to the window, drew aside the net curtain, and stood looking down on the square as if to assure himself all was well. Then he moved to his desk and sat down. His adjutant, an MGB Major, hovered at the far end of the room.

Abakhumov yawned. He had been awake half the night, like all Moscow *vlasti*, 'high-ups', waiting for that chance call from the Generalissimo which seldom came. He rubbed his eyes, looked at the paper laid before him, and grunted as always, promising himself one day to do something about the Ministry's bureaucracy. He flicked through, looking for anything stamped *Priority*: *Urgent*, always reading such messages first. That day, there was only one. It came from London Centre.

The news from Manjoulo puzzled the Minister. Meetings between intelligence services were common enough when their countries were allies, but seldom otherwise. Abakhumov and the rest of the Soviet leadership regarded relations with the West as a state of conflict, so why, then, was a man as powerful as the head of SIS requesting a meeting with the MGB *rezident* in London? There had been no indication of anything unusual. Abakhumov didn't like what he read. His senses told against it. Menzies disturbed him. Whatever he wanted, it couldn't be good. But what was it? The Minister felt a tightening of his throat, and pulled at its loose skin as he thought.

A minute passed and then Abakhumov scrawled a few words across the message, signed and folded it. There was no alternative. The meeting had to take place.

The barest sign to the adjutant, who clicked to attention, moving smartly to the desk as a ministerial arm held out the paper. 'Take this. I agree to the request – but no commitments. On no account. Just let them listen to what the British have to say. Send it priority. I want that meeting tonight.'

Abakhumov sat back, and wiped a thin film of sweat from his forehead.

Chapter Four

'You will drink, yes?' the old man asked. Nick accepted.

'I can recommend our vodka, made from grain. Or beer?'

Nick chose the beer. A white-jacketed waiter with the wide, open face of a Polish peasant took the order.

'And sandwiches, please?' suggested Lubienski, holding up an enquiring finger. Nick declined, successfully suppressing a smile at the man's quaint English. Lubienski's manner, too, was odd, rather picturesque. It was eleven-thirty in the morning, yet the old Pole had greeted him with an enthusiastic 'Good afternoon!'

Nick looked around. The Polish Club was a fine institution, full of mementoes of the old country, strong in faded glory, the sort of place where he expected to find the General of Cavalry-in-Exile earnestly discussing the future of the lance in combat with the Minister of Public Works-in-Exile, each with long, sad faces adorned with equally long, sad moustaches.

'Well, Mr Pelham, how may I be assisting?' asked Lubienski as he pulled at his tie with trembling hands.

'Your letter, Mr Lubienski, has aroused considerable interest in the Foreign Office. As I said on the telephone, I can promise nothing, you must understand, but I've been asked to have an exploratory talk with you.' That was a lie.

'Ah yes, quite,' Lubienski replied, his watery brown eyes smiling, his head on one side. 'You can promise nothing. But I must say, I find surprise at hearing from you at all. Our Committee had expected refusal.'

'Well, as you can see, Mr Lubienski, I'm here, so there's some hope.' Nick smiled too.

The beer arrived, but Lubienski only took coffee.

'I am old, Mr Pelham. Drink makes me sleep, and I have quite enough to do without that,' he explained.

Nick looked at the little man, obviously in his late sixties, a frail figure, with wispy hair and a toothbrush moustache, more like a portrait yellowed by time than a live Pole. His shirt-cuffs were frayed, and there were signs of rough stitching at the point where the cloth met the collar. But Lubienski had his pride. His head was held high, and his hands were placed neatly on crossed legs. His grey suit, double-breasted, was obviously pre-war, but held together and was clean.

The old man saw his guest surveying him, and gave a slight shrug of the shoulders. 'Ah, faded glory, Mr Pelham. I am a poor shadow, now. I have the Russians to thank for that.'

'You have no time for them, Mr Lubienski?'

'Not much, Mr Pelham. They once had no time for me.' Lubienski spoke simply, controlling himself, giving nothing away. He looked keenly at Nick. 'Or do you have some sympathy for these communists?'

Nick joked, hoping flippancy would suffice. 'No. Can't tell Karl from Harpo, I'm afraid'. But humour didn't work with the Pole. A frown clouded his face, and Nick felt suddenly ashamed. He became serious. 'But what do you hope to achieve by this memorial, Mr Lubienski?' he asked.

'Will we get it?'

'You might.'

'But will we get Poland?'

'That's what you're after?'

Again Lubienski shrugged his shoulders. Perhaps he alone of his friends realized such hopes were baseless, but still the dream of a decade came to the fore. He had nothing else, Nick could see that.

'One day we will rise, Mr Pelham. My people have no

love of slavery. We have risen before against foreign masters. The time will come again, and for that we shall be prepared.'

'And the memorial? How will that help?' Nick was genuinely interested.

'For myself, I care not so much about Katyn. I lost no son there. But I care for truth. And truth is that the Russians killed fifteen thousand of our best men in cold blood. Fifteen thousand, Mr Pelham, and no cross between them.' He paused, looking intently at Nick. 'It might not sound many to a world used to dealing in millions, but let me tell you, it is fifteen thousand meaning more to my countrymen than all others lost in war put together. It is a symbol, Mr Pelham, a powerful symbol of Russian tyranny over our nation . . .'

The old man's speech, begun haltingly, had become fluent, and he moved forward to the edge of his chair. But still his expression had its tiredness. He would never lose that.

'Yes, Mr Pelham, Katyn is a symbol, the best we have. And it can be recognized by the world.'

'It hasn't been so yet, Mr Lubienski. So why now?'

'Now? Because we live now, Mr Pelham. And, after all, is ten years so long? Not to old countries like yours and mine. It's a moment of history.' For the first time the Pole's hands moved, clutching the air to force home his point. 'Katyn lives, Mr Pelham, because it has existed as a lie, and lies never die until the truth is told. Never! And by allowing it to continue, Mr Pelham, you betray not only Poland – you betray your own country.'

'How's that?' But Nick was aware of what Lubienski was hinting, and found it difficult to look into the old man's eyes.

'How is that? Yes, it is all very well for an official of the British Foreign Office to ask that. All very well, Mr Pelham. But let me ask you a question. For what did Britain go to war in 1939?'

'To stop Hitler.' Nick sensed what was coming next.

'To stop Hitler destroying Poland, Mr Pelham, that is why. And how did Poland end war?'

'At peace?'

'No, Mr Pelham. It ended war shifted a hundred and fifty miles to the west, half its territory taken by the Russians, and with German land thrown at it in compensation. Then came a communist tyranny over a country that was smaller by almost a quarter. And all undertaken against Polish will, by her allies. That was our "peace", Mr Pelham. Is that what you fought for? Is that the result of your Mr Churchill's principles of freedom and justice?'

Lubienski slumped in his chair. His face revealed his agitation, the muscles in his jaw flexing and unflexing. 'Do you believe God suspended his commandments for Great Britain?'

Nick didn't reply. He drank his beer and fiddled with the glass, searching for excuses. Finally, he broke the silence, weakly, and despite himself, attempted a justification.

'But, Mr Lubienski, the fate of Poland was shared by the whole of Eastern Europe. We didn't want it, but what was the alternative? The Russians were on your soil with their armies – armies that had got there because they had fought the Germans, your conquerors. What could we do?'

Lubienski snorted contemptuously. 'What could you do, Mr Pelham? I leave that to your conscience. But do you think, for example, that by killing General Sikorski you "played the game", as you say? Murdering our Prime Minister – was that "British"?'

Nick looked blank. 'But we didn't kill Sikorski. It was an accident.' He paused. 'Wasn't it?'

'Accident? Accident, Mr Pelham? No, it was not an accident. Your British Intelligence killed our Prime Minister, and his daughter, and his Chief of Staff. Eighteen of them. That's who – British Intelligence.'

Nick's expression turned to disbelief. He remembered

Sikorski's death. He had heard the BBC's announcement while celebrating his own birthday in 1943. A minute or two of hushed conversation had followed, then more gin, and the tragedy was forgotten. It was war.

The accident took place on 4 July. The aircraft carrying the general had just taken off from Gibraltar when it inexplicably nose-dived into the sea, killing most of its occupants. Nick remembered how Nazi propaganda had made much of the incident, accusing the British of plotting Sikorski's death. But that, too, was war.

'That's what the Germans said at the time, Mr Lubienski. It's nonsense. Why would we have wanted to do it?'

'Mr Pelham,' said the old Pole slowly, sounding as though he pitied Nick his ignorance. 'Sikorski was the only man who could have prevented you British from making a deal with Stalin. He was an embarrassment. He had to go.'

'Many people were an embarrassment to us during the war, Mr Lubienski. General de Gaulle, for example, and he's still alive.'

'Just consider, if you would, why he didn't travel in Britain by aircraft.'

'Oh, absolute nonsense.' Nick was more dismissive of the old man than he wished. He felt uneasy.

'Nonsense, you say, Mr Pelham?' The Pole shrugged as he spread his arms wide. 'Well, perhaps. But the day before Sikorski's death he received a courier from Warsaw, a man by name of Gralewski, with information about Katyn. That gave the General sufficient proof to lay blame at Russia's door. The British couldn't risk it. So the Liberator aircraft – we know its code, Mr Pelham, AL 523 – the aircraft was sabotaged. It came down with Sikorski, his staff and baggage. All proof, all in one. Brilliant, Mr Pelham, and do you know how it was done? By a mail bag. Simple! Just one mail bag to jam the controls. Perfect crime. It left no trace. It dislodged on impact. That's British Intelligence for you.'

Lubienski paused. He frowned, as if wondering, sizing up Nick, then leaned forward. 'And do you want to know the man responsible, Mr Pelham, because we even know that. I will tell you. His name was Philby. Head of your Intelligence's Iberian Section. That much we know. Philby, with the initial "H".'

On leaving Lubienski that Wednesday afternoon Nick made his way back to Whitehall through the swathe of green at London's centre: Hyde Park, Green Park and St James's. Head down, he walked for an hour, kicking at stones, oblivious to the beauty around him, his thoughts sick of the world in which he moved.

Nick had finally understood. His disillusion was complete, leaving nothing of the enthusiasm with which he had once served his country in war – 'Hitler's War'. What had the dead died for? New suffering, injustice and violence? Lofty ideals, high principles – their words had ended on the dungheap, amounting to nothing more than another carve-up of Europe. Time and again, Lubienski's parting words returned: 'Tell me, Mr Pelham, what you think of Poland, and I will tell you what you are.' And the man's expression: quizzical, imploring, resigned.

Back in his office, Nick telephoned the Registry. The cockney who had so attracted him answered, but instead of coaxing her he came straight to the point.

'Nick Pelham here, PUSS's office. Can you send up everything possible on relations with the Polish Government-in-Exile for 1941 to 1944. Mark it for me personally, will you please?'

That done, Nick sat back to think. Philby. Who was Philby? And was Lubienski correct? Nick reached across his desk for his well-thumbed copy of the Foreign Office List 1951, and went to its index. There an agent's name might show up. It was worth a try. He found what he was looking for – Philby, H. A. R. Philby, a First Secretary in the Washington Embassy.

Nick got up and went to the bookcase. Taking out the Foreign Office List for 1950, he looked again for the man. Not in Washington. He turned to the index, and then back to the section dealing with the Embassy in Turkey. There was H. A. R. Philby, a First Secretary. And so Nick continued back to 1947. Philby had been in Turkey for three years. Thereafter, he vanished.

Nick picked up the telephone and called Jamieson in Establishments.

'Pelham here. It's late I know, but I've a request from PUSS. Can he have H. A. R. Philby's file as soon as possible. Send it to me, would you?' Nick paused, while Jamieson exacted the usual assurance of confidentiality.

'Of course,' replied Nick. 'We live by the proper procedure in this office, Jamieson. You should know that by now. Sir William's a stickler.'

Half an hour later, the telephone rang.

'Pelham, Jamieson here. Did I get it right? It was H. A. R. Philby you wanted, wasn't it? Well, we've no Philby in the Service with those initials. Where did you get the name from?'

Nick explained that it came from the list for which Jamieson's own department was responsible.

'Oh well, that's easily understood then. Philby must be an Intelligence johnny,' replied Jamieson in faded RAF slang. 'We won't have anything on him. PUSS will have to try elsewhere.'

Jamieson had confirmed it. Nick felt elated, like a bird who has found a juicy slug in the rubbish dump. But this mood died as swiftly as it had come: Philby was in Intelligence, attached to Embassy staff under cover – standard procedure – but that didn't make him the man responsible for Sikorski's death.

For a good hour Nick sat and thought, and only the

muffled chimes of Big Ben brought him back to the world and the paper on his desk. But suspicion remained, like the constant throb of toothache, and he knew it wouldn't go away. He reached out for a file marked PUSS, and rose.

Two-and-a-half inches below the collar stud – that's where it would go: the prescribed position for the Archangel St Michael trampling upon Satan.

The Cross of the Knight Commander of St Michael and St George was lifted gently from a velvet-lined case and fingers smoothed over its enamelled surface before it was raised and the blue and red ribbon clipped behind the neck. There it hung, a seven-pointed star, white on gold, surmounted by an imperial crown, with the motto, *Auspicium Melioris Aevi* – 'A pledge for better times.'

Sir William turned from the mirror as he heard the knock at the door. It was late, and he was in a hurry. Not expecting his preparations to be disturbed, he frowned as Nick entered.

'Yes, Pelham, what is it? Aren't you off yet?'

'Sorry, Sir William.' It wasn't a bad life, Nick thought as he looked at his chief: forty years of honours and self-deceit before a comfortable retirement. But not for Nick. 'Just some papers for tomorrow.'

'All right. Leave them there.' Sir William gestured at his desk. That was all. Time for the Assistant Private Secretary to scurry away. Nick went to the door, half opened it, and turned.

'Oh, Sir William, I was wondering, do you know anything about Philby in the Washington Embassy? I might have bumped into him in the past, but can't remember where.' He spoke slowly, deliberately.

Turning back to the mirror, Sir William didn't hurry to answer. In the reflection, Nick saw the man's face become wooden.

'Who?'

'Philby, Sir William. His initials are H. A. R. He's a First Secretary in Washington.'

'Ah.' A pause. 'No Pelham, I'm afraid I know nothing about the fellow,' and the head of the Foreign Service pulled at the cross around his neck.

At seven o'clock that evening of Wednesday, 11 April, five men gathered in the back room of a terraced house in Islington, north London. A table and high-backed chairs stood on bare floorboards, paper drooped from a corner, and paint peeled. Overall was a heavy smell of damp. Only the thick curtains were new, and as they were drawn light came from an uncovered bulb hanging from the ceiling, throwing the room into harsh relief.

Apart from restrained greetings, no words were exchanged until the men sat down. On one side of the table was Menzies, flanked by Vivien and Sir William Strang, incongruously dressed in white tie and tails, an enamelled cross glinting at his neck. Opposite was Zaroubin, with Manjoulo on his right, dabbing his face with a handkerchief. The Ambassador lit a cigarette; the MGB Colonel fanned the air.

'Good evening, gentlemen.' Sir Stewart put his hand to his mouth to stifle a cough, or a yawn. 'May I start by offering you some refreshment? I fear we are somewhat limited, but tea can, I believe, be rustled up from the kitchen.'

The Ambassador, without glancing at his companion, refused curtly. His nerves showed.

'Well then, perhaps we should get down to business. Introductions are not required. We all know each other by photograph if not by sight.' Sir Stewart smiled. His timing was exquisite. He let the silence fall before beginning again. 'I expect you are wondering why we should go to such trouble to arrange this meeting. This might help to explain, Your Excellency.' He handed the Ambassador the sheet of unheaded notepaper bearing eleven names.

Zaroubin permitted himself barely a glance, his heavy-set face betraying no reaction, and immediately passed the paper to Manjoulo, who bit deeply into his bottom lip as he read and re-read. When he had finished, the MGB *rezident* looked up, his face a mask.

'Only eleven, gentlemen?' he said in surprisingly good English, as he folded and pocketed the list.

'It's enough to be getting on with,' replied Sir Stewart, refusing to rise to the bait. 'No doubt more will fall from the woodwork when we knock again.'

The Russians made no attempt at denial. The game was up and they knew it. The men opposite weren't given to wasting time. Quietly, Zaroubin and Manjoulo waited for the next move. Again, Sir Stewart smiled.

'That list, gentlemen, is, as you can appreciate, a little embarrassing.'

'More for you, I think, than for us,' replied Manjoulo.

'We thought you might say that. I suppose it's really the reason we invited you here.' Sir Stewart was in command: his voice had authority. The Permanent Under-Secretary had often wondered how he had gained the highest office in the Firm, and now he saw why: the man was a consummate actor.

'You are correct. We have a problem. What to do with these men? But then, so do you. What will you do with this?' He pushed a second piece of paper over to the Ambassador. 'Sir William, I believe, gave you something similar yesterday.'

This time, Zaroubin lost his composure. He reddened, clenched his fists, then exploded. 'Monstrous! Lies! All lies!'

Sir Stewart said nothing, but watched calmly as the Ambassador thrust the paper in Manjoulo's direction, muttering something in Russian. The MGB chief's reaction was cooler.

'We shall, of course, maintain this is a forgery,' he said. His greasy face glistened.

'And the facts about the massacre? I suppose you'll tell the Poles they were all lies too?'

'They were.'

Sir Stewart leaned forward; his tone now was that of a schoolmaster. 'You sir, might take them to be so, but let me assure you that twenty-six million Poles do not, and nor will the world once this country takes up cudgels on behalf of truth and justice for Katyn's victims.' His face bore no trace of the embarrassment he felt. 'Have you any idea of the impact of that event?'

'I have some,' answered Manjoulo. 'I understand your point . . .'

'But you have no right to threaten like that,' blustered Zaroubin, riled by the Englishman's urbanity.

'No right, Your Excellency? And by what right did you recruit some of our best young men to your service? This is a dirty game, and we know how to play it as well as you. We'll get strong backing from the United States too, you can be sure of that.'

Manjoulo intervened, pouring his oil on the troubled waters. 'I think what the Comrade Ambassador was trying to say,' and here he smiled, 'was that we fully understand what you are about. The list with the names is bad for you. This . . .' he held up the paper, 'can be unfortunate for us. If we don't reveal the first, you won't do anything about the second. Is that correct?'

Sir Stewart nodded. 'It's all a question of Poland.'

'The point is,' Manjoulo continued, 'who will come off worse if we don't play your game?'

'You have a knack of putting things succinctly, Colonel,' Sir Stewart said approvingly.

'It does no good to confuse matters, I have found.' Manjoulo inclined his head in mock gratitude.

'At least we understand each other. These men cannot remain in operation for much longer. That's obvious. Colleagues of ours elsewhere are already on the track of at least one, so our little bargain will have to be completed within a month. We suggest by the end of April. You will just have to impress the urgency on Moscow. You've had an excellent run for your money. I congratulate you. It was quite a coup. But all good things must end sometime.' Sir Stewart smiled graciously. He had a talent for tossing out sweet, comforting words to sugar the pill.

'Moscow must decide,' added Zaroubin, unnecessarily.

'Quite. And now I think Colonel Vivien has something to say.'

Vivien cleared his throat, adjusted his monocle and began. In contrast to the studied amiability of his master, he was coldly formal.

'Presuming a bargain is concluded, gentlemen, the operation required to bring in these men will have to be delicately handled, and precisely. Not one of the eleven is to be alerted. We, for our part, will do nothing to alarm them – and that includes allowing full access to all information to which they are presently entitled. Is that acceptable?' Vivien looked at Manjoulo, who nodded.

'Unless it's imperative, you will not see the three of us together again. Contact should be made through this number.' Vivien pushed a piece of paper across the table. 'And I need hardly say that if anything leaks out about this meeting we shall deny it completely.'

There was silence.

'Anything more, gentlemen?' Sir Stewart asked courteously.

'Not at the moment. We've got quite enough to interest Moscow, I'm sure of that.' Manjoulo laughed silently, a wry laugh. His face quivered.

The Russians got up to go, and were joined by their hosts, who punctiliously ushered them out. At the door, the Ambassador turned to the Permanent Under-Secretary.

'And your political masters, Sir William? What of them?'

'What of them, Your Excellency?' Sir William assumed a blank expression.

'They do not know?'

'No.' Sir William's reply was brusque. There was a banquet to attend. 'But let me assure you,' he added, 'that for the purposes of the proposal we have just outlined, we three *are* the Government. Let there be no mistake about that.'

'And MI5? Do they know?'

'No.'

'Who else besides you?'

'No one, I assure you.'

'The Americans?'

'No – not yet, at least.'

'And that is how it will remain?'

'If Moscow consents, yes. Forever,' and Sir William adjusted his starched collar, which dug uncomfortably into his neck.

Once outside, Zaroubin and Manjoulo got into the back of a grey Rover saloon, its engine already running. As it pulled away and headed for the centre of London another car followed closely. Inside, not a word was spoken. Manjoulo, his face white by the street lights, turned to Zaroubin, raised his eyes to heaven, drew a finger across his throat, and turned away to face the darkness.

The weather in Washington that afternoon was dismal. Overcast and squally, with fine drizzle descending steadily, it was not the sort of day to be outdoors. John Anderson hated discomfort of any kind, and, returning from lunch, parked his car in the street opposite CIA headquarters, searching for the shortest distance between his car and the office. Pulling the collar of his raincoat up around his ears, and pushing his trilby still further down over his face, he ran into the building, head bent forward, eyes screwed up.

Had it been a better day, Anderson would have noticed a

blue and white Lincoln convertible pull away from the kerb by the CIA headquarters. It belonged to Simon Dyan, a member of the respectable end of the New York rag trade who worked as a front-man for Israeli Intelligence. The two men had had many dealings over the past years. Anderson, as head of the CIA's Soviet-Bloc Intelligence, had become closely involved with the Jews who, in return for CIA assistance, gave theirs generously. It was, therefore, no surprise when a few minutes after reaching his office a secretary came to him bearing a heavily-sealed blue envelope of the kind Dyan commonly used.

Anderson slit it open carefully and pulled out the contents – two sheets of thin paper, carbon copies of originals. One carried a short history of Jewish involvement with a Soviet Military Intelligence officer named Gregor Khopliakin, the other a list of twelve codenames – 'Atticus', 'Dumas', 'Elli', 'Hicks', 'Prometheus', 'Stanley' . . . By each was an indication of the information for which he was responsible.

At the sight of one, 'Homer', Anderson nodded. At another, 'Basil', he smiled as much as he ever did, and the corners of his mouth gave a twitch. He glanced at the heading – 'NKGB-controlled British Operatives, May 1944.' At the bottom in blue ink, were written the words: 'Passed to SIS, Tel Aviv, 19 March 1951.'

Chapter Five

Beria looked drawn, suddenly seeming much older than his fifty-two years. His podgy face, naturally devoid of colour, took on a greenish hue. He removed his rimless glasses and rubbed his eyes. Small and fish-like, they were discoloured, yellowing and so bloodshot that no white could be seen. Then, as if remembering he was a Marshal of the Soviet Union decorated with five Orders of Lenin, Beria drew himself up, putting his hands on the edge of the desk as he leaned forward – strangely delicate hands, almost feminine.

'How many did you say?'

'Eleven, Comrade Marshal,' replied Abakhumov who sat hunched on the edge of a hard chair. 'Almost all we've got.'

Beria put his head in his hands and his elbows on the desk. 'Who are they?' he asked, not looking up. There was a tremor in his voice, barely perceptible, but there.

'The best.' Abakhumov named them one by one, with their posts. Beria knew of them all.

'How the hell did this happen?' Beria's guttural Georgian accent became hard. He jerked his head up. His fist banged the table. 'How the hell did Menzies manage this?'

'I have no idea, Comrade Marshal. He didn't say.' Abakhumov blinked nervously, knowing that would not impress. He clasped his hands together.

'Hardly unusual.' Beria looked down his nose, becoming spiteful. 'But what about you? There aren't fifteen thousand men in your Foreign Intelligence Directorate for nothing, Comrade. Haven't you got even the merest suspicion?'

'No, Comrade Marshal. Nothing.' Abakhumov pulled at his tunic buttons. He paused. 'We'll be strung up for this, you know.'

Beria's expression changed. He smiled, baring his teeth. 'Correction, Comrade Minister. It will be you who'll be strung up. Fortunately, my direct responsibility for your Ministry ended in 1946. You are the man, Comrade. You.' And Beria pointed at Abakhumov with the little finger of his right hand, an affectation he had adopted long ago.

Silence descended on the Marshal's office. Situated deep in the Kremlin, little could be heard of the world outside. Only the clock, an ornate pre-Revolution affair ticking mutedly on the mantelpiece, reminded the men of a greater reality.

Seldom was Lavrenti Pavlovich Beria lost for words, and his silence unsettled Abakhumov further. The Minister of State Security had never been easy in the Marshal's presence, and that Thursday morning was no different. The outside world, he knew, thought them close – and, to a point, they were. After all, Abakhumov owed his post to Beria, and little of importance went on in the MGB about which the Marshal was not informed. But there was no warmth between them. Abakhumov was allowed to exist only because he served Beria's purpose, and he was never allowed to forget that any disagreement would end in his own downfall. For it was the Marshal who ran State Security. It was he, and not Abakhumov, who sat in the Politbureau and had the ear of Stalin.

Such power was well earned. Beria, the son of a peasant from the Black Sea coast, had played hard for it. Certainly, he was a brilliant linguist with a flair for secret activities, but that alone was not enough: he had forced himself to live without a conscience – that had been the secret. He had known just when to flatter and when to lie, when to cajole and when to kill. He had never allowed himself the luxury of goodness for its own sake, or evil. And that, as Abakhumov realized, could not have been easy.

'But what about this blackmail?' asked Beria slowly, coming out of his thoughts. 'Are the documents genuine?'

'Absolutely, Comrade Marshal.'

'How the hell did they get them?'

Silence. Abakhumov opened his mouth as if to speak. His lips trembled, but no sound came.

'Well?'

'I . . . We . . . It's a mystery, Comrade Marshal. A complete mystery.'

'Another? Not good, Comrade Minister. Not Good.' Beria looked with scorn at the cringing Colonel-General, hair greased down, smelling of French cologne. 'So, it's to be Katyn, is it? They wish to use Poland as a pawn in their game?' Again Beria took off his glasses and began polishing them with a square of white silk. 'It's clever of them. Very clever. We've had our worries about that country for some time.'

'Manjoulo assures me, Comrade Marshal, that should Menzies and Strang want to make Katyn a public issue, a matter of government policy, they can do so.'

'Of that I have no doubt. I know how these so-called democracies work.'

'The Americans, we believe, could be easily persuaded.'

'I can see that, too. You have a knack of stating the obvious.'

Another pause. Abakhumov searched for something to say, unable to bear the silence. Anything was to be preferred to that. 'But isn't Katyn too old to have any effect, Comrade Marshal? A point of history?'

Beria smiled contemptuously. 'No, my dear Abakhumov, not to the Poles. It's living proof of our attitude to their damnable little country.' He rose, and began pacing the room. He was a small man, squat, with thin lips, thin hair and small eyes. In the street he could have been taken for a bank clerk; but to those who knew him, Beria almost smelled the animal he was.

'Fifteen thousand were far too little, Comrade – they killed our good Soviet soldiers, after all. But we should have ploughed over Katyn's bones. It was our mistake.' He picked his nose. 'But that's not the point, is it? The point is that not only do the British expose eleven of our best agents, but they want to blackmail us into the bargain. Blackmail the Soviet Union!' He grimaced. 'I can just hear what our Great Leader will say about that.'

The Marshal looked intently at the Colonel-General with eyes which seemed endowed with the property of a rattlesnake's. Abakhumov couldn't take his own from them, however much he tried.

'You, my dear Viktor Semyonovich,' Beria continued, his use of the Minister's Christian name and patronymic sounding ominous, 'you will not be regarded in a particularly favourable light. Not particularly favourable at all.' Again his little finger poked the air towards Abakhumov.

Beria specialized in making people feel uncomfortable. Bullying, he had found, was generally to be preferred for quick results. It also reassured the bully – and Beria needed that. He was worried. In Stalin's Russia, marshals could be cast down with infinitely greater ease than they had been raised up.

'Malenkov will make great play of this, Comrade Marshal. We can be sure of that.' Abakhumov gave voice to Beria's fears. 'He'll push for a Party investigation, and for more Party control. He'll break us.'

Georgi Maksimilianovich Malenkov was a powerful man. Though only forty-nine, as Second Secretary of the Central Committee with the Party apparatus in his hands, he was already a likely successor to Stalin. Whereas in the late 1940s Malenkov had been Beria's ally, by 1951 he was his chief rival. So did power break men apart. Party versus Security – an old story.

Alone, Malenkov could have been dealt with, but his real danger lay in his allies. Foremost were the Politbureau members: Molotov, Kaganovich and Voroshilov were his men, and, in opposition to Beria, he could also count on Khrushchev and Bulganin, all united by fear of the Marshal and resentment of his arrogance. Only the wily Armenian, Mikoyan, stood by Beria's side. His speciality, however, was foreign trade – of little use in a power struggle – and, in any case, he had lost the confidence of Stalin. Any fight in the Politbureau, Beria recognized, would be unequal.

There were others, too: Kruglov, for example, Minister of Internal Affairs, bitter at Beria's transfer of the militia and frontier troops from his Ministry in 1950, and Vyschinsky, Foreign Minister, anxious to gain control of intelligence operations. And there was the Army, resentful of the civilian Marshal and angered by his purges of their ranks. General Zakharov, newly-appointed head of Military Intelligence, was particularly dangerous. Jealous of the MGB's dominance in espionage, and its powers over the GRU, he wanted to see a decrease in State Security's importance. And that demanded the removal of Beria.

In face of such opposition it was essential for the Marshal to retain control of Abakhumov's Ministry, which spread like a cancer through every sinew of Soviet Society. That, and the continued confidence of one man: Stalin. His trust was vital. If that were lost, the Marshal's enemies would drag him down like dogs a bear. Such was Beria's position. It was of a delicacy which SIS's blackmail could ruin.

The clock on the mantelpiece struck twelve. Beria looked up and stared at Abakhumov, who trailed off in mid-sentence. The Colonel-General shifted uneasily in his chair. Not for the first time, he became aware of the toad-like will of the man before him.

'So, State Security is being exposed and blackmailed,' said Beria. 'The question is, what will the Generalissimo say about it?' He paused. 'We must get to him first. The opposition can't have time to make its plans. That's essential.' He looked sharply at Abakhumov. 'And who have you told?'

'No one. Absolutely no one.'

'Not Svinelupov?'

'Especially not Svinelupov.' Abakhumov was vehement, appalled by the idea of telling his deputy even the time of day.

'Good. Then we only have to fear Comrade Ambassador Zaroubin. He's not on our payroll, is he?'

'There's no problem, Comrade Marshal. When we get to him he won't squeal. He's filth, absolute filth.' As with all weak men, Abakhumov liked to exhibit ruthlessness to those he feared. 'I've refreshed my memory. His file says it all. He's worth a fortune, and all from the black market in the war. Morphine.'

Beria smiled. 'Ah, yes. The Generalissimo does have his standards.' And he faked indignation, wagging a finger. 'Morphine! Tut! Tut! Just imagine how many of our brave front-line fighters must have died for lack of it.'

The theatre was over. Beria became serious.

'Get Zaroubin. Find out what he's done. Then we'll move.'

'Must we inform Comrade Stalin?' asked Abakhumov tentatively, nervously. What he was suggesting was treason, an automatic sentence of death. 'If Zaroubin hasn't filed his report, that is. There can be at most twenty men, all mine, directly involved with those traitors, and they can be silenced.'

'Eliminated?'

'Yes.'

'No good. You forget the KI,' replied Beria, referring to the *Komitet Informatsii*, run by Foreign Ministry officials and designed to co-ordinate espionage with foreign policy. 'We can't just shut down all those sources. They're the best we have in the West. They're gold. The KI would notice. No, we've got no alternative.'

Abakhumov blanched. 'Then it's the end?'

'Perhaps, Viktor Semyonovich, perhaps.'

'But Comrade Stalin would never take failure on such a scale without demanding our heads, would he?'

'Please, Comrade Minister, as I have said before, leave me out of this. It's your Ministry. Your head. I advise you to do some tidying up pretty quickly. Find some culprits. Find some answers. Have some other heads to present to our Great Leader on a platter.' Beria grinned. 'But then, I'm preaching to the converted, aren't I? As if Colonel-General Abakhumov requires lessons from me, a humble Marshal, in the art!'

Again, the play-acting, as a cat would with a mouse. Abakhumov feigned dead, and did not reply.

'They're going to crucify us, those bastards.'

General Walter Bedell Smith had lost none of the robustness picked up in the back streets of Indianapolis. As the first private in the US Army to rise to four-star general rank without the civilizing process of West Point, the manners of the rough-neck were always close to the surface. Now, as Director of the CIA, they broke out when he was worried.

'So what the hell do we do?'

The CIA's Deputy Director of Plans, Allen Welsh Dulles, looked up. He had been reading. 'Difficult to challenge in places,' he said. His voice had a calmness, but it failed to soothe.

'Difficult?' the CIA Director exploded. 'Difficult? Well it just happens to be your goddam job to find a way.'

Used to such treatment, Dulles smiled, and reached in his

pocket for a pipe. It didn't worry him: he was his chief's intellectual superior, and both knew it.

'Might take some time, Walter, and we'll almost certainly have to play dirty.' Dulles blew down his pipe, examined the bowl and began to fill it.

'Dirt you can have, but not time.' Bedell Smith sprawled forward across the desk, pointing at the paper that lay on Dulles's knee. 'They're not going to hold off for long.'

The contrast between the two men could not have been greater. Bedell Smith, small, wiry, was every inch the soldier, bustling with energy and command. Dulles, tall, gangly, dressed in tweeds and bow tie, was unmistakably a civilian, a manipulator. His training as diplomat, lawyer and spy made him an obvious candidate as the next chief of the CIA, and the General knew it.

'This is very effective stuff, Walter. Very effective.' Dulles tapped the four-page memorandum with his pipe. He was right. It was a devastating attack, hitting where it hurt most – at the possibility of communist infiltration within the Company itself.

The memorandum bore across its top the names of four men, the heads of the FBI and the three Armed Services Intelligence departments, and carried the lengthy title: 'Unified Views on the Urgent Reorganization of US Intelligence'. The date at the bottom indicated that it had been sent to the President nine days previously. It had only reached Bedell Smith, unofficially, the night before from the hands of a Presidential aide, a favour for past favours.

The authors began by detailing the failures of the CIA, laying particular stress on those that had directly affected the nation's security. In 1948 the CIA gave no warning that a revolution was about to take place in Colombia, the United States' 'back yard'. In 1949 it was taken by surprise when the Soviets exploded their atom bomb. And in 1950 it failed to warn of the North Korean attack, or, later, of Chinese intervention on such a massive scale.

Successive failures in the Company's subversive operations were also noted. First Romania, then Hungary and Finland, where anti-communist elements were betrayed, and finally Albania, where barely a year previously a joint CIA-SIS attempt to mount a coup had ended in failure. Moscow was warned. Of the five hundred Albanian émigrés sent over the border from Greece, only one-hundred- and-fifty had escaped. The inquest was still under way.

Finally, the memorandum pointed to proof of communist subversion within US Government agencies, and asked whether persistent CIA failures were solely the product of inefficiency. Guilt by implication. Unpleasant stuff, but a sign of the times.

'We've got an advantage with Korea,' offered the General. 'The President won't opt for a major intelligence reorganization while there's a war on.'

'Or shouldn't,' replied Dulles, whose opinion of politicians had suffered from close contact. 'I don't think we can make Truman out to be a man who always takes the most logical course. My guess is that our enemies won't hang on until Korea is stabilized.' He struck a match and began to suck at his pipe, momentarily obscuring his features in a cloud of white smoke, so that Bedell Smith was forced to turn to the third man in the room.

John Anderson had remained silent during the exchange, staring up at the plaque on the wall above Bedell Smith's head: an eagle's head above a sixteen-point compass – the CIA badge, symbol of strength and alertness on the radiating spokes of an intelligence system which covered the world. It might be a dodo's head one day, he mused. A dodo's head *rampant*, or would it be *passant*?

The head of the CIA's Soviet-Bloc Intelligence, generally recognized as one of the Company's most brilliant members, refused to get emotional. It was a trait for which he had no time, and as a spy it served him well. Anderson was a cold fish, introverted, disdainful – more like an Englishman, his colleagues said – and it showed in his nose, which was small and stuck-up, revealing its nostrils to the world. He sat hunched, arms folded, spidery fingers pulling at his chin.

But what on earth were they to do? The CIA's plight seemed hopeless. It was a new organization, born in 1947, and had aroused intense jealousy. The FBI, under the bull-like J. Edgar Hoover, was annoyed at being ousted from Central and South America, until then its operational area, and was frustrated in its desire to add intelligence-gathering to its counter-intelligence activities. The military spies, too, were resentful, and eager to find error. And now their criticisms gained greater credibility with every mistake the Company made. They were moving in for the kill.

'Well, John?' Bedell Smith was anxious to draw out the taciturn Anderson. He had come to rely on his opinions.

'I agree with Allen.' Anderson blinked behind thick glasses which magnified his eyes grotesquely. 'We can't bank on the war in Korea to bail us out. Hoover wouldn't have made this move unless he was pretty sure of it. And he's the favourite of Congress at the moment, too. You can bet he's lined up some Senators to lobby the White House. McCarthy will be in the forefront.'

McCarthy: the Senator and his supporters were active in rooting out communists wherever they could find them, and inventing others. It was a witch-hunt which could easily be turned against the CIA.

'Well, if we agree about the urgency of this, what the hell do we do?' General Bedell Smith was unused to the corridors of power that were his new battleground.

'Something spectacular,' returned Dulles. 'Something to make the President realize our potential.'

'Haven't we got anything on Hoover? Nothing to blast his ass?' Counter-attack – the General knew all about that.

But neither Dulles nor Anderson replied. The head of the

FBI had a private life as dull as it was blameless. In the stillness of the room the sound of rain against the windows was audible; the grey office block across the road seemed to melt, then became blurred.

'What have we got in the pipeline on operations, in that case? I'll pull the plug on any of our operatives to get the big one. But it's got to be big.'

There was silence, then Dulles spoke. 'We had been putting all our hopes on Albania.' He crossed and re-crossed his legs, his only sign of unease. 'If we had pulled that off, there would have been a gaping hole in the Eastern Bloc's flank by now. But all it's done is to make us look stupid. We're doing a fairly good job in Latin America, but that's long-term and no way can it be spectacular now. Korea is a shambles, and there's nothing in Western Europe – it's just routine. We've got a meeting with the British next month about an operation in the Ukraine to link up with the resistance there, but that will take at least nine months to produce any results, and by then it could be too late.'

Anderson nodded, and offered no comment.

'So the cupboard's bare?' said Bedell Smith.

'Quite bare,' replied Dulles with finality, again disappearing in smoke. 'Quite bare.'

Anderson remained silent. His manner, composed, betrayed nothing of his thoughts, which at that moment were in a tumult, racing ahead.

Dusk was in the room when Nick entered, and the pink sunset warmed the walls and was reflected in the mirror which hung over the fireplace. Through the windows, the bare branches of the plane trees could be seen, stark against the sky.

No light was on, and from a dark corner Sir William emerged. Nick knew something was up the moment he saw the man smile.

'Ah, Nicholas. Good of you to come,' he said.

The clock on the mantelpiece chimed six, weakly, and then began the deep echo of Big Ben. The head of the Foreign Service took out his fob watch, opened it, checked it, snapped shut the lid, then slipped it back into his waistcoat.

'Never loses a second,' he said with satisfaction. 'Have a seat.'

Things were unusual. Nick was on his guard. Sir William took an interest in people only when he was making trouble.

'Been meaning to have a chat with you, Nicholas,' Sir William continued, drawing up a chair opposite Nick to give the right impression of intimacy. 'Just want to see how things are. Trouble is, I never seem to get any time.'

He blew his nose with a large red-spotted handkerchief, then wiped his moustache. 'You can understand . . .'

Nick nodded. He didn't.

'Now, how's life been treating you here? Happy?'

Nick was unprepared, but kept his composure. 'Yes, Sir William,' he lied, unblinking.

'And the work? Fulfilling? Must seem a little dull sometimes.' Sir William's thumbs rolled over and over each other on his lap.

'Oh, it has its moments,' and Nick grinned, hoping that would suffice. The studiedly casual attitude usually did in the Foreign Office, but not this time.

'Are you ambitious?'

Nick hesitated, then replied that he thought he was.

Sir William appeared pleased. 'A good thing, ambition – but properly applied.' He raised a schoolmasterly finger. 'Shouldn't get too personal about it. The Service must come first – always. Don't you agree, Nicholas?'

Nick thought for a moment before replying. What was the point of arguing? It wouldn't change anything, it could complicate matters and would certainly be a waste of time.

Against propriety, too. But the devil rose. Discretion? It choked humanity.

'Ambition, Sir William? Or self-expression? I don't think you can stifle that – ever. It's too dangerous. You betray yourself, and probably become neurotic.'

The Permanent Under-Secretary snorted, and agitated his moustache. Those few words had shattered his complacency.

'Quite so.' That meant there was no sympathy. 'But don't get above yourself, Nicholas. Never think you know better than the Service. We've been at it a good deal longer than you, you know.'

The words were spoken in a kindly fashion, softly, as if by a wise man to a child, but they weren't advice, Nick knew that. They were a warning: no more about Philby.

'Just remember, Nicholas, that you serve your country, not yourself.'

'But what do you do if you start believing in causes, in "rights" and "wrongs", Sir William?' Nick hesitated, sensing the older man found him naïve. 'Even, perhaps, if you think your country has done wrong.' Secretly Nick cursed himself for being too open. 'Where does duty lie then? To the Service? Or truth?' The challenge was taken.

Sir William shook his head. Again, the smile – this time pity mixed with contempt. 'My dear boy, the way to hell is paved with good intentions. Cultivate a little pragmatism. Remember that we live in a real world. We have to compromise, to know how to get along with – how shall I call it? Evil?' He gave a short, hard laugh. 'You must learn to view it all with detachment, Nicholas. Let work glide over your desk. Don't get involved. You'll find life much easier.'

Again, a warning. Nick gave no reaction, knowing it was pointless.

'And you'll do well, too. That's really what I wanted to say, Nicholas. We're pleased with you. Keep it up. Keep your nose clean, and you'll make it to the top.'

It was the carrot, not the stick, Sir William was using – so far. But Nick knew he was the sort of man who believed the whip was a virtue.

'Remember, you're well on up the ladder.'

Perhaps, thought Nick. The trouble was, the ladder was against the wrong wall.

The interview over, Nick got up to go, and as he did, Sir William noticed for the first time the expression in his eyes. It was uncompromising, defiant, and he knew then beyond any shadow of doubt that Nicholas Pelham meant trouble.

It was on the fifth large Scotch that Nick decided – at the exact moment when the stripper hurled away her G-string and his friends shouted for more. The girl knelt down, offering her breasts to the audience as the curtains closed. The young diplomats, the men that were Great Britain abroad, clapped and whooped, then turned back to their drinks. A band struck up. Nick was nudged.

'Come on, old boy. 'Ave another,' a voice slurred, and a barely-attached head thrust itself into view. It grinned, as a cigar was pulled from its mouth. 'Did you see her?'

'Yes. Lovely.'

'I should shay sho,' and Delmaine, ear-marked for head of Chancery somewhere plush, looked back at the stage, stuck two fingers in his mouth, and whistled. Then the diplomats, five of them in dinner jackets, struck up a chorus of 'For He's a Jolly Good Fellow'. It was Charlie Repton's birthday, and he belched in appreciation. Back from behind the Iron Curtain on a flying visit, he was determined to have his fun.

For once, Nick didn't join in, but looked around, sizing up the clientele of The Lantern Club. The dirty mac brigade in bow ties. He smiled to himself. Could he have ended up like that, working out his frustrations in second-hand sex and alcohol?

But not now. Nick felt saved from all that. He suddenly

became elated, and as his mind cleared he saw for a moment his life with cold pin-point vision. Sir William Strang had been warning him, Nick was sure. Well, it was too late. He would call his bluff. This time, he wouldn't run away.

Nick felt something cold on his head, then wet, and champagne began to dribble down his forehead.

'Wake up, Pelham. The women are coming.' Delmaine giggled coarsely.

Nick raised his head to catch the champagne with his mouth. 'Eat, drink and be merry, for tomorrow we die,' flashed through his mind. But it would be nothing so dramatic – only the sack.

'And what's your name then?' Nick heard a girlish voice, and felt a weight on his knees as arms folded around his neck, blonde hair cascading over his face. Instinctively, his hand moved up the woman's thigh, and his lips searched for hers.

But suddenly the sight that had tortured his sleep for the past few days – the sight of shattered skulls, mouths open, choked with sawdust, row upon row, with their murderers standing at the edge of the pit, grinning – rose up at him.

Abruptly he pushed the girl away, got up and left the room. Outside in the foyer he found a telephone, pressed in some coins, and dialled. A man's voice answered.

'Johnny? That you? Nick here.'

He paused. 'No, of course I'm not drunk . . . Yes, I know the time, damn it. Look, how about a drink tomorrow lunchtime? . . . Come on, Johnny. You know I never bother you . . . Lunchtime then? Thanks, Johnny. Thanks.'

Nick replaced the receiver and paused a moment, his hand on the telephone. He had done as much as he could. There was nothing more, not at past midnight anyway. He took a deep breath, then straightened his jacket and pushed his hair back off his forehead. The girl would be waiting, as they all did for Nick. He could have had an easy life . . .

Chapter Six

Betrayal is an ugly word, and Nick felt unhappy using it about his country. But he did.

'My dear fellow, how can you say that?' The drawl was bored; arms spread themselves out languidly. 'We went to war to save the Poles, after all. How did we betray them? Oh no, that just won't wash.'

'But it does. Don't you see? We sold them down the river, one lie after another. We sacrificed Poland.' Nick raised his voice. His cousin was too stupid sometimes. It went with the chin, or lack of it.

'Do keep your voice down, Nicky. Please.' Jonathan Spencer looked at the waiter, who raised an eyebrow. The bar was fairly full, unusual for a Friday lunchtime.

Nick continued undeterred, but lowered his voice to the confidential whisper acceptable in the House of Commons. Gothic arches and heavy oak panelling seemed to demand hushed tones, an air of intrigue.

'Look Johnny, we went to war because Hitler invaded Poland. We gave a guarantee to safeguard that country's territorial integrity, and all its borders agreed by treaty. No one forced us, but we did. We recognized that the Soviet invasion had as little moral validity as Hitler's, and was indefensible in international law. Then we made public declarations that no discussion of Europe's boundaries should take place until we had defeated Germany. Churchill made the promise himself to the Poles at the beginning of 1942. All that's fine. But then, only a week later, he suggested to the American President that the Soviet Union's post-war borders should be the same as in 1941. That included half of Poland. More than half, actually.'

Jonathan Spencer nodded. He understood that. It did sound fishy. But Churchill . . . He wouldn't do that sort of thing.

'Not much he wouldn't.' Nick sounded rather too adamant for his cousin's liking. 'In early '43 Moscow claimed Eastern Poland and made all its inhabitants Soviet citizens, and the man did nothing. Didn't lift a finger. Nor did Roosevelt. Not even knowing what they did about Stalinist terror. They simply talked about giving Poland East Prussia in exchange. But the Poles didn't want that. They wanted Poland as it was.'

Nick finished off his whisky. The Member for Dorset East motioned to the waiter for another, and looked out over the Thames as if for reassurance. But the river was low.

'Then came Katyn. The Poles blamed the Russians. Highly embarrassing, and all that. "United front against fascism mustn't be weakened!" "The Soviet Union is blameless!" That was a lie, Johnny, and we knew it. The Russians were as guilty as hell. So what do we do? We threaten the Poles. Tell them to shut up and stop blaming our allies. We put pressure on them to withdraw their allegations. We orchestrate the press to demand they show more tact, and refashion their exiled Government to include men who would not play into the hands of the Nazis. We even consider closing down Free Polish newspapers, and we decline to look after Polish interests in Moscow when the Russians suspend diplomatic relations with them. We leave that to the Australians.'

Nick's voice trailed off as the waiter brought the drinks.

'Are you sure about all this, Nicky? It does seem extraordinary. The Foreign Office doesn't tell lies.'

'Nor does it always tell the truth, Johnny. Look at these. Copies of documents in the FO's archives.' Nick flicked through a pile on the table. 'It's all here. Betrayal in black and white. It's a bloody Foreign Office conspiracy.' He wouldn't tell him about Philby. Not until he was sure.

Nick's words had their effect: his cousin became eager. It was strange how normally inoffensive Members of Parliament loved a scandal. It ensured good coverage. They could reach out to their voters.

'Then Johnny, in November 1943, when we'd weathered all the fuss about Katyn, Churchill, Roosevelt and Stalin met and agreed that the Soviet Union should have the major share of the decision on Poland's boundaries. Poland was left out of the discussion altogether.' Nick had raised his voice again. 'So Stalin got all he wanted. We even gave him the decisive say in Poland's post-war constitution. In 1945 we completed the process by withdrawing recognition from the Polish Government in London, and giving it to Stalin's puppets. And so the end of the war, which began to save Poland, ended with her dismemberment and communist domination, all agreed to by us. We didn't even try to prevent it. Just as we had attempted to buy off Hitler with Czechoslovakian territory in 1938, so we bought off Stalin with Poland. Now if that doesn't stink, I don't know what does.'

Jonathan Spencer tugged at his cuffs. 'Must say, it's decidedly rum. But you know, "*real politik*" and all that. We had to keep Stalin fighting Hitler, didn't we? At least, that's how I see it.'

'That was their argument. But just tell me, Johnny, what good did it all do? Stalin would have kept fighting – he had no alternative anyway. Is the world a better place for Poland's sacrifice? Is Europe at peace? Are the principles for which we went to war better served? Or did we betray them? And perhaps, in betraying Poland, we betrayed ourselves.'

The Member for Dorset East looked glum. 'Well, what on earth do you want me to do about it? I can hardly bear responsibility.'

'Get the Foreign Secretary on the spot. Put down a few questions on Katyn. There was a cover-up there, and you can expose it. You'll get the FO on the run, and we can carry on from there. The press is bound to get on to it – they love a conspiracy.'

So did Jonathan Spencer.

At eight o'clock that evening, Friday the 13th, a black Zil saloon with two motorcycle escorts swept through the Russian capital. Down Kovybichev Street it went, free from obstruction in its special lane, at each junction a flashing amber light warning that a Politbureau member was on his way. By such means the servants of the people were kept from their masters. The car then passed through a deserted Red Square, with Lenin's red granite mausoleum on its right, driving up the ramp and through the Spassky Gate into the Kremlin. Passes were shown, guards came to attention and an officer saluted.

The Kremlin, standing on a group of small hills situated on the left bank of the Moskva river, is still the heart of the capital it dominates so completely. Once the centre of Tsarist authority, since 1917 it has come to represent Soviet power, housing the Council of Ministers, the Supreme Soviet and the Politbureau. But in 1951 the Kremlin was, most important of all, the official residence of Joseph Vissarionovich Dzhugashvili, known as Stalin, Secretary-General of the Central Committee of the All Union Communist Party of the Bolsheviks, Chairman of the Council of Ministers, Hero of the Soviet Union, and Generalissimo. It was to this high priest of Marxism-Leninism that the Zil saloon carried his most feared acolytes, Beria and Abakhumov.

Once inside the walls, thirteen feet thick and in those days impenetrable to the ordinary Soviet citizen, the Zil turned right, past the Praesidium of the Supreme Soviet and the Theatre. On its left were the Kremlin's three cathedrals, dominated by the belfry of Ivan the Terrible, imposing creations, black against the night sky. But even these did not get a second glance from the Minister of State Security, who sat slumped in the Zil's luxurious upholstery, staring vacantly. Beria, if he had his thoughts, revealed nothing of them. Instead, he sat expressionless, his podgy fingers tapping out a beat on the armrest.

The Zil drew up outside the classical Senate building, over whose green cupola flew the red flag, floodlit. Sentries came to attention and presented arms. The driver and bodyguard jumped out and held open the doors. Without giving them a glance Beria and Abakhumov ran up the few steps into the entrance hall. Two large marble busts, one of Lenin the other of Stalin, stood before them, and from behind the latter emerged the short, paunchy figure of Lieutenant-General Nikolai Spiridonov, MGB Commandant of the Kremlin. With the precision of the most menial guard, he came to attention to greet his superiors. Unlike his soldiers, he inclined his head as he did so.

'Good evening, General,' said Abakhumov coolly, preserving his distance. By contrast, Beria was warm.

'Kolya! Good to see you, my old faithful. You look well!'

Such was the difference between a Colonel-General and a Marshal of the Soviet Union, thought Spiridonov, who again bowed. Abakhumov noticed the man blushed with pleasure. Beria knew what he was doing. At any one time the Commandant disposed of at least three hundred well-armed guards, and one day their rifles could prove more persuasive than any amount of majorities in the Politbureau.

'The Generalissimo is waiting,' Spiridonov announced. 'In his study.'

'Good, Kolya, thank you. The Colonel-General and I shall walk – alone if you please.' Beria smiled, as graciously as he knew how.

Spiridonov bowed. 'The Generalissimo is a little disturbed tonight, Comrade Marshal.'

‘I understand, Kolya. Thank you.’ Beria smiled again. It was well to be warned.

In silence the two men began to mount the wide staircase, their footsteps echoing on the marble. Halfway, out of earshot to all, Beria cleared his throat and leaned towards Abakhumov, hand on his elbow as if to help him upstairs.

‘What, Comrade, is your knowledge of our Great Leader’s moods?’ he asked softly.

Abakhumov looked surprised. That was the last question he had expected so near to the Presence. ‘My meetings with him, as you know, are few and far between,’ he replied. So they were. As Minister, Abakhumov was called usually once a month for an hour at a time. Each meeting terrified him, though, as much as the first had done. He found those twelve hours a year a heavy price to pay for power. ‘But I have felt his moods.’

Who among the Soviet leadership hadn’t? Reporting to Lenin’s heir was like handling a detonator – one mistake, and it could be the last.

‘Well, remember, Comrade,’ advised Beria, ‘the Generalissimo is a child at heart. Be like Jesus, and suffer him.’

The Marshal didn’t laugh; nor did the Colonel-General. But Beria wasn’t finished. He halted and turned, placing his face close to Abakhumov, who, for the first time, smelled the brandy on his breath.

‘And keep looking in his eyes,’ he whispered, poking the Minister in his ribcage. ‘Whatever else, do that. Don’t turn away. Don’t lower them. The Generalissimo judges a man by his eyes.’

By the time the two men had reached the second floor, where the offices were situated, Beria was breathless and unable to greet the tall, immaculately dressed Guard major as he would have wished. A pair of highly polished jackboots clicked together, another head inclined, then, in silence, the security chiefs were led towards the presence of the All Powerful.

In the outer office they were met by Alexander Poskryobyshev, the final barrier between the dictator and the world. Whenever the bald, white-fleshed ex-veterinary surgeon spoke, even his suggestions were treated as orders. For as Chief of the Secretariat, he alone had constant access to Stalin. Although only a Lieutenant-General, he felt no deference to the Colonel-General in front of him, and it was simply because he possessed the soul of a servant that he bowed to the Marshal.

'Good evening, gentlemen,' he said, not even bothering to use the statutory 'Comrade'.

'Greetings, Comrade Poskryobyshev,' replied Beria, with a tone in his voice unusual for him, one verging on respect. 'Do we find you well?'

'In spirit as well as body, indeed you do,' the man answered, holding his hands clasped before him. Even his speech seemed out of place. A strange lackey, Abakhumov thought. Stalin had imprisoned his wife, yet there he was, the dictator's faithful servant still.

'And is the Generalissimo in good health?'

'A little poorly, today, thank you, Marshal.' Poskryobyshev spoke exclusively to Beria as if Abakhumov did not exist. 'I think you had better go straight in.' With that he turned the gilded handle of a heavy oak door. 'Comrade Marshal Beria and Comrade Minister Abakhumov to see you, Generalissimo,' he announced.

With palms sweating, the two men entered.

Strangely for the hour at which they had arrived, Beria and Abakhumov found themselves in the dictator's daytime study, a well-proportioned oblong room which caught the sun whenever it was out, bright in decor, modern in taste, and, by night, well lit – the Generalissimo had seen to it there were no dark corners. Comfortable enough, and functional, but to Abakhumov the study resembled a mausoleum, as much a memorial to its occupant as Lenin's tomb several hundred yards away. Around the walls were bookcases carrying the gems of Communist thought, prominent among them Stalin's own works, bound in bright red leather and embossed in gold. On the walls hung several large pictures, all of the dictator himself in various poses and uniforms. Abakhumov noticed that the curtains covered only the frames of the windows instead of reaching to the floor. They might look ridiculous, but were considered safer, he realized. No assassin could hide behind them.

Beside a desk bare of paper stood Stalin, small, white-haired, stooping, with an open book in hand. Undistinguished apart from his moustache, under which a cigarette hung, he appeared tired and feeble, his face pock-marked, quite unlike the portraits of the Great Leader surrounding him. He wore a simple grey military tunic, a row of medal ribbons, and black trousers. As the two men approached he removed his cigarette and showed his yellowing teeth.

'Welcome, Comrades. How good of you to come and see an old man.' The smile dropped away as suddenly as it had arrived. 'But why?'

Abakhumov stood to attention and said nothing. Beria, outwardly more relaxed in the company of the man he had seen almost daily for the past twelve years, moved forward.

'Comrade Stalin, we have come for advice,' he purred soothingly.

The dictator's beady eyes flickered from one man to the other, searching . . . Both looked at him, full in the face.

'Well then, let us sit.' Stalin gestured to the hard chairs around his desk.

In the silence that followed, Abakhumov had an opportunity to survey the man on whose confidence his life depended. Stalin was clearly ill – that much Abakhumov knew from the fact that a special Politbureau medical commission, composed of Beria, Malenkov and Molotov, had been appointed to look after him. Its proceedings were so secret that even he, Minister of State Security, had no idea of the facts. But he could see the listlessness of the seventy-one-year-old Generalissimo, a vacancy of expression alien to Stalin the Nation Builder that had once been.

That, too, was obvious to Beria, who knew the prognosis. A couple of years at most was all Stalin's constitution would stand. A couple of years – that was all Beria had to hold out. Then, the big battalions would decide the issue. Beria would be safe – and Secretary-General. But would this new crisis allow him the two years he needed?

'Well, and what is it?' snapped the dictator, as if suddenly remembering there was business to do. He stubbed out his cigarette in short, impatient jabs.

'Comrade Stalin . . .' began Beria, in a tone more suited to discussion of the weather. Abakhumov could not help admiring his nerve. ' – Comrade Stalin. I thank you for seeing us at such short notice.'

'So you should.' The interruptions were beginning. 'I had no intention of staying here tonight. I want to be back in Blizhny.'

'And it is much appreciated by myself and the Minister . . .'

'You could have come to Blizhny.' Stalin was becoming petulant. 'It's not far. Why didn't you come? Must it always be me who makes the sacrifice? Must it?'

'We weren't told. Of course we would have gone there had we known. It would have been our pleasure.'

'Well, ask next time. Moscow doesn't agree with me, you know that.'

'Of course, Comrade Stalin. We all like the country . . .'

It was like dealing with a child, Abakhumov thought.

'But the matter is of importance. We need your advice.'

'Yes, yes, so you've said . . .' The old man was irritable. Beria was off to a bad start. 'Get on with it.' Stalin reached for the silver case on his desk and drew out one of his favourite Troika cigarettes, pointedly refusing to offer them to his guests. The Marshal was relieved to see the dictator took no notice of his doctors.

'Comrade Stalin,' Beria began again, looking at his master full in the face. 'Comrade Abakhumov here has run into difficulty . . .'

The Minister of State Security had not expected that. The sweat ran along his back; his scalp prickled.

'The British, I'm afraid, know all about most of the traitors the Minister has in their service – eleven of them. They are the men who give us the best information we get from the West – by far. It's a major loss for the Minister.' Beria had said those words simply, without any emotion. Yet, by them, he had ditched Abakhumov completely.

The Marshal then went on to remind Stalin of the background to the affair. It had all begun in the early 'thirties, the result of a brilliant plan conceived by Litvinov, Commissar for Foreign Affairs. He had recognized that the strength of the British Establishment was also its weakness, and that the institutions basic to Britain's dominance in the world were built on a loose structure of trust, honour, and gentlemanly behaviour. The 'old-boy' network was not simply a catchphrase: it was reality.

But, Litvinov had argued, what if some of its members conspired to undermine that very structure they were held to support? How would such men be suspect in a country where good breeding was a qualification above question? The prime aim of Soviet espionage, therefore, should be to subvert the brilliant but disaffected among the British upper classes. And in the 'thirties, at a time of crisis for capitalism, of Fascism on the rise, and optimism for the Communist experiment, the Soviet intelligence services had found willing recruits. Undergraduates of the best universities were trained by their new masters in the art of deception, and took jobs where they could be of most use. By 1938 the process was complete, and information began to flow to Moscow, at first a trickle, then a flood. By the height of the Cold War, its value had never been greater. And now, all at once, it was over.

While Beria was talking, the dictator sat impassively, even at the news of the spies. But his steel-grey eyes narrowed, and turned from the Marshal to the Colonel-General, searching for signs of betrayal.

'And that's not all,' added Beria. 'Deeply wounding though that might be to the Comrade Minister's operations – and we cannot underestimate it . . .'

Abakhumov, sitting to attention, felt the sweat break out again. He tightened his fists but said nothing. Beria had the floor. A Colonel-General could only speak when spoken to.

'That's not the end. The problem is as acute to British Intelligence as it is to us. Were the extent of the treachery to become public knowledge, faith in British Security – indeed the whole government system – would take a severe blow. Co-operation with the Americans might be shattered. Western security would need years to recover.'

Stalin listened intently. All signs of illness were gone. Not for one moment did he take his colourless eyes off Abakhumov. The Minister began to feel uneasy about staring back. His head ached.

'So in a situation like that,' continued Beria, 'we should ensure the world got to know about these traitors. Highly embarrassing for us, it would be disastrous for the capitalists. The only use those men have got for us now is to destroy the British system.'

'So what's stopping us?' Stalin was menacing. He reverted his gaze to Beria.

'Blackmail, Comrade Stalin. Blackmail.' The Marshal's calmness underscored the drama. 'The capitalist pigs want to blackmail the Ministry of State Security.'

'What?' snapped Stalin.

'Blackmail. They are going to use Katyn. They are going to throw it in our faces. They will do all they can to lose us Poland.'

Silence followed, empty at first, but gradually filling as Stalin's anger gained authority over his initial incomprehension. His face, naturally red, became puce. His lower eyelids puckered. Beria prayed for rage; the dictator's silences were far more dangerous. He was in luck. Stalin brought down his fist.

'I will not have it. I will not allow another Yugoslavia. I will not!' he yelled, and pushed his chair back so violently that it fell to the floor. The two security chiefs jumped up. Stalin went round his desk.

'I hold you responsible,' he shouted, pointing at Abakhumov. 'Totally! It's incomprehensible. Blackmail! Blackmail of Soviet power! I will not have it!'

Going up to the Minister, standing quivering to attention, Stalin spat in his face. 'You! You!' His forefinger jabbed the man in the chest. 'I find *you* responsible.'

Abakhumov stood staring straight to his front, unblinking, his thumbs rigid along his trouser seams, letting the dictator's thick yellow-green sputum fall slowly down his face. Beria, no stranger to such behaviour, kept his eyes on his master, judging the moment to intervene. But for two or three minutes more Stalin raved. To many, this might have appeared a strength, the righteous indignation of the All Powerful. But not to Beria and Abakhumov. Both had been policemen too long; their noses scented human weakness, and they found it in Stalin. The Greatest Genius of History was afraid.

But this was little comfort to Abakhumov, who, unflinchingly, bore the brunt of abuse.

'And why, you fool, did you allow this to happen? Eleven men! Eleven! And all at once! There can only be one explanation. It's treachery! It's a plot. Your Ministry is riddled with spies. And you've just sat there, twiddling your thumbs, letting it happen. You and your gold braid.' He made a lunge at the Colonel-General's left epaulette. Fortunately for Abakhumov, its button held.

'And they want to blackmail us. Blackmail the Soviet Union! Me! With Poland! And all because of you, you brainless worm!'

Again he rushed at Abakhumov, and struck him on the chest. But the blow was weak: the storm had nearly blown itself out. 'I shall not allow another Yugoslavia. That fascist swine Tito will be the only one! The only one!' Stalin sank into a chair, exhausted. His arms hung limply. The rage was over.

Beria sensed his time had come and moved over to the All Powerful, leaving Abakhumov standing in the middle of the room, wiping the sputum from his face with his hand. He didn't dare get a handkerchief. The dictator, in his excited state, might have thought he was drawing a gun. It had happened before.

'Comrade Stalin.' Beria's voice was soothing. 'We must make decisions. Of course, you are right. There have been grave misdoings in State Security. But they can be dealt with.' Beria bent down and squeezed his master's shoulder. The old man looked up, his eyes grateful.

'We live in sick times, Comrade. Sick times.'

Beria smirked. He was now intimate, reassuring. 'But we can manage it. We've done it before, you and I.'

Stalin calmed. 'Yes, Lavrenti Pavlovich, we have. And we shall do it again.' His eyes became cold. 'How many was it before – two hundred thousand? Three hundred thousand? Well, it'll be twice that this time, eh?'

Abakhumov shuddered. He remembered those purges, when Beria had strengthened his hold over State Security. One of the victims had been its former chief, Yezhov, 'the bloody dwarf', shot in the same Lubyanka headquarters as Abakhumov now occupied.

'But that's not enough,' continued Stalin, struggling to sit up. 'The damage has been done. What are we to do? Poland must remain tied to us. I cannot allow it to go. I will have no more Yugoslavias.' He paused, becoming plaintive. 'But we can't submit to blackmail. We can't show weakness.'

The dictator's dilemma was real. Apart from Hitler's invasion in 1941, perhaps the greatest shock in twenty-two years of rule had been Yugoslavia's break with Soviet authority in 1948, an event which did irreparable damage to Stalin's prestige. His health never recovered, nor his confidence. The thought of Tito's defection tortured him. He tried to purge reality: in every one of his own portraits his Yugoslav decorations were painted out, and Soviet history was rewritten to exclude all but the meanest references to Tito. And thanks to the wonders of Soviet science, photographs were reprinted with the man's portly figure missing altogether. But failure made Stalin determined that no such thing would happen again. Nothing would be allowed to jeopardize the unity of the Socialist bloc, certainly not Poland.

But blackmail? Could the Soviet Union be shown so weak as to yield to the threats of just three men in Britain? Where, Stalin asked Beria, might one surrender lead?

After twenty minutes the dictator tired. His fatigue became obvious.

'Now I must rest, Lavrenti Pavlovich. We must discuss this in the Politbureau. Until then, do what you can.' Stalin turned to look at Abakhumov, still standing to attention in the middle of the room. 'And get that fool to do something.' With a burst of energy he flung his arm out at the Minister, a trembling finger pointing accusingly. 'I don't want to hear of him until he's got something useful to say. I want that viper's nest in his Ministry cleaned out.'

Abakhumov inclined his head in acquiescence.

'Now go, and send Poskryobyshev to me.'

Beria got up, and made his farewells to the dictator. His constancy was assured. Abakhumov clicked his heels and bowed, receiving not the slightest recognition.

Neither security chief spoke until they were outside the

Kremlin's gates. The drive seemed long, but only when they were crossing Red Square did the Minister's anger at his humiliation and betrayal break to the surface.

'Comrade,' he growled, 'if I go, I shall drag you down too, so help me, I will.'

Beria did not reply, made no movement, but kept staring out of the window. The silence pierced Abakhumov. He wanted to shout out, run, beg forgiveness.

Slowly, the Marshal turned his head.

'Comrade Minister, you have much to learn still,' he said quietly. 'And you have much to live for. It's foolish to hasten your end unnecessarily.' It was dark, but Beria could feel the man's terror. He smiled. 'But let's not quarrel. You might get away with your head yet. We shall talk about it.'

Beria needed Abakhumov – that was what would keep the Minister alive.

Chapter Seven

Blizhny, Stalin's dacha, thirty miles from the Soviet capital down the Mozhaisk highway, was a world apart. Closely guarded by walls, watch-towers and searchlights, no one could get in or out without a red and white pass approved by Stalin himself. He had come to detest Moscow: its vastness unnerved him so that only in Blizhny did he feel secure. By day he would sit and read, tend his roses in the fir-ringed garden, and feed the birds. By night he would curl up on a sofa, temporarily made up as a bed, the fire blazing, and stare for hours at the ceiling, uncomprehendingly, vacantly. At such times, those around him feared for his sanity.

But even there Stalin was prey to depression: loneliness haunted him and he craved for his comrades. Around him, they couldn't plot his downfall.

The Politbureau arrived, as summoned, just before midday on Sunday, 15 April. All came singly, none wishing to share their convoy with another. First to arrive was Molotov, former Foreign Minister, a man who lived by the clock, closely followed by Voroshilov, Stalin's whipping boy, a soldier and Marshal of the Soviet Union fully prepared to crawl on all fours in imitation of a nanny-goat to raise a smile on the lips of his master. Then came Kaganovich and Mikoyan, the Ukrainian Communist Party's First Secretary and the Party's trade specialist, arriving simultaneously, much to their annoyance. They were followed by Khrushchev, Secretary of the Moscow Party and the Central Committee. A slight pause, and then his great ally, the one-time Minister of Defence, Bulganin, arrived, and close behind his great rival, Malenkov.

The men were shown into Stalin's favourite downstairs room, bathed in sunlight, to be greeted by the dictator, dressed in his grey uniform, standing on a large oriental rug in front of a fire of pine logs. Above hung an indifferent portrait of Lenin, and opposite a reproduction of the famous painting, Repin's 'The Zaphorezhe Cossacks' Reply to the Sultan'. Around the walls were photographs of children cut from magazines, pinned there by Stalin himself. In the corner above the sofa on which he usually slept was his favourite – the picture of a young girl spoon-feeding a lamb.

As was customary at these meetings, each man received the greeting which Stalin's feelings demanded. For Molotov, the faithful robot, a smile and a handshake. For Voroshilov, a slap on the back in addition. For Mikoyan, a slight bow and a gruff good morning. Malenkov, as had long been customary, received a hug.

Midday struck. The men stood round, awkwardly, waiting for the last of their number to arrive. Beria, as so often, was late.

'He will come pleading pressure of work, I know,' declared Stalin, only slightly annoyed. He knew the Marshal chose to be late on purpose. It made more of an effect.

'It's not good enough, Comrade Stalin,' commented Malenkov, smiling nervously, 'keeping you waiting like this. Where is the man's respect?'

'Same place as yours, Georgi Maksimilianovich. In his arse.' The dictator exploded in laughter. 'But as long as I can kick it, I don't mind.'

The others smiled politely. It was too early to enjoy their master's humour. Better to save that for later, with the alcohol. Stalin sensed their reticence.

'Well, Comrades, can I offer you anything while we wait? A "worker's norm"?' he asked, referring to the favoured drink of the masses – a slug of vodka with a beer chaser. Only in this instance the vodka wouldn't be the cheap variety; it would be the expensive, odourless Stolichnaya.

'Or coloured water, perhaps?' Stalin again let out a roar. Malenkov and Mikoyan looked embarrassed. They remembered the occasion Stalin discovered they had bribed waiters to bring them coloured water instead of wine. His fury had been terrible then, but now he laughed. He could afford to – they had no alternative but to get drunk. It was a measure of his power over them.

At the dictator's command bottles were brought and placed on the large mahogany table. Beer and two types of vodka were supplied, the Stolichnaya, favoured by most of the men present, and Starka, a mature variety, more heady, preferred by Voroshilov. Stalin began the morning with Armenian brandy, a taster of which he ordered a waiter to sip. Cigarettes were also brought, Troika for the discerning, Belomor for the addicts. The men drank eagerly, the only way to overcome their nervousness. But, in any case, Stalin had demanded that they drink.

At a quarter past twelve Beria arrived, full of apologies as Stalin had predicted. The dictator greeted him, but without the usual warmth. The Marshal, as if not noticing, smiled, the selfish, hard-set corners of his mouth momentarily obscured in wrinkles.

'You have come, I see,' said Stalin sarcastically. 'So good of you, Comrade Beria, so good of you. Now perhaps the meeting can begin – that is, if you have no objection.'

Beria made no comment, but inclined his head as if in humility. To himself, he cursed his mistake and reached for the brandy: things were going to be difficult.

The eight men took their appointed places around the table. As Stalin sat down his manner changed. He became silent, brooding, and glared at each Comrade in turn, searching intently for the least sign of betrayal – a blush, a nervous tic, or eyes which looked away. All, to a man, stared back.

'Comrades,' he said at last, 'We are meeting today for a specific reason. Comrade Marshal Beria has some interesting news.' Stalin nodded towards his security chief.

Beria took off his glasses, rubbed his eyes, and began. His heart beat in his eardrums, his palms were sticky, but the others did not notice. To them his arrogance was overbearing.

'Comrades,' he began. 'Soviet power rests on its security apparatus. On that, we can all agree.'

'No, Comrade Marshal, we can't,' Malenkov interrupted immediately. 'It rests on the Party.'

So that was how it was to be, thought Beria: Malenkov already stirring up trouble. Had Ambassador Zaroubin got to him before he was silenced?

'Indeed, Comrade Malenkov. Quite so,' Beria replied, his lips pursed. 'Let me rephrase it. Soviet power does, of course, rest on the Party. The Party, without doubt, rests on the security apparatus.'

Stalin smiled. Khrushchev laughed out loud. Round one to Beria. A petty victory, but one worth having. It was the sort of thing which impressed.

Malenkov, a plump man with a Mongol cast to his features, sat still, but his dark eyes flickering over the others revealed that, for him, the fight had only just begun. A skirmish lost, there was the battle to win.

'We have, Comrades, had our failures . . .' Beria continued.

'Yes, you have had your failures.' Malenkov was venomous. 'But where does this confession, laudable though it is, Comrade Beria, get us? We are all only too well aware of State Security's flaws.'

Malenkov reminded Beria of a cat, crouching low, teeth chattering, ready to pounce.

'No more aware than Comrade Stalin and I, Comrade Malenkov.' The Marshal placed himself alongside the dictator in defence. 'That is why Comrade Stalin has asked us here today. Minister Abakhumov has had disturbing news from London.'

Beria explained the problem in as few words as possible, keeping his language simple in an attempt to play down the importance of what he was forced to say. It was useless. When he told of the eleven spies, several of his listeners gasped openly. When he broke the news of the Katyn blackmail, they reacted noisily. By the expression of incredulity on his face, Malenkov was surprised by the information. That was the only relief.

'But this is disgraceful,' stammered Molotov, pushing his rimless glasses to the bridge of his nose. 'The Motherland cannot be blackmailed. It's unheard of.'

'Never,' echoed Lazar Kaganovich, creator of the Moscow metro and destroyer of the Ukrainian smallholders. The hair on his square head bristled with indignation. 'Tell the British to run along and play games with somebody else. Not us.'

Voroshilov banged his fist on the table. His medals clinked – he always wore a full set. 'Generalissimo, the Soviet Army is behind you in any decision you make. We are prepared to resist blackmail with all the force at our disposal.'

'And what do *you* think, Comrade Khrushchev?' asked Stalin. 'You dealt with Poland during the war, didn't you?'

The burly Ukrainian who had 'Sovietized' annexed Polish-Ukrainian territory drew himself up. His innate caution revealed itself at once.

'Menzies and his crew can hit us hard on Katyn. We're weak, very weak.' Khrushchev breathed deeply, knowing that truth was not always wanted in Stalin's Politbureau. 'Poland is ripe for trouble. We should consider agreeing to their terms. No one but us and them will know about it.

How many? Twenty people? That's nothing to worry about, not if it saves us a great deal of trouble. After all, Lenin taught that we should occasionally sup with the devil.'

Stalin looked displeased; Khrushchev's argument did not appeal: it smacked of conciliation. So he took over. 'Poland, always Poland. We've had trouble from those swine ever since the Revolution. In 1920 they took land from us. In the 1930s they plotted against us. In 1939 we had to invade them. Then we had to liberate them. After that, we had to impose socialism. And with what thanks? Now, despite all precautions, we are still faced with trouble.' Stalin paused, gathering strength.

'For our people,' he continued, 'Poland is not just a question of honour. It's a question of security. Throughout history that mean piece of land has been the corridor through which our enemies have passed eastwards. Twice in thirty years the Germans have done so.' His fist hit the table. 'Twice! It is in our interest that Poland should be strong, a bastion, able to shut the door of this corridor by her own force. But, Comrades, that can only be if she is tied irrevocably to us. We cannot afford to let her go. I will not allow another Yugoslavia. That fascist Tito has taught me a lesson. Poland shall not go the same way. She cannot!'

The old man finished. He had spoken with force. The men around the table were silent. As usual, none dared disagree. On this occasion, however, Stalin had spoken for them all. Poland was vital and could not be allowed to weaken the Eastern bloc. That much was certain. But the question which still remained to be answered was: did the British threat pose a real danger? Could Katyn be the spark to set off the fire of Polish revolt?

The argument went back and forth across the table at Blizhny with an intensity and urgency few of Stalin's Politbureau meetings could match. The decision to support

North Korea had been the last occasion of similar drama, and that had been twelve months previously. Before that, there was the explosion of the atom bomb, the Berlin blockade, and Yugoslavia. Always Yugoslavia!

Stalin was still fretful. 'I've never trusted those Polish communists. In 1938 I had to accuse them of being agents of capitalist espionage. We abolished their Party, and shot their leaders. But, you see, they didn't learn. Those revisionists thought they knew best, and I had to deal with them in 1949. My only fear is that we've been too lenient. They haven't got the guts required to establish socialism.'

Stalin's fear was contagious, and it was Molotov who, in the absence of any other, finally summed up the dilemma before the Politbureau. Katyn, he argued, was a risk. In Poland's present circumstances it could either cause open disaffection or provide an excuse for the rulers to distance themselves from the Soviet Union – or both. Though knowing nothing of the conspiracy in the Polish Army, the threat, they all agreed, was real enough. But what to do about it? On one side was Khrushchev, backed by Bulganin and Mikoyan – give in to the blackmail. The loss of face was minimal and worth the trouble spared. If nothing else, any Soviet occupation would have to bear Poland's economic problems, which were considerable. On the other side were Molotov, Voroshilov and Kaganovich – accept the risk, they urged, expose the traitors. On no account should the Soviet Union submit to blackmail.

To the discussion, the two most powerful men after Stalin contributed nothing in the way of solutions. They listened, noting every subtle turn of phrase uttered by the others, but they were not ready to commit themselves. Rejection was to be avoided at all costs. Malenkov in particular had other matters to think over. At that moment the vulnerability or otherwise of the Soviet Union didn't interest him – not compared with the vulnerability of Beria. When discussion on Poland seemed to be nearing its end, Malenkov put the question the Marshal dreaded.

'But, Comrades, let us not forget the Ministry of State Security. How did they allow us to get in such a mess in the first place?' Without waiting for a reaction, he continued. 'Eleven spies. By Comrade Beria's account, long-term spies. Important men, not just flashes in the pan. Committed communists, not just mercenaries or sexual deviants. Clever men, not fools. Eleven – just like that.' He clicked his fingers. 'All at once, out of the blue. And Comrade Beria would like us to think it happened quite by chance. Comrades, that sort of thing doesn't happen that way. There's more to it than that. Much more.'

Malenkov stopped and looked around. His words had had their effect. All listened attentively, only Beria affecting unconcern. Malenkov continued, aware he had gained the initiative.

'And Comrade Beria likes to give the impression that Minister Abakhumov is responsible. Well, so he is. So he is. But remember, that man is Comrade Beria's creature. The two have worked in the same harness together, side by side. Comrade Beria, to whom the Generalissimo has given so much responsibility for our security, must provide us with information. There is more to this matter than he likes us to think.'

Malenkov had made his mark. He had gone as far as he could towards accusing Beria. All turned to the little Georgian. Mikoyan, his only ally, was silent. So too was Stalin, whose eyes had not moved from his security chief since Malenkov began speaking. A scapegoat would have to be found – Stalin had realized that from the outset. Until then, however, he had thought only of Abakhumov and his subordinates. But should retribution include the Marshal too? Was it time the executioner fell under his own axe? Beria and Malenkov guessed his thoughts. The battle was on.

But before swords could be fully drawn there was a knock on the door and the bald head of Poskryobyshev appeared.

'Generalissimo, luncheon is served. It is two-thirty, as you ordered.'

Stalin beamed. The day, for him, was just beginning. 'Thank you, Chief, thank you. Come and join us.'

The others groaned inwardly. The chief of Stalin's secretariat would be in attendance for the rest of the day, to be carried home dead drunk as usual. Nor was the meeting over. It was just postponed, to continue late into the night, through the eating and the drinking, the horse-play and the drunken anger, until a decision was reached.

Poskryobyshev's head disappeared, the door opened wide, and in trooped seven white-jacketed waiters carrying white linen, silver cutlery, gilt-embossed plates and ornamental table furniture. Behind them bustled the Chief, organizing every detail as if his life depended on it. The Politbureau members stood around in awkward silence, looking at Stalin's pictures on the walls, as they had done a hundred times before.

Next came food and drink. First, the bottles, prominent among which was Stalin's favourite – Kinzmarauli, a heady red wine from his native Georgia, injurious to his blood pressure. When he drank it by the bottle his Comrades rejoiced. Champagne, too, was brought in silver ice-buckets. Then, the food: savouries, two decorated sturgeon and Caucasian shashlik. Stalin rubbed his hands.

When the table was complete the waiters withdrew, leaving the Soviet leaders to help themselves. But before the door was finally shut, in bustled Matryona Petrovra, the dictator's old retainer, carrying an ornate wooden bowl filled with greens.

'Well, Comrade Beria, here's your grass,' the woman mocked in her nasal tone. She was one of the two people in the Soviet Union who didn't mind her tongue in Beria's presence. The Marshal, a vegetarian, always had his food brought over from his dacha. Whether he was genuine in this habit, none could determine. Certainly, it had the effect of marking him as a man different from the rest, but it also saved him from having to stuff his belly with unwanted food.

'Comrade,' Stalin would say to a man helping himself to food, 'neither men nor bulls can survive without mating,' and he would place another, larger, helping on his plate. Then with a glint in his eye he would add, 'But, come to think of it, two doesn't go far. God favours the Trinity.' Only Beria, busily feeding himself by hand, was immune.

And so the Politbureau continued, much as normal. Stalin succeeded, as he always did, in his aim of forcing each man to eat and drink more than he wished. But by six o'clock the feast was stalling. Stalin's guests, their heads swimming, struggled to keep their eyes open. The old stories, which had done the rounds of the dictator's table a thousand times, had had their customary airing, and on the carpet, flat on his back under Lenin's canvas gaze, Poskryobyshev snored. The time had come. The game would resume.

'And now, my blind kittens,' Stalin began contemptuously, looking slowly round the table, sizing each man in turn, his eyes malicious, bloodshot, fired by alcohol. 'We have some unfinished business, I believe. Comrade Beria, what was it? Remind us.'

Malenkov grinned menacingly, and remembered the verse by Marshak: 'I do not need the blood of sheep. I need the blood of men.'

'It was Minister Abakhumov's failure, Comrade Stalin,' replied Beria, his face expressing no emotion at such open betrayal. 'Comrade Malenkov here was asking what more we could do. I presume that he questions what you have done to maintain supervision of State Security.'

That was clever. The Marshal had sidestepped and

deflected the attack – for the time being. The dictator, not fooled by Beria's manoeuvring, allowed himself to be turned off course. It was Malenkov's turn to sweat.

'So, Comrade Malenkov, you were questioning my competence in keeping on top of the bunglers at State Security, were you?'

But Malenkov, likewise, did not bat an eyelid; he knew that for the moment the dictator was playing.

'Comrade Beria misleads you, Comrade Stalin, as, I fear, he misleads us all. I didn't question your competence. I would, however, suggest that your trust might be misplaced through the loyalty you have for old associates.'

'You mean, do you, that those who guard me might one day shoot me in the back?'

'I do. Indeed, I wonder whether they are not already squeezing their triggers.'

The drink had had its effect. The innuendo and suggestion had sharpened. Suspicion seemed to fall from the sky. The dictator looked at Beria, and noticed the sweat on his upper lip. Yes, there was something in what Malenkov said.

And so the cuts and thrusts continued, each man attacking and parrying with his wits, manoeuvring through the ritualized in-fighting of Stalin's Politbureau. A false step, and each knew Stalin would pounce. For a time the spectacle was enjoyed by all – Voroshilov, grateful to be free of persecution; Mikoyan, happy to have escaped it altogether; Khrushchev, disliking both antagonists, savouring each draw of blood; and so on, round the table. Even Poskryobyshev woke up to observe the proceedings, and, raising his back off the floor, tried to focus on each of the men in turn. His squinting, mobile face appearing above the table made a comic backdrop to the magisterial Stalin sitting in judgement below Lenin's portrait, but no one laughed.

It was Beria who made the first slip. In referring to the

blackmail, he called it an insignificant affair. That was fatal.

'Insignificant, you bloated little liar!' shouted Stalin, jerking forward, his hands gripping the edge of the table. 'Insignificant, you say? The blackmail of the Soviet Union, insignificant! Do you think I fought that man Hitler to have a worm like Menzies dictating to me? And you – you try to belittle your failures while I have to get us out of this mess. So that's how you go on, eh?'

Malenkov couldn't conceal his satisfaction, and the muscles in his face drew a smile. Beria fixed his gaze at the spot between Stalin's eyes. But the dictator wasn't finished. Building fear upon suspicion until his rage became uncontrollable, he pushed back his chair, nearly hitting the dazed Poskryobyshev, and advanced on the Marshal, lent over him and blew smoke in his face. A bizarre performance. It had been seen before, but never against Beria.

'And what have you done about that fool Abakhumov? He's still walking free, I suppose, letting our secrets leak away through that sieve of a Ministry of his. Perhaps he's punching the holes himself? Eh? A British spy?' Stalin put his face inches from Beria.

'Don't think I don't know about his antics during the war. Trainloads of booty – trainloads went back to our Colonel-General Abakhumov, rivalled, no doubt, only by your boatloads. Bourgeois thieves! And you say that blackmail is unimportant! Well, let me tell you, Marshal, you might only live for those little street girls you are so fond of, but I live for the advancement of our Cause. I have to concern myself with this blackmail, and I only want those about me who do the same. Clear?' He cuffed Beria viciously on the shoulder.

Malenkov exchanged a glance with Molotov. They scented victory. Beria felt the hounds closing in. The hunt had gone on long enough. The time had come to put on a turn of speed and leave the field behind. An old trick of his – by now, his pursuers might have spent their wind.

Jumping to his feet, he turned to face Stalin. The dictator, momentarily taken aback, fell silent. Beria took full advantage. Standing as much to attention as he was able, he addressed his master in stilted phrases, as a Sergeant would a Colonel.

'Comrade Stalin, I don't ask for forgiveness – you know that. I ask only to remedy my failings. In the name of our great teacher, Lenin, and of you, his great disciple, that is all I ask.' There was an expectant hush. Overblown sentiment often had its effect on the dictator. Stalin moved slowly back to his chair.

'And how, Comrade Beria, do you intend to do that?' he asked, looking sideways out of narrowed eyes.

'I can report on the measures already ordered, if you wish.'

Stalin, instead of asking why he had not done so at the beginning, merely nodded assent. Malenkov opened his mouth to protest, but too late. Beria had begun to salvage what had been lost.

'When I left you on Friday, Comrade Stalin, I gave orders for the return of the MGB *rezident* in London. He bears a heavy responsibility. All aspects of security there will be looked at. In addition, MGB operatives abroad who had anything remotely to do with Katyn or the Poles are being brought home. I have also instructed Abakhumov to set up a special investigation into his Ministry. I have given orders that General Eitingon shall head it.'

There was a whistle of amazement. Leonid Eitingon was a man to inspire respect, the brains behind the assassination of Trotsky. Beria had taken his task seriously.

'But that is not all, Comrade Stalin. I have given warning for three MGB Special Service divisions to stand by for your orders to move up to the Polish frontier, at Kaliningrad, Grodno and Brest. That's forty thousand men. In addition, I suggest that, should you wish it, we instruct Polish Security to arrest all potential leaders of any disruption. I have been in touch with our representative in Warsaw who assures me that, with reinforcements, he can do some useful things. Lastly, I have instructed Minister Abakhumov to place the VKR on the alert for operations against Polish counter-revolutionaries in the West who threaten to be a nuisance over Katyn.'

Again, the Politbureau members reacted – all except Malenkov. The VKR, the Organization for Counter-Infiltration of the MGB, were the successors to Lenin's Exterminators. Beria was obviously prepared for rough stuff.

'I hope, Comrade Stalin,' he concluded, 'that these measures will meet the requirements of yourself and the Politbureau. Finally, I request permission to lead the enquiry into the MGB myself.'

All the while, Beria had stood to attention. He now relaxed and sat down. There was silence. Malenkov, in a theatrical gesture, threw up his hands.

'Not good enough! Not good enough by half. So Comrade Beria suggests that the pigs of that Ministry are left to clear out their own sties. But how can we be sure they won't funk the job? They need supervision – Party supervision. And another thing. Is it right that we leave the organization that got us into this mess to get us out of it? Won't the same bungling stupidity and inefficiency that let the British find out about these spies also wreck our chances of dealing with this blackmail? I suggest control of the operation be given to Military Intelligence.'

Heads nodded in agreement. The Party and the Army, the great rivals of State Security, at last had the chance of power over Beria's empire. With that, the Marshal would fall.

The Politbureau waited expectantly. Beria and Malenkov had made their final bids. There was a long pause. Stalin turned to the Marshal.

'These arrangements – they are already in hand, you say?'

'Yes, Generalissimo. They await only your approval.'

The dictator was silent.

'But they do nothing to get us out of this mess.' Malenkov pushed home his point. 'Comrade Beria has conveniently forgotten about that.'

'And you – you have made little contribution on that score,' Beria reacted angrily. 'But you seem very good at gloating over other people's problems.'

'You think, do you, that I gloat at the mess you have got us in? You are stupid, like all policemen.'

The quarrel threatened to become petty. Usually Stalin would have enjoyed it, but not that day. Poland worried him.

'Enough, you two.' He raised his voice. 'I wish to make a proposal.' That was it. Only a brave man, or a fool, would vote against. 'Unless there is any disagreement.' The dictator looked round the table, daring anyone to speak. 'As I say, unless there is any disagreement, Comrade Beria's arrangements are to continue.'

The Marshal looked relieved. Malenkov's face was impassive.

'But the Ministry is not to have any dealings with the British on Katyn. They will be handled, as Comrade Malenkov suggests, by Military Intelligence.'

It was Malenkov's turn to look triumphant.

'And, further, I nominate Comrade Malenkov to supervise the operation. He is to have full responsibility.'

The Party had won – almost.

'And he is to advise me on security matters alongside Comrade Beria. In addition I shall be consulted on every move in the investigations of the MGB. General Eitingon will report to me. I want that nest of traitors rooted out. Remember, the finer the net, the more fish will be caught.'

'And the Minister and the Marshal, what of them?' Malenkov intervened before Stalin had finished – a measure of his confidence.

'Abakhumov will have to go, but not yet. I don't want the British to have the satisfaction of seeing our Security disrupted when it's their own that should be embarrassed. As for Comrade Beria,' – he sought out the Marshal's eyes – 'I shall judge his performance when the time comes.'

'And the British proposal?' Khruschev asked.

'Call their bluff. Do nothing and see what happens. I shall order the Armed Forces to hold themselves in preparation for an occupation of Poland. Comrade Beria's precautions might be sufficient. I hope so, for his sake.' He paused. 'Is everybody agreed?' Each man raised his hand. The battle was Malenkov's, and Beria had to comfort himself with the thought that there was still a campaign to win.

Over the following week the decisions of the Politbureau were put into force. The MGB moved with speed. By Friday, 20 April, five 'diplomats', all belonging to State Security, had returned to Moscow from embassies in Washington, Toronto, New Delhi and Khartoum. In addition, nine VKR agents were sent to London under the guise of trade and other representatives. In Moscow, Military Intelligence prepared to take over responsibility for the blackmail negotiations.

On the Polish border three MGB Special Service divisions began their assembly, and MGB Border Guards were strengthened. In Warsaw, MGB General Lalin received reinforcements from the MGB's Seventh (Advisory) Section, while the Soviet Ambassador, Lebedev, ordered Radkiewicz, Polish Minister of Security, to increase activities against potential opposition. As a precaution, Marshal Rokossovsky tightened surveillance within the Polish Armed Forces.

In London, the trio of Menzies, Strang and Vivien learned that Manjoulo had been recalled to Moscow, and waited anxiously for a reply to their proposal. But all they were given was the news that henceforth negotiations would be held with Soviet Military Intelligence. There was no further information and no reason given. They were worried.

Such were the activities of men who could see the sun and feel the rain. But in the Lubyanka, the cells began to fill with others less fortunate – men of the MGB's Foreign Intelligence and Internal Affairs Directorates suspected of espionage under Section 6 of Article 58 of the Criminal Code. The process began gently enough. Soviet Security was, after all, dealing with its own kind. In the interrogation offices, high-ceilinged, spacious rooms with large windows barred from the outside, General Eitingon and his assistants started their interviews at dead of night. Psychological methods were used – threats, promises, humiliation – but then, if guilt was not admitted, blood-stained canvas covers were placed over carpets, and the messy business of extracting a confession began.

For Soviet retribution, proof of espionage was not required. Its victims could just as easily be condemned for 'Suspicion of Espionage' – PSh in Security jargon; or 'Unproven Espionage' – NSh; or even 'Contacts leading to Suspicion of Espionage' – SVHSh. It mattered as little to the victim as to his interrogator for what he was sentenced: death would result, either quickly by bullet or slowly, serving a 'twenty-fiver' of hard labour. Only the numbers were important. The interrogators had their quotas to fill. It was more impressive that way.

Chapter Eight

It isn't easy to mistake the shadow of a mouse for an elephant, but after twelve days, and with nothing to show for them, Nick wondered whether he had done something similar. His cousin had proved useless. Before putting down his questions to the Foreign Secretary, the Member of Parliament for Dorset East had gone to clear the matter with his Party Whip – a needless precaution, but then Jonathan Spencer was ambitious. The Whip, an old hand, smelling a rat, had suggested he check with the Party's front-bench spokesman on foreign policy. Katyn had been bad news in 1943; it might still be in 1951. And the front bench agreed. Do nothing to rock the boat, was the advice. There might be a Socialist administration in office, but Conservative ministers had dealt with the matter in war. Anyway, it was never sensible to revive old skeletons. The front-bench spokesman thought that quite a good joke. So did Jonathan Spencer.

And Philby: despite his efforts, using every connection he could, Nick had learned little about the elusive First Secretary in the Washington Embassy. All he knew was that he was in Intelligence, of pleasing appearance and excellent company, had a stammer, drank like a fish and, when in London, frequented White's club. That was all. Nobody could, or would, say more, and not a scintilla of hard evidence had been uncovered to link him with the Katyn cover-up.

Lubienski had proved a disappointment too. Nick had twice arranged to meet him, and twice the old Pole rang to cancel. On the last occasion he had sounded agitated; something was clearly worrying him. He wouldn't listen, and hung up. There was nothing else for it: Nick would have to make his visit unannounced.

It was seven in the evening of Monday, 23 April, and the office was beginning to fill with the gloom of dusk. No light was on, the embers barely glowed in the grate, and in his chair Sir Stewart Menzies sat, eyes fixed on the ceiling, a paper-knife slowly turning in his hands, over and over. On the desk stood a whisky tumbler, empty. He stifled a yawn: it had been a hard day. Lunch with the head of MI5 was never enjoyable at the best of times. They had little in common, and Sir Stewart found the other's enthusiasms tedious. The man played his cards close to his chest, too, and skilfully. But Maclean's game was up, that much was clear. 'Homer's' end was just a question of time – and time was in short supply.

A knock at the door and Vivien entered, smoothing his hair as he always did, the crinkles bouncing back immediately.

'Sorry,' he said, 'but the green light was on and I thought you wouldn't mind. I've got some news.'

Menzies looked at his deputy chief, trying to focus. For a moment it seemed as if he had come from very far away. 'What was that, Viv?'

'I said I've got some news.' Vivien went up to the desk. 'Gregor Orlov's here.' He leaned over to switch on the desk-lamp. 'In London.'

'Who?' Sir Stewart frowned, shielding his eyes from the glare.

'Orlov. General Gregor Orlov. Soviet Military Intelligence. You must remember. He wound up our station in Prague two years ago with several well-placed hits.'

'Of course. Orlov. A clever operator. Did a neat job.'

'Well, he's here. Flew in yesterday.'

'What does he call himself?'

'By his own name. I suppose there's no need of deception. We've got nothing on him here. He can come and go as he wants, unless we put him on the black list.'

'Not till we have to.'

'The point is,' continued Vivien, 'that he could well be part of Russian reaction to Katyn.'

'Then we'll just have to let him do his worst. I don't want any open warfare between us and the Russians. That would ruin all our chances.'

'Let the battle ground be Poland, I suppose.'

'Something like that.' Sir Stewart smiled. He had brightened. 'So we can expect something pretty soon, eh?'

The Russians were reacting. They were playing for high stakes. It was all or nothing, as Orlov's presence in London indicated.

Suburbia, where even the disorder is neatly done, a place of regularity, of eight-thirty trains and five-thirty trains, of seven o'clock suppers, television and weekends in the garden. And yet . . .

By mid-evening, when it was dark, Nick reached Fallow Road, Wimbledon, conveniently situated near shops, an underground station and a park, and lined by semi-detached houses, typical mock-Tudor products of the 'thirties, uninspired yet practical, two storey with carefully tended gardens before and behind, surrounded by fences, low in front, high at the back. And at No 33 lived Lubienski.

No light could be seen in any of the windows, and even as he rang the bell Nick knew there would be no answer. He tried again, but heard no sound. Lubienski was out. Nick went slowly back down the garden path, taking an interest in his surroundings. The old Pole's poverty was clear. The garden was unkempt and choked with weeds, and even the vague light from the street lamps threw up the house's decay. Nick imagined the disapproval of the neighbours, and smiled.

Then he saw it: from the blackness of a car parked on the other side of the road, a little way down from No 33, a cigarette glowed. Instinctively, Nick stopped and fell to his knees, pretending to tie his shoelace, then raised his eyes. There it was again: a cigarette. He stood up, and on reaching the pavement turned in the direction of the main road, his back to the car. The street was deserted, the air still. Nick felt uneasy. He turned the corner into another quiet street. Behind, an engine started. Fear took him by the throat. His mouth dry and his heart beating loudly in his ears, he began to walk faster, looking over his shoulder with every fourth or fifth step, the sweat breaking out along his back. His instinct had come into play. He knew he was unprepared for what that car could mean.

As the sound of the engine grew louder, Nick broke into a trot. When he reached the white light of a street lamp, he ran, hesitantly at first, then frantically, his one thought being to get away. He reached the main road, bathed in light, with the underground station almost opposite. There was an evening paper seller packing up his stall, and a gang of boys lounging against a wall, laughing. Nick skidded to a halt. He was hot and panting, embarrassed at his obvious panic and annoyed by his fear. He looked back, but saw no car – the road was deserted. He waited for a minute, secure in the gaping company around him, and seeing nothing suspicious, went to buy a ticket home.

When he was safely on the train, alone in a carriage with no stranger near him, he thought back on his stupidity, and laughed out loud, as a man does who is at ease in his own company. Then he fell silent. He had seen the glow of a cigarette. Someone had been sitting in an unlit car, waiting. But why? For him, or Lubienski? Or was it entirely innocent, a father waiting for his daughter, perhaps, or a lover for his mistress? Not until he fell asleep much later that night, did Nick end his wondering.

* * *

The next day, Tuesday, Nick woke to the rays of the sun piercing the curtains. Rising immediately, he went to shave, and looking in the mirror remembered the events of the night before. He had behaved like a fool, and all because of two glows from a cigarette. It was ludicrous. And he had completely forgotten to leave a note for Lubienski. He cursed as he cut himself. The day hadn't started well.

Work passed slowly that morning, and Nick was kept busy with fiddling tasks for the Permanent Under-Secretary. Then, just before lunch, came the final blow: he was called in to his chief.

'Ah, Pelham,' Sir William said in a business-like fashion, his gimlet eyes on his Assistant Private Secretary. 'You will be relieved to know that, henceforth, you have no further responsibility for Katyn. I doubt whether we'll be proceeding much further up that particular road.'

'But, Sir William, what . . . ?'

'Yes?' An eyebrow was raised.

'What about the truth – about Katyn?'

'The truth?' Sir William gave his answer cynically, thinking he was clever, the supreme diplomat. 'Time has a way of dissolving good intentions, Pelham. What seems right one moment, may become foolish the next. Time even changes the truth in our trade.'

'But Katyn, Sir William. The truth can do nothing but good now. Russia's the enemy . . .'

There was steel in Sir William's eye. His voice grated like a file. 'Don't make the mistake of thinking the Foreign Office owes you a living, Pelham. It owes you nothing. It was here first.'

Nick opened his mouth to protest, but too late.

'Thank you, but the matter is closed. I've given it a lot of thought. It's best forgotten.' Sir William felt his anger suddenly rise, but he checked it, becoming cool, with non-committal eyes, his voice smooth, almost a whisper, but precise. 'That's what I advise anyway, Pelham. It's safer.'

There was no curt nod, and the Permanent Under-Secretary didn't turn away as usual, but sat staring dumbly at his subordinate, daring him to continue. Katyn was finished, and another warning given, the last.

Nick said nothing. There would be little purpose in it yet. So he accepted Sir William's decision, smiled and left. He could work for the man with enjoyment, he decided, if he were his grave-digger.

Outside was different. Getting back to his office, Nick kicked the door shut and sent his waste-paper basket flying. Lubienski had been right. The Foreign Office didn't have the guts to admit its mistakes. But he had been expecting it, and felt relief at the certainty. He knew now he was in the presence of a single, brutal fact, and he could either walk away or stay with it.

There was no hesitation. Nick picked up the telephone and dialled a number he had come to know by heart. But all he got was a dialling tone.

Nick reached Fallow Road that evening when it was dark, but again there was no sign of life at No 33. He went back down the path, and then further up the road, checking the cars as he passed. All were empty. He returned, rang the doorbell for a second time, but without bothering to wait turned to the right side of the house, where the darkness was unrelieved by street lamps. There he found a small wooden door which opened easily on to a narrow concentrated area between house and fence. Nick put his hand out to guide himself along the wall. After a couple of yards he touched wood, then a pane of glass. Below, his fingers gripped a handle, and he turned it. Unexpectedly, the door moved.

It was pitch black inside, and the first thing that struck Nick was the smell – strong, pervasive, a mixture of lavatory and decay out of keeping with the Lubienski of his memory. Had he got the right address? Nick flicked on his lighter. He was in the kitchen, a greasy affair, the product of a bachelor life. Going through, he came into a hallway, illuminated by moonlight coming from the windows at the side of the front door. Here, the smell was stronger. On one wall Nick could make out a picture of the Pope and, next to it, an old Polish flag. On the doormat he noticed a newspaper, folded just as it had dropped. Lubienski either hadn't been home the night before, or had left very early that morning.

The hall was typical: narrow, unprepossessing and functional. Uncertainly Nick opened the door nearest him. It was the dining room. Even the dim moonlight was unable to hide the shabbiness of its furniture. The walls were covered with views of Poland: a farmer's barn, a cathedral, mountains, typical photographic studies of the 'thirties long since out of fashion. Sad, too. There was nothing of any significance, but as he was leaving Nick noticed the sideboard. Its doors were open and the contents littered the floor. He was surprised. The Pole had struck him as a neat man.

Going upstairs, Nick went first into the bathroom, then to the front bedroom, and finally to the back room which served as a study. Fearing to switch on any of the lights in case they drew the attention of neighbours, he could see little, but the untidiness was clear. The study in particular, full of filing cabinets and bookcases, was a mess, with drawers half open and folders lying at all angles across the desk. But a superficial check showed up nothing of interest.

Downstairs, Nick went towards the kitchen. There was only the back room left. He opened the door, and put his hand to his nose. The stench was unbearable. Inside was pitch black. The curtains were closed so that there was not even any reflected illumination from the garden. Nick searched for the light switch, found it, and flicked it down. Nothing happened. He moved into the room, fumbling for his lighter, then stumbled and fell forward, throwing out his arms in protection. He crashed into something firm yet yielding, and felt the cold surface of a button brush his cheek.

Nick rolled over, arms protecting his head, expecting a blow, but none came. There was no sound, no movement. He waited, then got out his lighter. There, almost directly above, was the body of a man, hanging limply from the wire of the ceiling light, pirouetting in a slow dance of death. Scrambling up, he held the flame close. Distorted and with eyes bulging, he saw the colourless face of the old Pole, Lubienski. His tongue, sticking out from his mouth, was black.

The police were everything Nick expected of them: late, sympathetic and non-committal. Their lateness, however, gave him an opportunity to go through the dead man's house with the lights full on. It had been ransacked. Even the pile of old newspapers in the study had been gone through. A *Daily Telegraph* dated 5 August 1949 lay on top, while the most recent issue was at the bottom. Newspapers, Nick remembered from his wartime training, were good for hiding letters and notes: most searchers were too lazy to check each one, page by page. But the men who had been through Lubienski's house had been expert. Even the mess had been kept to a minimum, giving the impression it was Lubienski himself who was untidy. Nick didn't know what they had taken, but in the files he could find nothing bearing the title 'Katyn' or 'Sikorsky', the only words he would recognize in Polish.

Twenty minutes after Nick had telephoned, a Detective-Sergeant and two Constables arrived. The Sergeant was sympathetic. 'Nasty business,' he said knowingly, and took a statement.

'Well, Mr Pelham, sir, you'll be relieved that we can't begin to suspect you for this. He must have been stiff for at least twenty-four hours. Look.' His torch scanned the body, and with the end of his pen he pointed to the dried saliva around Lubienski's mouth, and to the almost dry mixture of excrement and urine staining his trousers and the floor beneath. 'Unpleasant, isn't it? The smell's always the worst thing, so I say.'

Nick looked at the body still swaying, mouth wide open in a fool's gape, and found it hard to link that limp, stinking jumble of skin and bone to the gentle old man of his memory. He saw how the wire had been yanked down from the ceiling to produce sufficient length to form a noose, how it had cut deep into the neck without drawing blood, and how a chair had been kicked away in the final seconds before strangulation. A look of uncomprehending horror remained on Lubienski's face, and deep scratch marks on the side of his neck showed where he had tried to free himself. His fingers, bloodstained, bore evidence of their struggle.

'It can't have been suicide, can it?'

'Oh, you can never tell. Not just like this, sir.' The Detective-Sergeant was non-committal, peering at the marks left scarring the wall by Lubienski's kicks. 'Could have been, but, then again, might not. You haven't seen a farewell note anywhere, have you?'

Nick hadn't. 'That shows it wasn't suicide, doesn't it?' He was reluctant to say the word 'murder'.

'Oh no, not necessarily, sir. Most go without saying goodbye, you know. That's why they go, because there isn't anyone to say it to. Ever.'

'But what about these?' Nick asked pointing to the bloody gashes on his neck.

'That can happen. Last minute regret, too late. Death this way isn't quick, but it's certain.'

Nick didn't bother any further. He left. Outside on the street, when he saw the parked police car, he remembered he hadn't told them about his visit the night before.

That might have been about the time Lubienski was dangling, alive, at the end of the wire. And then he recalled the glow of the cigarette, and his inexplicable sense of fear.

Chapter Nine

Wednesday, 25 April. It was raining that afternoon, a London rain, thin, constant and sooty. Sir William had been caught and was already wet when Sir Stewart offered him his umbrella.

'Didn't know you knew him,' the head of SIS whispered in the Permanent Under-Secretary's ear. Sir William nodded. 'Ranson was in the Department for a time,' he said. 'A decent chap.' He had died a decent death, too, in bed.

'. . . ashes to ashes, dust to dust, in sure and certain hope of the Resurrection.' The parson intoned with indecent haste, unreconciled to the wet. A few pebbles, thrown by the widow, could be heard bouncing off the coffin. Mourners huddled round the grave side, coat-collars up.

'Poor turn out,' hissed Sir Stewart. 'Must be the weather.'

The priest hurried the ceremony. Not having known the coffin's content when it was a man, he saw no reason to prolong the acquaintance now it was a corpse. '. . . and the love of God and the fellowship of the Holy Spirit be with us evermore. Amen.' The blessing over, he left, but the mourners, their lack of intimacy with the Almighty making them more a prey to guilt, stood for a moment in silence, none wishing to be the first to move yet all anxious to begin the return journey through London's traffic. With a loud 'Amen' an aged woman broke the spell, and strode off among the slabs and the mounds of the cemetery.

'Well, that's that,' said Sir William, the relief making him sigh. 'The only decent thing about a funeral is that it's one step better than a wedding.' His humour plummeted like lead. 'But it's sad to see the old boy go,' he added hurriedly. Sincerity had never been his strong point. He replaced his bowler on his sodden hair. 'Anyway, Stewart, let's take this opportunity for a chat.'

The two men moved away from the grave, away from the exit, and further into the cemetery. It was old and neglected, blackened by London's grime, tombstones at all angles, some fallen on the ground, with, overall, a thick undergrowth of evergreen. 'Time's not on our side, you know, Stewart.'

Sir Stewart did know. Moscow's silence was disconcerting. So far, the arrival of Orlov in London had signified nothing. For three weeks they had known about the traitors, and for three weeks MI5 had been getting closer to Maclean. The Permanent Under-Secretary voiced his fears.

'If the Snoopers get to Maclean before we do, Stewart, he'll blow everything.'

'Then we're left with no alternative,' Menzies replied, pausing to look at a gravestone. *John Edward Meacher of this Parish. Born 6 July 1886. Died 29 April 1938. With my Saviour, I Rest in Peace.*

'Optimistic sort of fellow,' he commented, smiling.

'More than I am, Stewart. What do you propose? Our cousins?'

'Them, William . . . and the Poles.'

Requesting support from the CIA over Katyn had already been agreed as an option. The Company would be asked to further the demands of the American-Polish community for a Congressional enquiry into the massacre. They wouldn't need much persuading. At a time when bullets were flying in Korea, it was good propaganda against Communist maltreatment of prisoners. And SIS's request would be sent via Philby, liaising with the CIA in Washington, so Moscow would know about it in twenty-four hours. It was a plan Sir William liked. He hadn't much time for Americans, and it was good to make the United States dance a British tune. But Poland?

'What do you mean, Stewart, "the Poles"?'

They were picking their way through the Victorian section now, where tombstones gave way to crosses and statues. Huddled together under Sit Stewart's umbrella, the two men were an odd sight, one tall, the other short, both in funereal garb, lost among the monuments to death.

'The Polish military, my dear William, are teetering on the edge of a coup, and we can provide them with that little jolt they need. You see, they trust us.'

The head of SIS explained. Much had happened over the past few weeks. The conspirators in the Polish Army had taken their SIS contact into their confidence. Their plans were well advanced, far more so than Sir Stewart had at first suspected. The coup would begin with the assassination of the Defence Minister, Marshal Rokossovsky, an event which they expected would temporarily paralyse the Polish high command and provide a chance to co-ordinate the forces of revolt. The Warsaw garrison would move first, occupying government buildings and radio installations and eliminating all opposition within the capital, while officers in the General Staff co-ordinated activity in the provinces. It was a good enough plan, Sir Stewart acknowledged. But the conspirators were hesitating. Activity by the Security Police had unaccountably increased over the last week, and the officers feared detection. Only a guarantee of support by British Intelligence could goad them into immediate action.

'Steady on!' Sir William nearly stumbled, recovered, and, as he always did when he was anxious, dug a finger into his ear. The more he thought about it, the less he liked the idea of any destabilization of Poland. Better to have Soviet domination than a flare-up which could spill over into Eastern Europe. Attitudes would have to be struck for and against a free Poland, and that could only lead to trouble. Threat of an uprising was one thing; its reality very different. His finger made its excavation.

'You know the consequences if this comes off, don't you, Stewart? They could be disastrous.' The Permanent Under-Secretary didn't bother to hide his agitation. 'There'll be a bloodbath. Central Europe will be in turmoil. And what chance our blackmail then?' He hoped he had found a flaw. 'Moscow won't be in the slightest bit interested in our bargain after they've flattened Poland.'

Sir Stewart gave one of his reassuring smiles. 'Don't worry, old boy. Vivien and I have got it all worked out. There'll be some fine tuning, that's all. We'll make sure there's no uprising. Just a little jolt to Moscow. We've a man out in Warsaw now – he knows what to do. In two or three days it could all be over.'

'And the conspirators?'

Menzies didn't reply. The rain had stopped and he lowered his umbrella. The two men separated. Sir Stewart peered at a gravestone. '*Loved by all who knew him, respected for his works before God*. Most of the lies in this world are on graves, William. You would think mankind's only hope lay in resurrecting the dead and disposing of the living.' He bent to look at another slab. '*I have fought a good fight, I have finished my course*. Which reminds me, William, what about that man Pelham?'

The finger went back into the Permanent Under-Secretary's ear as he stood stock still and looked at a bunch of spring flowers that had been left at the foot of the new headstone. *In Loving Memory*. He preferred that; less sententious.

'Still rooting around asking questions about Philby, I'm afraid.'

'What about a cosy chat, William?' The head of SIS specialized in those, and always preferred them as a solution.

'I've tried, given him enough hints, but anything heavy

would be counter-productive. Pelham's pig-headed when he wants to be. Too ambitious in my opinion.'

'The last refuge of failure, or something, eh?' Sir Stewart smiled. 'Well, anyway, Vivien's got him under some sort of surveillance.'

'Yes, he's ambitious,' Sir William continued, as if talking about Pelham could exorcise the man from his thoughts. 'His background is sound – Harrow, Cambridge, that sort of thing – which is what makes his behaviour so odd. And intolerable.'

'Even the best blood gets into mosquitoes, William.'

'And he's got a fairly good war record. Infantry service in North Africa, then recruited for Special Operations and used in Holland. Something pretty unpleasant happened out there, I believe. But this must be coincidence. He can't be on to the blackmail, can he?'

'Mmm.' Sir Stewart looked at the Permanent Under-Secretary with mild concern. But then, his concerns seldom appeared more than that.

'Anyway I'll leave Pelham in your tender care, Stewart, if I may. You know best how to hush these people up.' Sir William looked away, across the graveyard. 'Dreary place.' A commonplace remark, indicating that the subject of Nicholas Pelham was over as far as he was concerned. 'And anyway, apart from him, we're safe. The only others to know are in the Kremlin.'

Sir Stewart read another inscription. '*Until the day break and the shadows flee away*. That could be our epitaph, William. We won't have much longer to wait now, I promise you. We can't lose, not with Poland.'

In 1951, CIA headquarters were situated in Washington's 'Foggy Bottom', and that was a long way from the Kremlin. Between them there were no connections, not even any of the informal contacts which abound in the world of espionage. That was a strict rule, basic to

American Intelligence, and one handed down from the White House itself. But rules are made to be broken.

Dulles coughed. Bedell Smith sat up. Both looked at each other in amazement. Here, before them, was the CIA's head of Soviet-Bloc Intelligence advocating a gamble which, should it prove false, would end Anglo-American co-operation on security for at least a decade, and their careers for ever. But if successful, it could save the Company from extinction.

When Anderson had first seen Khopliakin's list eleven days previously, one codename among the twelve had special significance for him. It was 'Basil', belonging to John Calder, a British nuclear physicist working in Washington. Anderson had known him as a Soviet spy as early as 1948, and since then, when he had been 'turned', his identity had been a closely-guarded secret. His value as a double agent was immense, feeding false atomic secrets to the MGB, as well as helping track other spies. By 1951, information provided by 'Basil' had hardened American suspicions as to the identity of 'Homer'. He was, they were sure, Maclean. In addition, 'Basil' had implicated Philby, though nothing was proven.

The CIA chiefs, cautious by nature, had not informed the British, regarding both SIS and MI5 as unreliable, penetrated by other traitors, so instead they preferred to wait. Khopliakin's list, however, was a different matter. It not only confirmed the identity of 'Homer' and the treachery of Philby, but pointed to Soviet penetration of the British government and security services on a scale Anderson had never suspected. The question was, what to do with his discovery?

'It is known,' said Anderson dryly, 'that SIS was given Khopliakin's list on 19 March. That's five weeks ago. With the information they've got at their disposal, I would give them three at most to work out who the traitors are. But, as far as we know, they've done nothing. Calder hasn't been troubled. Philby is still here in Washington, and Maclean is at his desk in London. No bother at all. Nor have we been warned by SIS of anything out of the ordinary. Nothing – just dead silence.'

'What the hell are those Limeys playing at?' Bedell Smith asked angrily. 'I mean, they surround us with goddam traitors, and when they find out they just leave them alone. For Chris-sake!'

'Put yourself in their shoes. What would you do?'

'Lock the bastards up,' said the General, slapping the desk. 'Give'em the chair!' He was a straightforward man.

'And destroy yourself?'

Dulles nodded vigorously. 'I see your meaning, John. Carry on. Don't keep the General in the dark.'

An unhelpful dig, Anderson thought, typical of Dulles, but he continued.

'Menzies has got no alternative but to cover up. Can you imagine the British reaction if treachery on that scale got out? Or ours? It was bad enough with Fuchs and the other boys. But this – it's incredible.'

Anderson, for the first time the other two had known, showed emotion, and hit the paper bearing Khopliakin's list. 'It's unbelievable. We're blown wide open. Would you admit to this if you were British?'

'Put like that, no,' said Bedell Smith.

'Quite. So what do you do? Trot along to the Russians and say, "Well done, chaps, but let's call it a day"?' Anderson faked an upper class English accent. 'Hell, you would. The Russians would laugh in your face. Moscow will use those traitors. They'll expose them to screw up the British.'

'So what are the Brits doing? Just letting the bastards louse up the system as if nothing has happened?'

'No. More than that, General. They're not gutless, those Limeys, whatever else they are. They're blackmailing Moscow, that's what.'

Dulles whistled through his teeth. Bedell Smith swore.

'There have been some strange happenings recently,' continued Anderson. 'First, there was the unscheduled movement of Soviet diplomats back to Moscow. From London, there was Manjoulo, head of MGB operations there. And the five others have something in common – all were concerned with internal security in the 1940s, and three were known positively to have dealt with the Poles. Second, the Polish Prime Minister was called to Moscow five days ago, and spent some time at the Kremlin. Third, this morning, SIS has asked us for everything in our files on Katyn, and has requested us to push the investigation into the massacre that some Congressmen have been wanting. The British simply gave foreign policy revision as a reason.'

'Okay,' said Bedell Smith, interrupting Anderson's flow. 'So you've got some coincidences, but that doesn't make a story.'

'Not by themselves,' Anderson agreed. 'But there's a pattern. Three or four reference points is enough for most Intelligence guesses. And there's another. The request on Katyn came through Philby. Now, normal channels for such a low-level exchange would be through our own London office, not through their liaison officer here. So why did they do it that way? So the Soviets would get to know they were involving us in Katyn, that's why.'

Anderson paused, letting his words sink in.

'And what do we see happening on Poland's border? The Soviets are moving up Army units and MGB special service divisions. In Poland, security is being increased. Our Embassy has just had movement-restrictions tightened, and there are reports of the MGB reinforcing their men in Warsaw. It all adds up.'

'So Menzies is having a go at bargaining those twelve against Katyn?' There was a hint of respect in Dulles's voice. After dealing with them in the war, the English weren't his favourite race, but he could appreciate the blackmail.

'Yes. They're after persuading the Russians not to risk unrest in Poland. It's a clever choice, and if I were Stalin, I would be windy about it, especially after Yugoslavia.'

'But what the hell do we do?' The General looked perplexed.

'Don't you see?' Dulles said with sudden enthusiasm. 'It's our coup, ready and served up to take along to the President on a plate. It's perfect. Twelve names and the Limeys' cover-up. The greatest Intelligence scoop in history, and all ours. He'll be impressed. The opposition won't stand a chance after that, and the Company will be safe.'

'But how do we go about breaking the codenames?'

'Simple, General,' Anderson replied. 'A deal with the Russians: we shut down on Katyn, and they give us the names. It'll serve their purpose – they'll appear blameless, the British will be embarrassed, and there'll be no trouble over Poland.'

'It's a bastard thing you're proposing, John,' said Dulles, grinning.

'It's a bastard business we're in, Allen. And the Brits haven't exactly been angels, have they?' He paused. 'Well, have they?'

The decision taken, the CIA chiefs moved fast. Within hours Allen was in a down-town parking lot, seated in a car with the Soviet Ambassador, Panyushkin, who doubled as the MGB's Washington *rezident*. The proposal was made, and an evasive answer given: by the weekend, a response from Moscow might be forthcoming, but there could be no guarantees.

In the event, no reply came. Moscow was undecided.

Chapter Ten

Kowalski squinted down the sight, and grunted. There was no need for further adjustment. The view was good, the range manageable. Putting down the rifle, he tightened its sling and, looping it around his arm, tried the aim again. It was perfect. His arm, the rifle and his shoulder were rigid, with not the slightest tremor. A single shot, and he would put a hole through his target's shoulder – of that he was confident.

Kowalski regretted only that his instructions didn't allow him to place the bullet elsewhere. Like most Poles, he would have liked to see Rokossovsky dead, but orders were orders, and the Centre had been clear: on no account was the target to be eliminated. The Polish officers with whom he had been in contact since his arrival in Warsaw two days ago might have other ideas – about that, too, the Centre had warned him – but their expectations wouldn't be fulfilled. It was all very unusual . . .

A sharp command echoed from the parade ground below.

'Regiment! Attention!'

The time had come. Picking up the rifle Kowalski pulled back the bolt and inserted a bullet. One shot was all he was allowed. One shot – that was all SIS was prepared to give the Poles.

'Regiment! Present arms!'

Kowalski went to the low table he had positioned well back from the open window, and climbed on it. There was a crash of booted feet outside as he brought the rifle up to his shoulder.

Sixty feet below, a band struck up the Polish national

anthem. Diagonally across the square appeared the slight figure of Marshal Rokossovsky, recognizable from his photographs, surrounded by a posse of staff officers.

Kowalski aimed. The Marshal obligingly paused on the steps leading down from the *Kommandantura* to survey the brown ranks of the 5th Rifle Regiment. That was enough. Kowalski squeezed the trigger. The shot echoed around the square, and Rokossovsky was sent hurling back. The 5th Regiment stood stock still.

Kowalski threw down his gun and made for the door. His escape was well planned. He must leave his homeland for ever.

The shooting took place at eleven o'clock precisely on the morning of Saturday, 28 April 1951, at the Lenin Barracks in a southern suburb of Warsaw. As a result of the bullet aimed at the right shoulder of Marshal Rokossovsky, turmoil in Poland, erosion of Soviet power, and a realignment between East and West was for a short while a possibility.

But as those men in London who had planned the fake assassination expected, the crisis soon passed. Although in great pain, the Marshal remained conscious and able to give orders. The conspirators hesitated too long. Polish Security, stiffened with MGB agents, went into action. Army officers and likely dissidents were placed in protective detention, government buildings, radio stations and all sensitive areas were put under heavy police guard, and after forty-eight hours of intense activity, the critical stage was judged to have passed. The search for the conspirators continued, but restrictions were eased and Poland returned to what passed for normality. No information of the attempted assassination was given, no publicity, no broadcasts, and the world remained in ignorance of what had been.

SIS's gamble paid off, producing everything Menzies had

predicted: a potentially disruptive military coup in Poland was nipped in the bud, the precarious state of that country was underscored, and the Soviet leadership was forced into a decision on the blackmail – or so it appeared.

It was not London that was informed first of Moscow's reply, but Washington, late on the evening of the 29th. As Anderson had predicted, the CIA's offer was accepted, although, unexpectedly, Soviet Military Intelligence was to take over liaison. As for the British, the Russians requested that for the time being the Americans co-operate fully on Katyn and whatever else they were asked for. Absolutely no grounds for suspicion should be given, a condition readily accepted.

That done, London was notified, by means of a signal sent to Major-General Orlov at the Embassy.

The powerful Abakhumov fiddled with his buttons; the mighty Beria stared at the ceiling, signs of dribble on his chin. Both slumped in their chairs. The Minister sighed. For days now he had lived with the certainty of his downfall, and it had done little good to hear the Marshal reaffirm it. Only the exact time when General Eitingon would respectfully request his presence in the interrogation cell remained unknown. Abakhumov took a large sip of brandy and stared down at his shoes. He wished it would be soon.

Beria was equally depressed and more drunk. He belched and reached for a bottle. The previous day, in the dictator's study, he had lost out to Malenkov, who had urged the acceptance of the American offer in the light of Rokossovsky's shooting. The man was taking seriously his new role as security adviser. Beria had urged caution: he didn't trust the Americans – they were either too stupid or too unreliable. A deal would be dangerous. There were other ways of causing the British embarrassment while appearing to accept their blackmail. Malenkov, however, disagreed, and Stalin had listened to him. Both the British and the American proposals would be accepted. It was a blow to the Marshal from which he had not recovered.

Beria fumbled, the bottle dropped to the floor, and he swore feebly as its contents stained the carpet. He felt listless. Even the thought of a girl repulsed him. The MGB, his security, was slipping from his control. Stalin, his protector, was losing confidence. Malenkov was winning. The end, if not certain, was in sight. He cursed. The hoods of his eyes began to fall. Then he shouted, picked up his glass and hurled it against the wall, a final act of defiance which signalled his weakness. Abakhumov looked up. He coughed – he had been smoking too much – then chewed the phlegm, swallowed, and felt worse.

There was a knock on the door, and Beria's adjutant appeared, coming to attention as he spoke.

'Comrade Marshal. We have just been informed by Military Intelligence that General Orlov is taking care of the blackmail negotiations with the Americans as well as the British. I apologize for disturbing you, but it might be of interest.'

The adjutant clicked his heels, and left.

Beria pulled himself up and went over to a cabinet. He picked out a bottle of brandy bearing Napoleon's name. The little Corsican was a man the little Georgian admired, and he always drank that brand in the mistaken belief that it had been Bonaparte's favourite. He moved back unsteadily to the fireside, and dropped into his chair. He looked for his glass, then remembered it was shattered. Grunting, he put the bottle to his lips and drank greedily, letting the brandy run down his chin and on to his shirt. Then slowly, almost imperceptibly, his top lip curled.

'A clever man, Orlov,' he said. He took another swig. 'Too good for the military.'

Abakhumov nodded, still looking at his feet. Another's brilliance held no interest for him now.

'An able man, General Orlov,' continued Beria. 'A strong man. A good spy. Able. Malenkov's choice, you know. Approved him personally.' And again brandy poured into his mouth. 'But I wonder, my dear Abakhumov, whether our Orlov is a good Communist?'

Abakhumov looked up, a flicker of understanding on his face. And admiration. Few men are able to know all the ill they do, but Beria was one of them. He measured it precisely; and the more he drank, the more precise he became.

'Do you know, my dear Minister, whether this General is a good Communist? Can you make some enquiries? Not too discreetly.'

Beria might be drunk, but he knew what he was saying. So did Abakhumov. In Comrade General Orlov's commitment to the principles of Marxism-Leninism lay their hope for the future.

'The whale room?' Vivien had been disbelieving. 'The Natural History Museum? You must be joking.'

'Afraid not, old boy,' Sir Stewart had replied with obvious amusement. 'That's how Orlov operates.'

So at four exactly that Monday afternoon Vivien entered the dimly-lit room, deserted except for an old attendant snoozing on a bench, and dominated by the life-size replica of a giant Blue Whale in plaster. He snorted contemptuously. It all bordered on the farcical.

But he didn't have long to wait. Almost immediately two men entered. Orlov was recognizable from a photograph: large, in his early fifties, grey-haired, broad, dressed in a well-fitting blue suit, his face red, almost jolly, with beady eyes – a figure of fun, yet deadly. He was accompanied by a squat, pug-nosed bodyguard. Vivien, not knowing quite what to do, turned back to look with his monocle at the skeleton of a Steller's Sea Cow, now extinct. He heard Orlov click his fingers, and out of the corner of an eye saw the guard obediently sitting down on the bench next to the attendant. Without hesitation, the Soviet General walked up and held out his hand.

'Colonel Vivien, how pleased I am to meet you in person.' Orlov spoke good English, although his accent was guttural. 'You are warmly spoken of.' His eyes were mischievous, and his face had that strange quality Vivien had observed in drunks: amiable, but at a stroke turning ominous.

The two men shook hands. Vivien, conscious of the other's iron grip, smiled icily. 'Shall we sit, General?' was all he could say.

They chose a bench as far from the attendant as possible, from where they could view him and the bodyguard under the white belly of the whale.

'I have to tell you, Colonel . . .' Orlov began with little hesitation, 'that Moscow has accepted your offer of, how shall we put it, "co-operation".' He was not a man to waste time.

'They took long enough to come to a decision.' Vivien was ungracious, trying to hide the relief he felt.

'Moscow has much to take into account, Colonel. For you it was easy – either you blackmail us or you lose your heads. For us, it is very different. It takes time.' Orlov's lips spread wide. 'But come, Colonel, all this political business is no affair of ours, no reason why we professionals shouldn't get on with the job as far as we are able. Let's walk.'

Orlov helped Vivien up by the arm, an unnecessary gesture which surprised the Englishman. They began to stroll, Vivien with his hands clasped behind his back, Orlov with them in front, gesticulating whenever he spoke. Up in the gallery another man, with the face of a Russian, stood watching.

In front of a cast of the False Killer Whale, they paused. 'Now Colonel, what about the handover of our men? You don't want any ripples coming to the surface, I presume.' The Russian touched Vivien's arm in reassurance. The Englishman froze imperceptibly.

'At the moment things are complicated by three of them being on holiday,' he replied. 'And we've also got to bring two in from America. That will take some organizing. So you see, we shall have to wait for several weeks. It's unfortunate, but inevitable. We'll move in early May.'

'You operate under many obstacles, Colonel. You should join us!' Oblivious of the attendant, Orlov let out a loud laugh and slapped Vivien on the shoulder. Vivien smiled faintly.

They moved on to the jawbones of three whales, soaring arches standing sentinel. There were other reasons why a delay was inevitable, but Vivien didn't reveal those to the Russian. SIS would have to call home operatives skilled in fieldwork, twenty-two of them. The agents, unknown to each other, would all come from different parts of the world and be briefed, individually or in pairs, by Vivien. They would then bring in their appointed man, and return immediately to their overseas stations. That way, the chance of gossip around a bar coming up with any coincidences would be minimal. Many years should pass, Vivien reckoned, before there was the least hint of any suspicion as to what had happened on that day in May 1951.

'And how do you want the handover to be made?' Orlov asked casually as he looked up at the jawbones towering above him. He reached out to touch the smooth white bone.

'Your controls should proceed with business as normal until the very last moment, then get their agents to a rendezvous predetermined by us. It has to be exact. There can be no room for slippage, no chance of the alarm being raised through one mistake. We attach the greatest importance to that, General. Everything must be exact.'

'I understand completely, Colonel,' said Orlov as he led the Englishman to the next exhibit, the cast of a Bottle-nosed Whale, an ugly creature. Vivien barely glanced at it.

'But now let me ask you a question, General. Why have you taken over from Manjoulo?'

'Colonel Manjoulo is no longer with us.' Orlov looked at Vivien. His eyes were blue, and they shone with amusement. 'He has been promoted out of sight,' he added with another guffaw. This time Vivien could not even manage a smile, and he suddenly felt very sorry for Manjoulo.

'I see you do things differently, General,' said Vivien as his arm embraced the room.

'Ah, you like it, I hope. I have always loved whales. My father and my grandfather used to kill them. But tell me, where else do you find such a public place for cosy discussions in London, one that is not light enough for, let's say, photographic records to be kept?'

So that was Orlov's reason. He had no wish to be compromised. Unnecessary, thought Vivien, but prudent.

'There is something more, General. Your "activities", shall we call them, since you came to London have not exactly gone unnoticed. Your surveillance of the Poles is quite strong, isn't it?'

'You obviously know the answer.'

'But was it really necessary to kill that man Lubienski?'

'Ask yourself, Colonel Vivien, what you would have done in our place.'

'Perhaps, but I warn you that clumsy action may be dangerous. If MI5 get on to it you can expect trouble. And so can we.'

'One death will serve as a warning. There will be no need of others, I trust.' Orlov took care not to wear his brutality on his sleeve.

'Good. Well, I think we've squared the police on Lubienski. They won't be pursuing the matter – there's not much in suicide, is there?'

Orlov smiled.

'But that doesn't mean there are no complications. We've got someone poking his nose into everything – a Foreign Office official called Pelham, Nicholas Pelham.'

'Pelham.' Orlov toyed with the name as they moved on to the nine Common Dolphins plunging through a plaster sea. 'Not tall and slim, with dark hair sticking up. Bobs up and down when he walks?'

'Yes.' Vivien tried to hide his surprise at the Russian's knowledge, but couldn't. 'How do you know?'

'Oh, he's come up in our "activities", as you call them.'

'Well, he discovered Lubienski's body. Seems he must be pretty thick with the Poles. He's also on to Philby – God knows how. Could be coincidence, but he's unpredictable, this man Pelham. A danger.'

'And why, Colonel, do you tell me all this?'

'So General, you won't think we bear any responsibility for him.' Vivien removed his monocle and bent down to scrutinize a Leathery Turtle stranded on a plinth. He was avoiding the General's eyes.

'Then why don't you deal with him?' Orlov was puzzled, unused to that sort of problem.

'It's not easy over here. We've done about as much as we can. We watch his movements and we've taken him off Katyn. But that's all. Even a phone tap is difficult. He's still a danger.'

'May I take it, Colonel, that you are not entirely happy with this young bull remaining in the china shop?' The flesh around Orlov's eyes puckered.

'You may.'

'And that you would not be upset if he were to meet with an accident?' The corners of Orlov's mouth twitched.

'It would, of course, be unfortunate.' The irony in Vivien's voice was not lost.

'Do you wish us to take over, Colonel?' The Russian was beaming, though not with good nature. It amused him to think of Soviet Military Intelligence taking in SIS's dirty washing.

Vivien was embarrassed. Apart from anything else, he found it demeaning to ask a Russian to eliminate a loyal British citizen. He looked fixedly at the lower jawbone of a Sperm Whale, its ivory teeth the size of a man's fist. Finally, he replied. 'Nothing messy. Make it natural – and quick.'

Chapter Eleven

The Soviet Embassy in London, No 13 Kensington Palace Gardens, is a fine building, built in the Gothic style of the mid-nineteenth century for the fifth Earl of Harrington – one of the biggest mansions in a road popularly known as 'millionaires' row'. The hospitality given there, in true Russian tradition, matches the surroundings. Under the high ceilings, stucco mouldings and dripping chandeliers in that part of the house that was once the picture gallery, diplomats talk, moving from one table heavy with food to another, taking their glasses from white-gloved waiters on the way.

Into this brightly-lit world, Nick stepped in the early evening of Tuesday, 1 May, accompanying his chief. He was greeted, as were all the guests, by His Excellency Monsieur Georgi Nikolaevich Zaroubin, resplendent in black and silver uniform. The reception marked May Day. It was a touching gesture, but then the Russians didn't miss any opportunity to pour alcohol down the throats of their enemies.

There must have been at least three hundred guests. Nick reckoned, all members of the 'circuit' who had probably seen each other the night before and were dreading the inevitable repeat. He looked at them with jaundiced eye. Honest men, all of them, who wouldn't dream of cheating at cards, and yet there they all were, lying for their country.

'God rot them,' he muttered, and reached for a glass of vodka, downed it with one gulp and had another before the tray disappeared. The Russian waiter, a military-looking young man, gave him a wink. That amused Nick.

He drained the new glass as quickly as the first, took one more and winked back.

Nick moved into the throng and came up against a Soviet Third Secretary he had met before, who began addressing him on the subject of the weather. Only the appearance of Harrison, the sickly Principal from Protocol, made him abandon the Russian and go to one of the side-tables. Picking up a plate, he helped himself to as much as he decently could, trying not to appear greedy but intent on having sufficient to avoid cooking a meal later that night. His plate full, Nick wandered back into the multitude, food and drink in both hands. Avoiding Harrison, he bumped up against a Russian who bore down on him like a battleship on a destroyer.

'Good evening,' the man said in a heavy accent. 'You have everything?'

Nick nodded, and smiled. His new companion was in his early fifties, large but dressed in a dapper dark suit, with red tie and a red banner lapel badge. Not much interest there, thought Nick: all production quotas and Five-Year Plans. 'Everything I can wish for, thank you,' he replied as he tried to sidestep.

But the Russian proved persistent. With a deft move, he blocked Nick. 'Everything! No man has that,' he joked, 'not even in the Soviet motherland!' As he laughed his body heaved. A man with an odd sense of humour; Nick liked that. He had a merry face, too, and his fingers were covered in rings which glistened as he flourished his hands when he spoke.

'You are English, I think?' the Russian asked. 'I like your country, but not your rain,' he continued. The weather again, thought Nick; it would be fog next. 'Your famous English fogs. We know all about them in Russia.'

'Peasoupers,' replied Nick automatically. He expected to have to explain exactly what that was. It always kept a conversation going. But the Russian switched tack.

'And what is your name?'

'Pelham, Nicholas Pelham. I look after Sir William Strang, if you know him. He brought me along tonight.'

'Ah, Sir William.' The Russian paused for a moment. 'My name is Penkovsky, Gregor Penkovsky, on attachment from our Ministry of Economics.'

Probably a spy, thought Nick, only half in joke. They shook hands, and the Russian's was clammy.

'Not that we have much to do with economics in our country,' Penkovsky added, and burst out laughing again. 'It's more a question of persuasion.' He poked Nick in the ribs.

Nick was lost in wonder as he watched the man's powerful shoulders shake up and down, and hoped that, for Penkovsky's sake, none of his colleagues had overheard the remark.

'Tell me,' asked the Russian when he had calmed himself, 'do you like your job, Mr Pelham?'

Nick replied that it was like any other, but did not add, as he had done before, that it was an honour to serve his country.

'And one day you will be like Sir William, yes?' Nick answered, with feeling, that no, he didn't think he would ever end up like Sir William.

'And what did you do during the war?'

Quite an interrogation. Nick was about to answer that he had been in Special Operations, but thought better of it.

'Medically unfit, I am afraid, Mr Penkovsky. My chest.'

'We did not recognize such things when the fascists invaded us. We had to fight, chest or no chest.'

Now it would come, Nick thought, the Great Patriotic War as fought by Gregor Penkovsky from beginning to end. Middle-aged Russians delighted in that. But no; again, the man abruptly changed subject.

'You are married, Mr Pelham?'

'No, I've avoided that so far. As they say, it would be a triumph of hope over experience.'

The Russian broke into laughter again, this time a positive gale. 'You suffer like us all, eh, Mr Pelham?' he spluttered. 'That is why we drink, is it not so?' He signalled to the waiter for more vodka. 'Ah, my Katerina. Well, you see my grey hairs.'

And so the conversation continued. No politics, no economics, no work, not even the weather, just life as seen by a Russian and an Englishman in the warmth of alcohol. But after five minutes or so, another Embassy official came to join them, a man Penkovsky clearly disliked. Making his excuses, he shook Nick warmly by the hand and moved away. Conversation became strained, and Nick, conscious that he was a little drunk, felt on edge. Not wishing to let his good spirits get dampened, he left the Embassy and walked down to Kensington High Street where he slipped into a telephone booth. He dialled a London number and a girl answered.

'Hello, Teresa. It's me, Nick.'

There was a pause.

'Oh yes, you sod.' Her voice exuded permafrost.

'Sorry I haven't called recently. Been hellish busy at work. But I've got off unexpectedly early tonight, thank goodness, so how about a late supper to celebrate . . .'

Nick started, sat up, emerging from his sleep as from a long tunnel, uncertain of where he was in the dark. He felt stifled, clutched at his head, full of the suppurating shriek that wouldn't die down. He pushed his bedclothes away, and the girl. But still he could hear it, the shriek of a man with a bullet through his head, falling. He blinked, trying to push back the dream which refused to go away, and the vision, fading only to return, of a pit, a writhing sea of bodies, blood-soaked, spattered by brain, mouths gaping, a fool's gape, Lubienski's gape.

For lunch on Wednesday, 2 May, Dulles joined Anderson at his table at the Colony Restaurant, late. Anderson looked up, his mouth full. 'Well?'

Dulles said nothing as he sat down and picked up the menu, putting it down with barely a glance. He always had lobster at the Colony, with a bottle of Chablis he never finished. Anderson took water.

'We've got a new name,' Dulles began, while Anderson ploughed his way through his steak. 'Orlov. Gregor Orlov. A general in the GRU. He's got the task of co-ordinating the Soviet side of things.'

'Never heard of him. But I'll do a check.'

'All will be ready in about ten days. That's sooner than expected.'

The waiter came to the table to take Dulles's order. It was given, curtly.

'We'll be getting the final date through any time now, they reckon,' Dulles continued when the man had gone. 'But it's got to be Vienna. That's where they'll do the deal.'

'Vienna?' Anderson nearly choked. 'What the hell is wrong with good old Washington?'

'Agreed, but as I said, this Orlov has taken over the show. I suppose he doesn't want to travel all this way – that, or his masters won't let him. You know how they are.'

Anderson nodded as he pushed a potato round his plate to soak up the bloodied juice. The suspicions of Soviet Security were legendary. They mistrusted even themselves.

'It's a damned nuisance, John. But look at it this way. It'll mean a pleasant little jaunt for one of us.'

'If you can call Vienna pleasant nowadays. I'll willingly not go.'

'Well, there it is.' Dulles leaned back to look at the bottle the waiter brought him, then waved his hand in approval. 'Everything through Orlov, and he'll be in Vienna.'

'Do you know where in Vienna?' Anderson was still uneasy.

'No. But they'll tell us.' Dulles swilled the wine round his mouth and nodded. The waiter poured, and left. 'So I can't see that they can pull a fast one. We can saturate the area with our men, just to make sure if you want. But don't worry. I really don't expect any trouble. I think they're just windy about their man, as I say. That, and wanting us to go halfway to meet them. It's a deal, after all, and we can't expect to have it all done in our own living room. I don't think that going to their back yard is too much, eh, John?'

Anderson didn't answer, but busied himself with extracting a piece of gristle from his mouth.

The lobster arrived, a fine specimen, covered with Mornay sauce, and Dulles tucked in.

'What do they say about this Congressional investigation into Katyn?' Anderson asked. 'Things are hotting up on the Hill. We'll get it unless we put the stops on now. So what do we do?'

'That goes ahead. Moscow confirmed. They don't mind any enquiry providing we prevent the Administration taking it up. I think we can manage that, don't you?' Dulles ate his lobster and swilled it down with wine. 'It'll be the usual dead duck.'

Anderson smiled. 'A little cynical, isn't it?'

'Sure, what's changed?'

Over the past few days, the Company had done its research on Katyn, and the results hadn't improved Dulles's faith in human affairs. During the war the US State Department had come into possession of a considerable amount of information concerning massacre, all pointing to Soviet guilt. It originated from a number of sources whose variety and authority was impressive: reports from British and Polish Intelligence, from the US Ambassadors to Moscow and the Polish and Balkan Governments-in-Exile, the US Special Emissary for Balkan Affairs, a US liaison officer to the Polish forces, and a special research group set up by the President. All, either by implication or in plain language, blamed the Soviets.

However, at no time did the State Department ever come near to condemning the Russians, and President Roosevelt remained adamant that the Germans were responsible. Indeed, such was the conviction of the US Government that when, towards the end of 1944, a new Ambassador to Poland was preparing to assume his duties, he was not allowed to see any of the incriminating evidence. All he was given was a report written by a twenty-five-year-old American girl who had visited the graves during Soviet investigations. Other requests for information, including those from Senators, were also rejected. Katyn was, to the State Department, a matter for secrecy.

The cover-up, however, took other forms. In late 1943, for example, the US liaison officer to the Polish forces was sharply criticized by the US War Department for the biased information he sent, while as late as March 1945 the Emissary for Balkan Affairs was expressly forbidden by the President to write an article on Katyn unfavourable to the Soviets. The press was severely muzzled, and a government-inspired editorial line imposed in which the US Office of War Information took an active part. Later, at the Nuremberg War Trials, only a small, unrepresentative selection of the available evidence was given to the American prosecutors. Even as late as 1950, when a former Polish officer visited the United States, officials of the 'Voice of America' eliminated all references to Katyn in the Polish language broadcast of his interview.

Then there was the Van Vliet report, written by an Army Colonel and presented to Army Intelligence after the war. When a prisoner, he had visited Katyn as a guest of the Germans and had been allowed free access to the site. To his satisfaction, Soviet guilt was conclusively proved. But as one of his last acts before his death, Roosevelt ordered Van Vliet's report suppressed. It was classified *Top Secret* to keep away prying eyes, then went missing altogether.

'Katyn's a can of worms.' Dulles wiped the sauce from his mouth, and stifled a belch. 'But it's going to do us a lot of good, I can see that.'

Chapter Twelve

The title came easily enough: 'Katyn: A Foreign Office Conspiracy?' But what next? It had to be snappy enough for the newspapers, yet detailed, leaving out nothing.

Nick leaned back in his chair, tilting it on its legs, and chewed on his pen. His thoughts, as so often over the past week, turned to Lubienski, a man he had liked, even admired – and that was rare for Nick. Had he unwittingly caused the old man's death? Had he, by shouting Philby's name from the rooftops, caused British Intelligence to act? If, after all, they had murdered Sikorski, they would hardly hesitate at Lubienski. That would explain a lot. The thought was staggering, yet disturbingly plausible. But what was the truth? Nick realized he had to do something to provoke a reaction: fighting the British Establishment was like punching putty. Perhaps a press article would make them a little more brittle.

Nick was a stubborn man. A set-back, and he followed Wellington's maxim, tied a knot and began again. So the death of Lubienski, the elusiveness of Philby, the impossiblility of Parliament – all that he could cope with, as well as, now, the certainty of losing his job. There was no turning back, no compromise – not this time. Nick had made his judgement and found he possessed a loyalty greater than just to the Service. Relations with his chief were already strained. Conversation had become clipped, confined to business or current meteorological conditions. Another false step, and Nick knew he would be out.

He turned back to the paper and began. 'The massacre of fifteen thousand Polish officers is burned on Polish memories, yet few Britons remember Katyn – or care to.'

He grinned. That would make them turn in their ruts. 'It was a major crime . . .'

Just as the flow had begun the door-bell rang. Nick looked at his watch: ten-twenty. Who the hell could it be? He had few casual callers, a breed of acquaintance he discouraged. Getting up, he went into the hall and opened the door. Two men stood there, framed by the doorway, their bulk obscuring the light from the passage.

'Mr Pelham?' came a foreign accent, which Nick couldn't determine. The tone was disarmingly polite.

'Yes,' he replied guardedly.

The taller of the two moved forward, and with full force slugged Nick in the stomach. He doubled up, then reeled back with a knee in his face. His head hit the wall, and he slumped on to the floor as two boots smashed into his chest, sending him sprawling, gasping for breath. The pain became unbearable. He couldn't even cry out. The two men moved in and shut the door, and for a split second Nick saw them with an unusual sharpness of vision, before they became dark blurs, merging with the blackness that dropped from the ceiling.

Nick came round as he felt himself being hauled on to his bed. His head was swimming and he had difficulty in focusing, but slowly he became aware of what was happening. The two men were going through his flat, emptying the contents of drawers on to the floor, clearing out cupboards, ripping up carpets and tearing the spines off books. They were thorough. Nick tried to get up, but couldn't. His left ankle was handcuffed to the bedstead.

After what seemed an age, but can have been no more than ten minutes, the men turned their attention to Nick. The smaller, whose face was badly pock-marked, picked up a pullover from among the heap of clothes on the floor, and flung it at him.

'Come, my friend. We go.'

Nick opened his mouth to reply, but found it too painful. He moved his tongue, and tasted blood.

'Come. Hurry.'

Nick sat up, his ankle still manacled, and slowly eased the thick pullover over his aching body. When he had finished, his overcoat was thrown at him, hitting him full in the face. He kept silent, remembering his training: say nothing, watch, listen.

'We go,' the smaller man hissed, holding Nick's keys out to him, while his companion, a burly brute with a squashed face, bent down, unlocked the handcuffs, and pulled Nick up by the arms. Nick cried out with pain. The little man took him by the chin, pulling it from side to side.

'Now listen, friend. Not a word. One squeak, and you die. Understand?'

Nick nodded. He had worked out the man's accent. It was Russian.

Nick was hauled out of his flat and down the stairs, stumbling as he went. His head ached, was almost bursting, and his feet dragged as if they were lead. He wanted to vomit. Outside, the street was deserted. Pausing a moment to check the way was clear, the two men flung Nick across the pavement and into the back of a waiting car. Someone was there to grab him, and he was pulled roughly inside, followed closely by the larger man. The smaller went round to the driver's seat. Another, also burly, sat in front, hat over his eyes, not once turning to look at the captive. The car started up, turned out from the kerbside, and accelerated off into the night.

Nick, still dizzy from the blows, saw the lights of Kensington High Street, then shut his eyes as waves of nausea enveloped him, and he dropped his head to his chest. It was only by a miracle of concentration he wasn't sick.

Time was not easily measured, but Nick reckoned that the journey could have lasted only twenty minutes, not half long enough to get out of London. The car came to a halt, and when he managed to focus he saw they had parked on a hill in a deserted, dimly-lit road lined by houses. The driver remained by the wheel, with the engine running, while Nick was bundled on to the pavement, a guard at each arm. The man in the front passenger seat got out awkwardly, stood for a moment, concealed by his own shadow, then moved close. The dim light from the street lamp was barely sufficient for Nick to make out his features. The man smiled, a broad, almost friendly smile, which Nick thought he recognized. Then he spoke, in a thick Russian accent. It, too, was familiar.

'Mr Pelham, good evening. I must apologize for the manner of our second meeting.'

Nick, unsure, remained silent. Fear rose in his stomach, but he controlled it with his breath.

'You do not remember me? Yes? Surely?' There was a flash of rings as he removed his hat.

Nick's confusion amused the Russian, who burst out laughing.

'Come,' he said, taking Nick by the shoulder as the other two men moved back into the shadows. 'We must talk.' He hugged him, like an uncle. Then Nick remembered.

The Russian slipped his grip to Nick's arm and led him up the hill, the heavies following at a distance of about five yards. Nick looked around for an escape, but saw none.

'What the hell do you think you're bloody-well doing?' he turned on his captor.

'I need to talk.'

'There's no need for all this. Christ, those bully boys might have killed me.' Nick pulled away, but was restrained.

'I doubt it, Mr Pelham. They are a little brutal, but quite expert.'

'Well, what do you want to say that needs all this, then?' Nick jerked his arm, almost ready to lash out and risk another battering.

'Mr Pelham, please, just listen. Save your anger for later, I beg you.'

The Russian changed his tone. It was almost pleading. Nick, taken by surprise, listened.

'You have an interest in Katyn, yes?'

'Yes.'

'And an interest in Philby, yes?'

'What's all this got to do with you?'

'Never mind, now. We haven't time.'

They reached the top of the hill where the road ended, and beyond was grass stretching into blackness. Nick realized where they were: Hampstead Heath – over two square miles of open land and thicket where anything could happen. He felt the grip on his arm tighten as they walked on, their way illuminated only by a moon half obscured by passing cloud.

'Now listen, Mr Pelham. Our interests coincide. Only I know more than you.'

'That's not difficult.'

'Just listen, will you?' The Russian was getting angry. He controlled himself. His tone quietened. 'I can give you everything you want to know. And more. But in return I need your help.'

'Who the hell are you?'

'My name is Orlov. Gregor Orlov. I'm a General in Military Intelligence.' Nick was not surprised and didn't reply. Orlov continued. 'As I say, I need your help.'

'What?'

'I want to defect.'

Nick didn't know what to say, whether to laugh or cry. It was bordering on the ridiculous.

'Well, do, then. Why bother me?'

'Because, Mr Pelham, you are the only man I can trust.'

'What about our Intelligence services? I'm sure they would be delighted to receive you.' Nick was sarcastic, too suspicious for anything else.

'But that's the point, Mr Pelham. I can't rely on them.'

'Why the hell not?'

'I can't explain, not now. Time's too short. You will just have to trust me. It's dangerous, that's all I can say.'

'But why me?' Nick stumbled on a tuft of grass. 'Shit.'

'Because I know you. I know you have no connections with British Intelligence. And I know you have good training for this sort of thing.'

'What do you mean?'

'You were in Special Operations during the war. Let's not play games, Mr Pelham. I know a lot about you.'

'How the hell do you know that? Even my parents weren't told.'

'I tell you, I know. That's all.'

'But I still don't see why you can't just knock on MI5's door here, and announce yourself. It's what they're there for.'

'You don't understand. I can explain later, but not now. You just have to trust me.'

'Shall I take you home with me now?' Nick found it hard to believe the Russian.

'No. There's no chance here,' and Orlov jerked his head backwards. His men were less than six yards away. 'It will have to be elsewhere. In Vienna.'

'For Christ's sake!'

Orlov looked back anxiously at his men. 'Keep your voice down, please, Mr Pelham. One of them understands English quite well enough. Just listen, I beg you.'

Repressing his disbelief, Nick listened. In a few short sentences, obviously well rehearsed, the Russian gave his plan. He was leaving London in two days and would be in Vienna in twelve. That was certain. He would bring with him incriminating documents about Katyn, and much more besides. The mystery of Philby would be cleared up, he promised. They would then leave Vienna together, and Orlov would hide while Nick arranged for his defection. Money would be no object; the Russian would bring sufficient. But again, he repeated, all explanations would have to wait until Vienna.

Nick thought quickly. What if it were a trick? But then, why should it be? A mere Assistant Private Secretary in the Foreign Office was hardly a pawn worth playing in the Cold War. Though if it wasn't a trick, and Orlov really did want to defect, why turn to him? Why not to a senior diplomat or the Intelligence services? Why Orlov's fear?

Nick found no answers. The Russian prompted him.

'Hurry, please. We have no more time left. They will be suspicious.'

'Why Vienna? Why not now, here in London?' Nick persisted.

Again, Orlov checked behind him. 'I am not ready yet. I don't have all the information. It must be Vienna.'

Nick hesitated before replying. 'All right,' he said. 'I'll help.' There was nothing else for it. And anyway, the Russian's story, or lack of one, was so absurd that it just might be true. 'But I want everything on Katyn and Philby. And if I change my mind, I'll keep the curtains of my flat drawn during daytime. So before you leave London, check.'

'And not a word to your security services? To anybody?'

'No.'

'Good.' Orlov let out a sigh of relief. He put his arm around Nick's shoulder, and Nick felt something slipped under his lapel.

'Details of our meeting,' whispered Orlov. 'Any day between 15 and 19 May. And there are photographs. I need a British passport. Don't lose this. Put it in your pocket now.'

He withdrew his arm. Nick straightened his coat, catching hold of Orlov's folded paper, then put both hands in his pockets.

'Just one thing more, Mr Pelham. Trust nobody. Act as if you were being watched.'

'Who on earth . . . ?'

'Just do as I say. Now listen: you are here to receive some rough stuff, meant to keep you away from Philby – permanently.'

Nick stiffened.

'Don't worry. On your right, through those trees, there's a bank. Down it there's a path. We were to use it for our escape. Follow it to the left.'

Nick nodded.

'Now, hit me in the stomach,' and Orlov gritted his teeth.

Nick lashed out with his right arm, and Orlov doubled up in real pain, for Nick had hit him hard. He wrenched his left arm free, and ran for the trees, bursting through the undergrowth and falling down a steep bank. Winded, his face bleeding, he picked himself up and sprinted along the path. Shouts came from behind, and Nick could distinguish Orlov's voice abusing the guards. He kept running, his heart exploding in his ear-drums, for all the world to hear.

Chapter Thirteen

He swore stealthily, letting out his 'fuck' as a puritan would a 'damn'. Trying to avoid the Permanent Under-Secretary, he put his hand to his forehead, to the wound left by Orlov's men, now six days old. But too late; Sir William had got him. There was a glint in his eye.

'Nicholas, dear fellow. I hear you're off.' News travelled fast. 'I'm so sorry.' It was what passed for sugary sweet, but to Nick the man couldn't hide the elation he felt. He was a diplomat, used to making cream from cheese, only in this case the cream was sour.

Nick had been intending to see Sir William before he left, but at a time when he was ready, and he felt off guard, though that only added to the impression of illness. He mumbled his apologies, hoping his absence wouldn't be inconvenient.

'Jaundice, eh? Nasty.'

Jaundice affects the liver, making the urine brown, excrement white and the face yellow, all to the accompaniment of a deep depression. Catching it is not pleasant, even when manufactured, as service in Special Operations had taught Nick. As a precaution, he had learned how to take the digitalis tablets necessary to reduce his heart-beats to sixty a minute; to stuff himself with chocolate and raw eggs before going to bed; to keep his teeth unwashed – all with a gram of picric acid at the end. Three or four days of that, accompanied by complaints of diarrhoea, then constipation, itchy skin and stomach pains, and the symptoms were clear: jaundice.

'How long will you be away?'

'A month. Perhaps six weeks.' Nick looked his chief

straight in the eye. 'I might not come back.' To fool a diplomat, he had to speak the truth.

'Ha! Where are you going?'

'My mother's, Sir William. Surrey.'

'Ah well, we'll struggle on without you.' Sir William smiled, not knowing how close Nick had come to staying. What had happened to his Assistant Private Secretary was the sort of thing that occurs only to others, and Nick had been unready for it. There was so much he didn't understand. Continually over the past five days he had asked himself what he was doing, preparing to go to Vienna to meet a Russian spy who said he wanted to defect, knowing nothing more about him than that. Was he taking leave of his senses? But indecision lasted only until he remembered Lubienski's words: 'Tell me what you think of Poland, and I will tell you what you are . . .' Nick had no choice. If he wanted the truth about Katyn he had to go to Vienna, and trust Orlov. Pigs, he knew, were needed to find truffles.

Nick wiped imaginary perspiration from his forehead, and tried to straighten up.

'You don't look after yourself, that's the trouble, Nicholas. You bachelors are all the same.' Sir William obviously believed that sympathy should be tempered with blame; and advice. 'Take a wife. Settle down.'

Nick, his play-acting finally over, left the Foreign Office at midday that Tuesday, 8 May, but not by the main entrance, where, in the lobby, the man would be waiting, as he had been for the last few days. Instead he used a service entrance, now familiar to him, squeezing between vanloads of paper and linen, and only when his business was completed an hour later, did he return the same way to leave the Foreign Office by the front door. He didn't bother to check whether the tail was following; he just presumed. And he didn't care. In his pocket he had all he needed, without anyone getting to know.

Over the past five days Nick had been busy, though

obtaining the passport for Orlov had proved surprisingly easy. He had known two ways, both illegal. One was to search for the grave of a boy who had died before the age of holding a passport, but who, had he lived, would be in his middle fifties – Orlov's age. Once Nick had a name and a birth date, obligingly given on the tombstone, he could go to the Central Registry of Births, Marriages and Deaths at Somerset House in London, and purchase a copy of the child's birth certificate necessary for the passport application. It was safe, but the other method was less trouble, and that was the one Nick chose. All he had to do was find someone who had never held a passport – an easy enough task – then obtain their birth certificates and proceed from there.

It hadn't taken long for Nick to decide on his man: his uncle, crippled in the First World War, who had just celebrated his fifty-eighth birthday. Service for King and Country had left him such a hatred of foreigners that he made it a point of honour never again to leave Britain's shores. Nor had he, as a simple telephone conversation confirmed. With the birth certificates, the passport application was easy. Henderson's name was entered, his age and place of birth, as well as Orlov's height, colour of eyes and hair, and profession. He was to be a businessman. For a referee, Nick gave his own name and address, and made up another. And that was all, except for Orlov's photograph, which showed a man as unlike the Russian as possible, given his distinctive features. The new face had spectacles, moustache and dark hair. A ladies' hair dye, mid-brown, obviously unobtainable in the Soviet Union, had been requested in Orlov's list of instructions.

At the Passport Office in Victoria Nick had used his connections, and the passport was ready for his collection within forty-eight hours.

And then there was the 'biography'. For the new man Henderson, Nick had kept bus and underground tickets, had bought a complete range of men's toiletries, a pen and wallet with 'Made in England' stamped prominently on them, and had even sent Henderson a postcard of Trafalgar Square thanking him for a party, addressed to his London flat – all to be given to Orlov.

Travel had proved a little more difficult. As a penalty for being incorporated into the Third Reich in 1938, post-war Austria was a country under occupation, and the victorious powers had not only divided her land between them, but also her capital, Vienna. That made formalities complex. Although British citizens didn't need a special visa, entry to the Soviet zone which completely encircled Vienna required what was known as a Grey Card, entitling her bearer to cross the border zone by train or car at Semmering, a mountain health resort sixty miles south-west of the capital. Only a special authorization allowed crossing at any point. If the traveller were to fly to Vienna, using either the Schwechat or Tullin airfields, both in Soviet territory, a Grey Card was unnecessary. However, as Nick had found out, there were no civil flights between London and Vienna. A change at Paris was essential.

The total time by air, the girl at the travel agency informed him, was eight hours; by train, also via Paris, it would take thirty-three, and by car roughly forty-eight of hard motoring. For that, however, yet more paper was required. Apart from an international driving licence and an international automobile circulation permit, Nick would need an entry permit valid for ten days only. He had even enquired about bicycles; they were dutiable at the border unless a deposit was paid. In the end, Nick decided on a second class train ticket, to leave early on Sunday, 13 May, and requested the travel agency to obtain the necessary Grey Card from the Soviet Embassy for an extra charge. In addition, he asked for comprehensive details of train and air departures from Vienna, as well as a map of Austria and its capital. That, as well as drawing £200 from the bank, completed Nick's preparations before jaundice took him to Surrey.

At his mother's home, a rambling Georgian manor set apart from the village, Nick took to undergoing rigorous physical exercise for the four days remaining, but always in the house. Not once did he go into the garden, and even practised target shooting with his old service revolver in the cellar. Although she tried, his mother couldn't understand the reason for his activity. On one occasion she caught him sitting among a pile of clothes, ripping out the makers' tags, but all he gave was a wink and a smile in reply to her questions. Only when, on Saturday night, Nick told her that he would be leaving for Vienna the next day, did he explain why he had been poring over maps and guide books of Austria. She was never to understand the rest, especially why he left at five o'clock on Sunday morning by the back gate which led into the fields.

Chapter Fourteen

Vienna in 1951 was a city still shattered by war, the headquarters of an enemy occupation, with each victorious power in its zone, marked by wire or notice board. Half of Austria's capital was divided between the Americans, the French and the British, with the Russians holding the rest. Only the centre, the *Innere Stadt*, two miles in circumference, came under joint control, each power taking the lead for a month at a time. Here, the last visible sign of co-operation between East and West was to be seen – the International Patrol, four military policemen in a jeep, one from each nation.

To this divided city Nick's train arrived on a grey evening of Monday, 14 May at the Westbahnhof terminus. There, from charred remains, a new station was rising, made of concrete and glass, a palace which the enthusiastic Austrian who sat next to him was sure would be better than the old. But the presence of British, French and American soldiers in large numbers made Nick doubtful how long it would last.

Outside on the square he found a taxi. The driver, a surly individual in an old German Army forage cap without insignia, nodded at the destination and asked in broken English for a cigarette. Nick had none. The man spat and cursed softly in German. Nick understood – he had been called a 'damned Jew'.

The taxi made slow going for the Austrian drove carefully to save petrol, and purposely took an indirect route to increase the fare. But Nick didn't mind. It gave him a chance to see Vienna for the first time. His immediate impression was of the scars of battle left by the Allies.

Whole rows of houses lay in ruins, testimony to indiscriminate bombing, their walls, like broken shells, still blackened from the fires which raged in the final months of the conflict. Twenty per cent of the city had been destroyed, mostly by British and American aircraft, the rest by the Soviet and German armies in the bitter fighting of April 1945.

Through the older quarters they drove, the rabbit warrens of the working class, brown with the dust of burned coal, until they came to the Vienna of legend, with its tiled mansard roofs and walls of yellow ochre, soft pinks and whites. Here, on the outskirts of the centre, Nick first caught sight of the broken spire of St Stephen's Cathedral. Battered and truncated, the '*Steffel*' still dominated the city, a symbol of its suffering.

It took fifteen minutes for the taxi to reach the *Innere Stadt*. Girded by the Ring, the wide road on which Vienna's public buildings stand, this inner city is a maze of narrow, ancient streets, palaces, houses and shops, the historic centre of what had once been Europe's greatest empire. Here lay the Dorotheergasse, and at No 6, the Aclon boarding house, small and unassuming, recommended by the girl in the travel agency, and just five minutes' walk from the rendezvous with Orlov.

The taxi driver asked for twenty schillings. Nick looked at the meter. It read just four, but before he could argue, the man gave his explanation: the price had to be multiplied by five. It was all a consequence of losing the war, he said; inflation. Nick made a rough conversion, made the cost five shillings, fair enough by London standards, and paid. Giving the driver a tip, a broad smile and a '*Guten Abend*', he picked up his suitcase and went inside the Aclon.

The interior was quiet, cosy and bourgeois. The walls of the hall were painted deep yellow, a highly polished mahogany counter lined one side, chairs and a small table the other. Delicate lace curtains covered the windows, and the air was fragrant with spring flowers. On the walls were paintings and photographs of old Vienna and a portrait of the Emperor Franz Josef, the top edge draped in black, greening round the edges. A sprig of evergreen had faltered lopsidedly across the frame. A wireless playing sombre classical music was switched off, and a little old man, bent almost double, emerged from behind the counter and bowed as low as he was able. His hair was brushed up and across and around, but still couldn't hide the fact that, on top, his head was as bare as an egg.

'May I be of some assistance, *Excellenz*?' he asked in a soft Viennese accent full of musical cadences.

Nick replied in almost-fluent German that he required a room.

'For how long, may I enquire, *Excellenz*?' The old man asked, smiling sweetly.

'A week at the most. Perhaps less, I don't know.'

The old Austrian returned to the desk and opened a heavy book. The effort seemed to take all his strength. Putting on his spectacles, as ancient as himself, he squinted at blank pages, obviously having difficulty focusing, and it took him some time to come to a decision. Nick suppressed a smile.

'Yes, *Excellenz*, that will be possible. You will follow me, please.'

Nick's bedroom was on the second floor, its window overlooking the street. The highly polished wooden floor was bare except for a rug, and the walls, freshly painted light blue, naked except for a crucifix above the double bed. In a corner stood a wash-basin, and next to it, opposite the bed, a large wardrobe. Through the floor-boards seeped a sickening smell of cooking, but Nick showed his appreciation and, leaving his baggage, returned downstairs to sign the book. His offer to deposit his passport was declined, the old man merely noting its details. Passports, it seemed, were essential for movement in occupied Vienna.

He didn't go out that evening, and after a light meal of beer and sandwiches, went to bed. The mattress was hard, but Nick, exhausted after his travelling, slept well.

His alarm gave its high-pitched buzz at seven the following morning. Downstairs, in the little back room that served as a dining room, coffee and rolls were brought by an elderly lady who had one eye hermetically sealed, and giggled like a schoolgirl at the Englishman's accent, while the old man, her husband, fussed round, bowing and '*Excellenzing*' for all he was worth, continually rearranging his hair to cover his baldness. Nick liked them. Perhaps they were a little overbearing, but, as he seemed to be their only guest, that was understandable.

After breakfast, Nick went back to his room and took off his jacket. Burrowing beneath the clothes still in his suitcase, he took out a throwing knife – flat-handled, about ten inches long, in a thin leather sheath – and thumb-tested the blade, sharpened on both sides. Then he pulled a short length of string through two holes in the sheath's neck where once there had been a strap to secure the handle, and tied it round his back collar stud. The knife hung down his upper spine. Tucking it beneath the Y of his braces, he put on his jacket and examined himself in a mirror. There was no sign of the weapon he carried, except when he hunched his shoulders.

Nick looked at his watch: eight-twenty. Stuffing a guide book in his pocket, he went downstairs and out into the street. He had the rendezvous to check.

For their meeting, Orlov had specified the main entrance to St Stephen's Cathedral, and the gateway to the Hofburg Palace in the Michaeler Platz. At the first, eye contact would be made; at the second, words exchanged. Two times were stipulated: nine o'clock and seven past nine respectively in the morning, and seven and seven minutes past seven in the evening. If either man thought he was being followed, he would keep both hands in his pockets.

Nick had checked the rendezvous with a map. Orlov was clever: the two places seemed near enough to cover the distance between them in the seven minutes without suspicious haste, and far enough to tell if either was being followed. Orlov had not forgotten the importance of timing. Waiting, as Nick remembered from his wartime training, was a dangerous occupation. More importantly, both locations gave wide angles of view and several choices of exit, essential for a safe rendezvous.

His stroll through the *Innere Stadt* that morning brought Nick into his first real contact with Vienna. Though the early morning air was cold, the city's atmosphere was warm, intimate, so that he imagined the place full of violinists, soulful, gay, romantic . . . But the only music he heard was jazz, whistling with atmospherics, played over the radio of an International Patrol.

Through the narrow side streets Nick wandered, past the round-arched double doors of courtyards, with their covered stairways and cage-like balconies, the fading baroque fantasies of noblemen, half-decrepit shops, and then on to the main roads, the lively Graben, already full of traffic, and the Kohlmarkt, a narrow, elegant shopping street, together forming the route between the Hofburg and the Cathedral. The vast, domed gateway to the Imperial Palace was impressive, dominating the Michaeler Platz, decorated by ornate ironwork, classical columns, and vast sculptures symbolic of power long since gone. And finally the Cathedral, which had miraculously survived the fire by retreating SS troops, dwarfing all around it, a vigorous Gothic edifice with an uncompleted north tower and the other, once a needle, now truncated; the steep diaper-patterned roof; the water-spewing gargoyles; Christ and the Virgin.

At St Stephen's, Nick found he had ten minutes to spare,

so went inside, to be struck by the vast interior and the mass of candles lit by the pious before the Madonna. Slowly shapes took form in the gloom: columns, statues, the pulpit, altars, and, everywhere, the signs of reconstruction, with hoardings, drills and bricks lying scattered. In the All Saints' Chapel he found a quiet corner and sat down on a rickety chair opposite the fifteenth-century masterpiece, 'The Man of Sorrows'.

But at that moment the Cathedral didn't interest Nick. At any other time he would have been absorbed, lost in the magnificence of its Gothic, but not then, not with a bellyful of butterflies. In just a few minutes he expected an event which, whatever its outcome, might change his life irrevocably, and could even end it altogether. There he was, alone in a city at the centre of the Cold War, stiff with security officers from four nations, intending to spirit a senior office of Soviet Military Intelligence back to Britain. And that was if everything went according to plan. What if it were a trap?

The pain of his finger-nails digging into his palms made Nick realize how frightened he was. He unclenched his fist, though inside he remained shivering. But he knew he had no alternative – not if he wanted to live with himself. He flexed his back and felt the knife lying between his shoulder-blades. It was little comfort, but would have to do. It was all he had.

At nine precisely, Nick left the Cathedral and looked around the square like a tourist. Groups of Viennese stood talking while others bustled past on their way to work. Visitors gazed heavenwards at the spire, a group of military policemen lounged against their jeep, and a man turned a barrel organ, whistling its melody, something by a Strauss. But no Orlov.

Lingering longer than was wise, Nick moved off in the direction of the second rendezvous. Down the Graben he went, turning left into the Kohlmarkt, not relaxing until he came to the relative calm of the Michaeler Platz. He looked at his watch: six minutes past nine. A minute early. In his excitement he had walked too fast. He stopped, took out his guide book and pretended to read. The sixty seconds went agonizingly slowly, but at seven past exactly he looked up and began to walk through the archway and into the Hofburg. Still no Orlov. Nick stopped again. The gateway was deserted. He looked at his book. Another minute, but nothing happened. Turning back on himself, he slowly retraced his steps up the Kohlmarkt. Passing a door inscribed *Demel's Sohne, Confectioner to the Imperial and Royal Court*, Nick stopped, hesitated, then went in.

A pair of frosted-glass swing doors gave way on to a piece of old Vienna – a traditional coffee house with tiled floor, mirrors, brass and crystal gas lamps, court pictures, painted plasterwork, and, directly in front, a large mahogany buffet on which a waitress was arranging cakes. Around marble-topped tables sat the Viennese, silent and engrossed in journals and newspapers. Overall, the bitter, pleasing aroma of ground coffee.

Nick found a seat and waited to be served. An operatic bosom towered over him, belonging to a severe Frau compressed within a black uniform, decorated by frills. Nick smiled, but met with no response. He ordered a *grosser Brauner* and a slice of *Sachertorte*, which he had not tasted since before the war, and the waitress left without a word.

The order was long in coming. Nick flicked through an art journal but couldn't concentrate. It had been a blow. Orlov's non-appearance. Although Nick had known of the possibility, he hadn't really reckoned with it, and all his plans had envisaged the two of them on the midday flight from Vienna to Paris. Now, he had to face the certainty of a day in the city, and the possibility of a week spent there, perhaps fruitlessly.

When the coffee and cake was finally brought, Nick polished them off quickly, and ordered the same again.

Disappointment always made him eat. Above her bosom the waitress lifted an eyebrow. Appetite clearly impressed her, for she permitted a smile. His second helping eaten, Nick paid and left, and as he did so he became aware that he felt a little sick.

The pelican opened a pink eye, blinked, then shut it, deciding the world was not worth staying awake for. His neck sank into his feathers, he fidgeted, and his belly settled itself firmly in a clump of daffodils. Sir Stewart Menzies looked away, then at his watch. Two thirty-five. The man was late.

He got up from his bench and to kill time sauntered on to the bridge, hands in pockets, stooped, looking tired and alone. In the middle he halted, and resting on the rail gazed at the view. Across the lake of St James's Park, through plane trees and weeping willows, massed buildings rose, piled one on another, capped by towers and cupolas and Union Jacks. The illusion was of a city of dreams. Reality was Whitehall.

'Afternoon Stewart!' called the Permanent Under-Secretary as he strode briskly on to the bridge, broadening his mouth in greeting. Lunch at the club had clearly been well lubricated. 'It's good to see spring at last, eh?' he remarked, jabbing at the sky with his umbrella. Sir Stewart looked up, and for the first time noticed the weak sun. 'Yes,' he said. 'Very.'

Tossing a pleasantry or two, they moved off the bridge and on to the grass, away from the lunch-time walkers.

'Well? What's up, Stewart?'

'Saw Dulles this morning, William.'

'Oh yes? How was he?'

'Well enough, but he's a supercilious sort. Can't say I warm to him.' It hadn't taken long for Dulles's pretensions to annoy the aristocratic Sir Stewart.

'What's he doing over here?'

'Didn't say.'

'Well there we are then.'

'He's on his way to Vienna, William.'

'Vienna?'

'Yes.' Sir Stewart was beginning to look embarrassed, unusual for him.

'Ah . . . What's wrong with Vienna? A good place for a spy.'

'Yes. And . . .' Sir Stewart hesitated.

'And . . . ?'

'Pelham's in Vienna.'

'God!' The conviviality of lunch vanished as Sir William choked on the name of his Maker. 'But it's a coincidence, surely?' He tried to laugh. 'And anyway, Pelham's ill, isn't he?'

'No, William.'

'What's going on? You did have your men on him, didn't you?'

'Yes.'

'Well?'

'He gave us the slip. I'm sorry.'

Sir William reddened, but checked his anger as a pair of lovers strolled past, nose to nose. Sir Stewart took advantage. 'All I can say is that we saw Pelham safely to his mother's, we kept watch, then when we made a routine phone check yesterday, he wasn't there. And he didn't leave by the front door.'

They had arrived at a bench, and sat down. Sir William took off his bowler. 'When was this?'

'He left the country on Saturday.'

'How do you know he's in Vienna?'

'Last week he went to a travel agency. Said he was finding out about holiday arrangements in Austria. All perfectly respectable. This morning we checked with them again. Seems he returned there several times without us knowing and bought a ticket for Vienna.'

'Why on earth couldn't you have found this out earlier?'

'Pelham was planning a holiday, we knew that. He was telling everyone. And . . . well, we just did our best.' Sir Stewart's words trailed away as he realized their insufficiency.

'Are you telling me there is a connection between Pelham and Dulles?'

'No, William. What connection could there be? It's just coincidence. Has to be. We've alerted Vienna Centre for Pelham. They're . . .'

But Sir William was hardly listening. He was remembering the sinking feeling he had felt in his stomach that Friday morning ten days ago, as he saw Pelham arrive at work with only his face marked, when he should have been lying dead in a ditch on Hampstead Heath.

'And we've got a lead,' Sir Stewart continued. 'The travel agency recommended several boarding houses. They're worth a try.'

'So we could have him nailed by tomorrow morning at the latest?'

'Yes.'

'Thank God.' Sir William rose, and stood looking at the ducks waddling incongruously on dry land. He opened his mouth, hesitated, then finally spoke. 'This time, Stewart, if you find that Pelham is up to something, take care of him properly, will you?'

From behind came Sir Stewart's voice, calm and reassuring. 'Don't worry, old boy. That sort of thing is easy to arrange over there.'

Chapter Fifteen

Spring in Vienna was more advanced than in London. The brilliant sun, the air crisp from the Alps, the pink and white blossoms of the chestnuts, the scents of goulash and kümmel, the drunks and the dark-eyed girls – those were the lingering impressions of that Tuesday for Nick. Those, and the evidence of war – the blackened hulks of the Opera and Burgtheater, the ruins of the Dianabad, the destruction of the Prater amusement park.

By early evening Nick was tired, but he still felt the excitement mount as he went, first to the Aclon for his knife and then to the Cathedral. Seven struck as he walked on to the square, but again no Orlov. Without waiting, Nick continued on to the Michaeler Platz, carefully judging his pace to arrive exactly at seven minutes past. The palace gateway was deserted. Nick took a sharp turn left, and headed for the Dorotheergasse. As he entered the Aclon five minutes later, he was unaware of the man in the shadow across the street, watching.

There was no sign of Orlov again the next day, or the next. Nick kept faithfully to his times, did nothing to risk exposure, and kept his suitcase packed ready for escape. But the tension was beginning to tell. Only when sleeping did he relax, and then his knife was never more than half an arm's length away. Just as soldiers cannot forever be held in readiness to go over the top, so at last Nick sought release from the strain. On Thursday night, after dinner at the bustling Rathauskeller, where he drank more wine than was good for him, he set out for a night club and excitement. There happened to be one next door to the Aclon, the Casanova, and when he had asked about it earlier Herr Stulpnagel, unable to say much in the presence of his wife, had rearranged his hair suggestively, then nodded and winked. The pickings, Nick hoped, might prove good.

The Casanova lived up to its name. It was small, with a bar at one end, tables and chairs grouped around a dance floor, and comfortable seating along the walls. In one corner stood a piano, silent when Nick entered, behind which a man sat filing his nails. The furnishings were from the Gay Apocalypse, all glass, burnt gilt and velvet the colour of champagne, their shabbiness obscured by the dull glow of red light. The club was full, its clients unambiguous as to their intentions. Most were servicemen, officers and Americans with wives far away, and the women, all Austrian, were the type who wanted a good time and money spent on them. Of the two, the latter was probably the more important.

Nick sat down at a small table, drank the cold beer brought by a waitress and ordered another. The pianist began to play some American jazz, and couples moved on to the floor. There was little that interested him. Most of the women seemed to be attached, and those that were free were the sort of obvious tart he found attractive only when very drunk. It would probably come to that, he thought, but until then he preferred his own company. A woman in her late forties came and sat at his table, leaning forward to allow him a better view of her cleavage. He accepted the offer, but declined conversation. She was over-painted, and it disgusted him. Nick looked away, trying to avoid contact with the woman's eyes which blinked repeatedly, and caught sight of a young blonde sitting at the bar, legs crossed, thighs hugged by her dress, smoking. He got up and moved towards her.

Her name was Anna. She had blue eyes and a turned-up nose and pert, unsupported breasts which showed through her silk blouse. But it was her legs that fascinated Nick:

they were long, slender, constantly crossing and uncrossing in an elegant display. And she was available, so they stayed together at the Casanova until one o'clock, then left. Herr Stulpnagel, roused from his sleep to open the door, was delighted. A room with two in its bed was worth half as much again than with just one.

Nick got on well enough with Anna. Apart from the obvious physical attraction, she was amusing in her empty-headed way, laughed at everything because her teeth were good, and didn't ask questions. When he went to his rendezvous the following morning, she waited happily enough at Demel's eating her helping of cream-laden *Sachertorte*, and when he returned she smiled sweetly and asked for another. That would do her until lunch, she said, and they could have that in the Prater.

At midday, among the white-flowering chestnuts of the park designed by the Hapsburgs, they stopped at a garden restaurant, *Zum Stillen Zecher*, To the Quick Drinker, a picturesque, wooden building with painted walls and an old woman playing a zither by the side of one of the windows.

'Now,' said Anna as they sat down, 'I'll order, you pay,' and she giggled. That was her philosophy. It suited her, and at that moment Nick too.

After lunch, they strolled through the Prater to the amusement park at its north-west corner, destroyed by war, whose desolate chimneys and rusting girders were all that was left of the marionette theatres, shooting booths, roundabouts and beer taverns that had stood on the spot for over a century-and-a-half. But a part of this magical world had been resurrected, and the huge ferris wheel, standing over two hundred feet high, was again revolving.

With Nick's money Anna bought two tickets and paid a bit extra on top for a car by themselves. As the wheel began to rise they looked down on the figures disappearing below, until the Danube and Vienna lay before them, and beyond the Wienerwald the foothills of the Alps. At that moment it was difficult for Nick to imagine Orlov out there, waiting. Katyn, Lubienski, Philby – they all seemed so far away.

He turned to Anna. He was beginning to notice her moods, her mannerisms, how she would wrinkle her nose when she laughed, how she looked at him with her large, trusting blue eyes, her head up and slightly to one side like a bird's. She reminded him of someone in his past: the same hair, the same carefree toss of the head, the flash of teeth and the laughter. And Anna's silences: deep, wistful, signalling there was more to her than she would give away. As the ferris wheel made a full circle, Nick thought he might want to know.

That evening, after another abortive rendezvous, Nick rejoined Anna, and they took a taxi to the Upper Belvedere. There, in front of the pond that reflected the baroque palace, they looked down on the centre of Vienna, framed between the green cupolas of the Karlskirche and the Salesianerkirche, and watched as the city was bathed in successive gradations of orange, pink, mauve, purple and blue. Again, the thought that a Soviet General was somewhere below, waiting to defect, seemed absurd. Not until the sun had gone down behind the hills to the west, and the air had taken on its night chill, did they begin the walk down the city. It was dark, but by the curb near the palace, Nick spotted a Packard saloon, a man lounging behind the wheel. Normally he would have taken no notice, but not now. That same car had been with them earlier at the Prater – its wheel had hit the curb and the hub-cap had shot off. That was why Nick remembered it. He said nothing to Anna, but it unsettled him.

That night Anna took Nick on his money to all her favourite places. They began in the Twelfth District, in the French zone, at the little *Heurige* tavern where they drank the new wine and listened to a *Schrammel* quartet play old

Viennese songs. They continued at the *Café Sperl* in the Sixth District, under American occupation, the haunt of rebel artists in the 1890s, where they ate and played French billiards, and afterwards returned to the *Innere Stadt* for a hot chocolate in the 'Old Vienna', before bed. And by this time Nick knew he was being followed.

On Saturday morning he woke early and heaved the protesting Anna out of bed. She had to go. Nick was fearful she would become caught up in his life, perhaps be killed because of him. His dream of that morning in a Dutch town seven years ago had ended, and he didn't want it replaced by another. So they left at eight, when the streets were deserted and footsteps could be heard in the stillness. At first there was nothing, no sound except for Anna's chatter. Nick tried to quiet her but she just giggled and hugged him harder. They turned a corner, and from behind came an echo of shoes on cobbles. Hurrying, Nick pulled Anna along until they reached the Graben.

'You've got to go now,' he said. 'I'm moving on.' She pouted, reached up and kissed him, then walked away, her hands in her coat, throwing an *Auf Wiedersehen* over her shoulder as Nick headed off in the opposite direction.

Nick knew expert tails were difficult to detect: they could work in pairs, change regularly, and use any vehicle they wished, but to Nick, who had been trained in their ways, a sixth sense took over. So when he finally walked past the Cathedral at nine that morning, his head was lowered and his hands were in his pockets. And again at the Hofburg. Orlov, if he were watching, would be warned.

Nick returned to the Aclon. He had some sleep to catch up on and anyway the sky was lowering; a deep grey, and the whole city seemed to be running a temperature, so there was nothing to do except go to bed, alone, and wait.

A knocking at the door woke him.

'Herr Pelham. *Excellenz*. A guest for you.'

Nick heaved himself out of bed, shook the sleep from his head, and looked at his watch. A quarter past twelve. Wrapping a sheet around his nakedness, he opened the door. There, towering over Stulpnagel, was Orlov. Nick felt shock, then relief, and smiled.

'Nicholas,' roared the Russian, arms outspread. 'How good to see you, my friend. Welcome to Vienna. Welcome.' Advancing into the room, Orlov closed the door on Stulpnagel. His manner changed abruptly; the smile dropped away and he held his finger to his lips. Then, going over to the window and hiding behind the curtains, he peeped down into the street. Only when he heard the old man's footsteps recede along the corridor, did he speak.

'We're in trouble,' he said, turning.

'I know. Who is it?' Nick remained standing as the Russian sat on the bed and got out a packet of cigarettes.

'You want one?'

Nick declined. 'I've been followed for at least a day. Perhaps more.'

'Three days, Mr Pelham. I have seen. That is why I did not move until you had your hands in your pockets. Then I felt it was at least possible you were not betraying me. So here I am.'

'Who is it?'

'Your side. It always has been.' Orlov lit a cigarette, not taking his eyes off the Englishman. He was still suspicious.

'My side?'

Smoke curled from the Russian. 'You know, I only smoke when I'm worried. And I do it now, just when I need all my breath to run – it's crazy.' He screwed up the packet in his hand, and dropped it to the floor.

'I want some answers, General – or whatever you are. I'm not going to risk my neck without knowing why.'

'You have already risked your neck, Mr Pelham. It's too late.'

Nick got up. 'To start with, how did you know I was here?'

Orlov forced a smile. 'You ask a General in Soviet Military Intelligence that? Nothing is impossible in Vienna.'

'And what are you doing in this city in the first place? Why didn't you defect in London?'

'Here.' Orlov pulled out a piece of paper from his pocket. 'Read this.'

Nick took it, and saw eleven names, all British, each with a codename. When he read 'Harold Adrian Russell Philby – Stanley', the expression on his face reminded the Russian of an owl blinded by too much light. Orlov could not suppress his amusement. He was relieved too. The chances were that Nick was not deceiving him.

'He's a traitor, your man Philby, along with all those others,' Orlov chuckled. 'In the service of Soviet State Security. That's what it's all about.'

Nick shook his head. 'But I don't understand. These are traitors? These men?' He caught sight of the names Gould and Maclean. 'I don't believe it.'

'Please . . .' Orlov was pleading. 'We don't have time for explanations now.'

'But why here, Vienna, for this?' Nick held up the paper.

'Later, please. Later.' Orlov rose and paced the room, grinding his cigarette into the floor in his agitation. Nick, still in his sheet, sat down heavily on the bed and put his head in his hands.

'You'll have your answers – but later, Mr Pelham. You have little understanding of Soviet Security. If I'm not back at the Imperial by two, they'll notice. I'm supposed to be leaving for Moscow today. I've delayed as long as I dare.'

The Imperial was the hotel on the Ring which the Russians had commandeered as their administrative head-quarters.

'But aren't you too senior to be bothered by such things?' Nick looked up, unsure of his man.

'No, Mr Pelham. In matters of security, we are all equal

in the Soviet Union.' Orlov peered out of the window again. 'We must get to the Westbahnhof by two-thirty. I don't dare risk it any later. We can hide there.'

That gave them only two hours.

'We're going by train?'

'Yes. The stations are watched, but not so closely as the airfields. They are impossible. Now, burn that.' Orlov pointed to the paper crumpled in Nick's hand.

'But the names. It's proof.'

'Burn it. I have all the proof you want.' Orlov fumbled in his pocket and produced a small metal phial, opened it, and carefully drew out a stick of paper, tightly rolled. 'It's all here. That and much more. Everything I could get my hands on of importance. All on microdots.' And from the same pocket he produced a packet of condoms. 'I've just bought these.' He grinned. 'From an American. Have you ever seen them used for this?'

Orlov unravelled a condom, cleaned it, and popped in the stick of paper. Then he twisted the rubber over the top and folded it down back over itself, twisted again and brought it back up. Sufficient was left at the top to tie a knot, and with a small pen knife he trimmed the excess. Nick watched in silence, intrigued.

'And now for the difficult part.' Going over to the wash-basin, Orlov filled a glass with water and swallowed the condom as if it were a pill. It took several attempts, but finally he managed it.

'There. Safe for about twenty-four hours.' He laughed. 'But it's always unpleasant poking through the shit.'

Nick looked at the Russian. He admired him for that. It couldn't be easy, swallowing those things.

'Now, Mr Pelham, are you with me or against?'

'With.'

'And the passport and the hair dye?'

'They're here.'

'Good. I've left a small case in a locker at the Westbahnhof, but I've brought the cosmetics.' Orlov patted a pocket. He seemed more at ease now, pleased they were getting on their way, and he started undressing as Nick put the passport and bottle on the bed.

'Right, Mr Pelham. While I do this, why don't you take a look outside? Have a walk. See what they are up to.'

Outside the storm clouds had gathered, and already a thin drizzle filled the air, but Nick was oblivious as he walked the maze of little streets, listening, watching. He was confused, too, by what he had just heard and wanted to work it out, but couldn't. There were still too many questions.

After ten minutes, seeing and hearing nothing suspicious, Nick returned to the Aclon, anxious to be off. Stulpnagel, as usual, greeted him.

'The Fräulein has come back, *Excellenz*. She's gone up to your room,' he said, and winked, but his expression changed abruptly as he saw Nick rushing upstairs like a man possessed.

At the top of the landing, Nick heard a stifled scream. Bursting into his room, he saw Orlov and Anna on the bed, she with arms flaying and feet kicking, he bare-chested, hair wet and streaked with dye, pressing down hard on her throat. Her face was distorted.

Nick jumped on Orlov, clawing at his body, tearing at his face – anything to make him let go. Leaving Anna gasping for air, the Russian grabbed Nick's arms and forced him off his back, turning with the Englishman until both were standing, locked together. Orlov heaved, and sent Nick flying back against the wardrobe, his head cracking against the heavy wood. The Russian followed up with a rain of blows, thudding down on Nick's skull. Blindly Nick lashed out, kicking between the man's legs. The Russian gasped with pain, but didn't stop. Slowly, Nick sank into unconsciousness, but not before he saw Orlov turn to deal with Anna.

Chapter Sixteen

Dulles walked into his chief's office. He looked tired. Bedell Smith removed his feet from the desk.

'How do you feel, Allen?' he said.

'Washed up.'

'Got them all?'

'Good as. All except one. Apparently SIS couldn't identify him from Khopliakin's list. It's the man called "Hicks".'

Dulles dropped a piece of paper in front of his chief. Almost immediately, Bedell Smith let out a whistle of amazement.

'Jesus Christ. Just look at that! Who knows about it in London?'

'Just three men – Menzies, Vivien and the head of their Foreign Service, Strang.'

'No one else?'

'No one.'

'Not even MI5?'

'Especially not MI5.'

Bedell Smith was silent.

'Scoop, eh?' said Dulles, triumphantly.

'Yeah, thanks to Anderson.'

Dulles didn't reply. Bedell Smith re-read the list. 'We're busted wide open by these bastards,' he said.

'Not for long now.'

'Too right. How long?'

'Four days. On the 23rd. Wednesday. That's when SIS is going to pull those men in. The Russians insist we do nothing until their deal with the British is complete. They won't have us jeopardize that.'

'And what's to stop us?' Bedell Smith's word did not bind him to Soviet Intelligence.

'The Russians have been clever. They know we can't just trot along to the President with the names and no back-up material. It looks too suspicious. And if it gets out that we had a deal with the Soviets, we're done for. Can you imagine Hoover's reaction, or McCarthy's – the President's even? No way we can weather that. So immediately after the 23rd, Orlov is going to give us the information we need to build up a case against each of those men. Without that, we can do nothing.'

'What's this man Orlov like?'

But Dulles was more interested in filling his pipe. 'Oh, the usual sort. They never vary, do they?'

Nick was brought round by cold water thrown in his face, to see Orlov towering over him, dripping with sweat, bloody scratches on his face and chest. Nick shook his head to clear it, and got to his feet with the Russian's help. Steadying himself by the wardrobe, he looked over at the bed. There lay Anna, skirt around her middle, pillow over her face dead. By her side was Stulpnagel, his neck broken, his baldness now revealed for the world to see.

Nick felt sick. He stumbled to the wash-basin and retched, but no vomit came.

'What the hell did you do that for? What did they do to deserve it?'

Orlov said nothing. He pointed to his hair, streaked with dye.

'So?' Nick moved over to his suitcase which lay open on a stand by the door.

'So she saw me dying my hair. So she knows the two of us are together. So she could ruin everything.'

'She had to die?'

'Yes.'

'And who would she tell – the Kremlin?' Nick slipped his hand inside his case, feeling for the knife.

Orlov shook his head. He thought the Englishman naïve. To him, death on suspicion had been a fact of life since childhood. In Vienna, with its network of spies and informers among the occupied as well as the occupiers, no chances could be taken.

'And the old man?'

Orlov shrugged his shoulders.

Nick found the knife. His hand closed around it.

'You bloody murderer!'

'Don't let that blind you, Pelham. You need me. Those,' Orlov growled, as he jerked his thumb at the two bodies, 'Those make you a wanted man. You have no choice. You've got to get me out, back to England. I'm your insurance.'

Orlov's words rang in Nick's head. He paused. It was not just a question of Katyn now, but his life, he realized, as he loosened his grip and let go the knife. There was a noose behind him, and no known destination in front.

By two o'clock the men were ready, both with their cuts mended as far as possible. Nick had on a sports jacket with the knife down his back, a precaution which impressed the Russian, who was now with brown hair, fake moustache and glasses. In addition to a passport, Nick had given him his 'biography', with the postcard addressed in his new name, a pen, a diary, London bus and train tickets. His coat had a new label quickly sewn in, as did his shirt. He had more labels for the clothes in his suitcase at the Westbahnhof. Such precautions would not, Nick admitted, fool an experienced security officer since Orlov, when he opened his mouth, was so obviously not the Englishman he pretended to be. They might, however, deceive the ignorant or the rushed.

The Soviet General was complimentary. Nick had done well – even obtaining an Austrian entry stamp in the

Henderson passport by some deft acting at the border in the train's lavatory. Nick, however, was distant. The violence of the man had disgusted him: he only wanted his secrets now.

A final check from the window that the street was clear, and they left the room. It was tidy, with no evidence of the struggle an hour previously, or of the bodies now stacked one on top of the other in the wardrobe like pilchards. Downstairs, the hall was empty. Clearly Frau Stulpnagel was out. For a moment Nick wondered whether to put the money for his room on the counter, but decided it was pointless, and went outside on to the street to join Orlov. The wind had got up, rain came in heavy gusts, but the way seemed clear and they set off, turning left towards the Graben to find a taxi.

They had only gone five yards when two cars, black Mercedes, appeared from nowhere and drew up, tyres squealing, one in front, the other behind them. Doors swung open blocking their escape, and before Nick and Orlov could run, four men had jumped out, two from each car. As they closed in Nick felt something hard in the small of his back. He was grabbed by the arm and his suitcase snatched as he was pushed to the first car, while Orlov was dragged to the second. It was all over in less than thirty seconds. Doors slammed shut, and the cars accelerated off.

Once past the Ring, Nick lost all sense of direction and found the blue plaques on the side of the houses too small to read. It was almost black outside, blinding rain blurred vision, and a gun in his ribs didn't allow for concentration. After fifteen minutes of what had obviously been a circuitous route designed to confuse the prisoners or shake off followers, the cars swept in at a large house standing in its own grounds in a residential area.

Nick and Orlov were bundled out and pushed at gunpoint to the back door, half-soaked on the way by the storm. Going through the kitchen and down to the basement, they were frisked, their passports taken, and their hands bound behind their backs. The door shut, a key turned, bolts slid home, and they were left alone.

Their prison, small and windowless, was bare except for two mattresses. The walls were of rough brick but in good condition, and the door looked strong. There was no sound, not even of the storm outside, except for the hum of an electric light that hung from the ceiling, and it was cold, damp running from the walls in patches of slime. Nick shivered.

'Who the hell are they? Austrians?'

Orlov shook his head, doubtfully, and nodded towards the walls. 'Bugged,' he mouthed.

'Well,' said Nick out loud, winking. 'We'll just have to sit back and wait, won't we?' and he wriggled over to the Russian, then lay on his side.

Orlov understood. He moved so that they were back to back, and with his hands, cupped together by the rope, he pulled up Nick's jacket, wriggling his body along the ground to do so. It was a long and painful job. Several times they stopped to listen or rest, but finally Orlov found what he was looking for. As he lay on his stomach holding the knife, Nick sat up and pulled the blade into an upright position. The Russian gripped the handle firmly, and Nick began to rub his rope against the blade. One by one the strands broke. Twice his hand was cut, but after three minutes it was over. He rubbed his wrists to get back the circulation, then taking the knife freed Orlov.

After hiding the rope under a mattress, Nick knelt next to Orlov and whispered in his ear. The Russian nodded, and they settled themselves to wait, huddling together for warmth.

It was to be a very long time, hours, before they again heard footsteps in the corridor. Orlov tensed, but Nick felt calm, his mind cutting through fear like a searchlight through the dark, almost as if he were indifferent to death – now, that would be the only way to survive, he knew.

The door opened, and two men stood there, both in their early thirties, pistols raised. Seeing the two prisoners against the far wall, lying uncomfortably, hands behind their back, they put away their guns and moved forward, making as if to drag them to their feet.

One towered over Nick, his face in shadow, so that Nick couldn't see the look of astonishment as he thrust the knife under his ribs to his heart. He fell dead. Orlov, meanwhile, grabbed the other by the throat, pulling him to the ground just as Nick's blade slid into his side. It was all over in seconds. No cry for help had been made, nothing but strangled gasps.

Hurriedly, Nick went through the men's pockets, finding two pistols and identification, including United Kingdom passports. He turned the pages to look for the men's occupation: Government Service. That could be anything. He flung the passports over to Orlov, standing by the door, gun at the ready. The Russian nodded, and his expression showed no surprise. Impatiently, he pointed to the passage.

Nick motioned to Orlov to go first. The Russian, surprisingly agile for his age and weight, ran to the bottom of the stairs and squatted, gun aiming upwards. Nick joined him, then moved past, climbing noiselessly up the stone steps to the door. It was ajar. He opened it slowly, checked the way was clear, and let Orlov slide through into the kitchen, then followed.

The room was empty, with the remains of a meal and the contents of their pockets, minus passports and wallets, on the table. They scooped them up, and were just about to snatch at some food when voices came from the corridor. They darted to the back door. The key was in the lock. Orlov turned it, the door opened, and in a second they were free.

It was dusk, and the storm over; the streets were heavy

with the rising smell of damp. Putting away their guns, Nick and Orlov walked from the house, not too fast, doing nothing to arouse suspicion. Keeping at least five yards from each other, they turned into street after street, distancing themselves from their kidnappers. Only after a quarter of an hour did they stop. They had arrived at a main road.

'Careful!' Orlov moved close. 'I know where we are. It's a border between the zones. Over there,' he nodded across the street, 'it would be very dangerous.'

Nick peered across. In the gloom, he could just make out a giant portrait on one of the houses. It was Stalin.

They turned back, and headed into the darkness of the French sector.

'Sorry to call you so late,' Vivien had said, sounding agitated. 'But we've just got some more news in from Vienna. I think you should come as soon as possible.'

It was past eleven-thirty when the head of SIS arrived back in his office to find Vivien and the head of the Austrian-German section, Tom Cunningham, waiting. Sir Stewart knew he would have to choose his words carefully.

'Well, what's up?' he asked.

'They've escaped,' said Vivien, knocking his monocle against the palm of his hand, making a hollow smack. 'Killed two of our operatives in the process.'

Sir Stewart made an effort to control his dismay. 'And when was that?'

'At about seven – just when Vienna Centre received clearance for Pelham's elimination,' replied Cunningham. 'How they got free is a complete mystery. They used a knife.'

'That makes four killings today,' commented Menzies. 'They're active.'

'And now they're armed. They've got the dead men's

guns.' Cunningham looked drawn, shocked by what had happened. 'But we've got their passports. And we've identified the other man, Henderson. It's Orlov, a General in the GRU. His passport photograph has too many similarities, except he must have dyed his hair. He lost his moustache in the cellar.'

'Ah, Orlov.' Sir Stewart raised his eyes to the ceiling, and screwed them up, pretending to think. 'Orlov. Yes, I've heard of him.'

It was seven hours since the message had come from Vienna Centre which informed Sir Stewart that his instructions of the previous day had been carried out. Pelham had been taken. The risks of his remaining free were considered greater than those involved in his disappearance, however mysterious. In the event, a bigger fish was also caught. And now they had both gone.

'So what does this leave us with?' mused Sir Stewart.

Cunningham jutted out his jaw. 'May I ask why this man Pelham is such a danger? It may make things easier if I knew.'

Sir Stewart looked his subordinate full in the face, unblinking. 'Sorry, Tom.' He smiled. 'But don't let me keep you. Get everybody in Vienna on the scent, and bring in the military boys. We might as well inform the Austrian police, too. Give them the passport photographs. They'll be looking for Pelham anyway, I should think, so put on the pressure to get him handed over to us if they catch him. We'll have to get the diplomats on that, and I'll make sure the Foreign Office acts first thing tomorrow.'

Cunningham got up to go. 'Will do,' he said stiffly, and with a goodnight, he was gone.

'Well?' said Menzies when the door shut.

'Well?' replied Vivien, hunching his shoulders.

'Are the Soviets pulling a fast one?'

'Could be. A defection stage-managed with one of our

chaps who can take Orlov straight to MI5 or, worse still, a politician. It makes sense. That way they'll have their cake and eat it. But God knows how Pelham is involved.'

'What else?'

'A bona fide defection. But again, why Pelham?'

Sir Stewart thought for a moment, finger over his right eye to control its flicker. 'Perhaps Orlov needs someone to bring him in, to liaise with our side, pave the way. He couldn't just trot along to MI5 himself. After all, he must know what happened to Volkov.'

In 1945, Konstantin Volkov, MGB *rezident* in Istanbul, had wanted to defect to Britain. Negotiations were conducted through normal SIS channels, but before he could be brought out he was arrested by Soviet Security, drugged, trussed up in a stretcher and flown back to Moscow. Not until Khopliakin's list revealed the traitors, did the SIS chiefs realize what had happened: Philby, then head of Section Nine, concerned with Soviet Intelligence, had warned his MGB masters. Clearly, Orlov would not risk similar betrayal.

'Any other reason?' asked the SIS chief. 'How does Dulles fit in?'

'Perhaps he doesn't. Could have been coincidence. If Orlov was defecting to the Yanks he wouldn't use Pelham. So if Dulles is involved, I can't see how.'

'Then there's no reason to believe our cousins are on to us, is there?'

'None. Unless they've got Khopliakin's list as well.'

There was silence as doubt seared through both men. Neither had considered that the Israelis would pass on the list to the CIA at the same time as handing it to SIS. Washington had given no indication; the Americans had continued to deal with Philby and Maclean as if all was well. There had been nothing unusual, nothing – except Dulles's visit to Vienna.

'The Israelis are close to the Yanks, you know that,' said

Vivien. He felt sick. The more he thought about it, the more likely it became.

'We've got a lot of thinking to do.' Sir Stewart shrank visibly into his chair as a premonition of disaster crashed down upon him. 'One's thing's clear, though. We can't bring in the traitors. Not until we've got Orlov and Pelham. We can't commit ourselves until then. It's too risky,' and his right eye began to twitch violently.

Nick and Orlov sat in the anonymity of a bar in the French sector, positioned near the lavatory for a quick exit. Over beer and rolls they discussed their next move. Their assets were few: about five pounds in Austrian schillings and the key to Orlov's locker in the Westbahnhof, where there was a change of clothes, two automatics, a small supply of ammunition, and roughly four hundred pounds in Austrian, German and French currency. Against that, the men were stateless, homeless, on the run from two security services, wanted by the Austrian police for murder, and isolated in an occupied city within the occupied Soviet zone of Austria.

'Well, where to tonight?' said Nick when their calculations were over and the beer drunk. 'The Ritz?'

Orlov shook his head, not understanding the Englishman's wry humour. 'No hotel will take us – not without passports.'

There were only the wet streets left, and their gloom was no cover, deserted by the inhabitants and patrolled regularly by police, military and civilian. Now they would also be stiff with security men.

Orlov paid and they left. Outside, the night air was chilly, and Nick pulled up the collar of his jacket. The Russian beat his arms around his body. They walked, four or five yards apart, up the street, away from the lights. Suddenly a car turned into the road, headlights blazing. Both men flattened themselves against the doorways. The car passed slowly, and went on out of sight. They emerged from the safety of darkness and continued, walking faster whenever they came to the dim gas lamps. Another car – another dive into the shadows. A pedestrian, and Orlov crossed the street; yet another car – and so it went on.

For half-an-hour the two men kept to the back-streets, weaving their way across Vienna, searching for cover. A bombed-out building would do, though cold and probably open to the rain, but before they came across one which was suitable, they were brought up short. Their street, the Linden Gasse, ended. Across the road stood an American military policeman in a distinctive white steel helmet. Perhaps he was watching for them. But as they were wondering, they saw a notice: the 'snowdrop' was guarding a barracks used by US Military Police. From inside, they could make out an anti-aircraft tower rising to about three hundred feet, one of the many put up by the Nazis in the last years of the war and now probably used only for storage – ideal for hiding. The problem was the sentry.

They had stopped in a narrow street. On the other side, by the corner, several cars were parked, probably belonging to Americans. Nick pulled out the tail of his shirt, ripped it off, and took the Russian's lighter. With that in his pocket, and twisting the white cotton into a long, thick fuse, Nick sauntered over to the cars, knelt in the shadow of the one nearest the main road, undid the petrol cap and inserted the cloth. Lighting it, he returned to Orlov.

A minute passed. Half a minute more. Had the cotton gone out? Two minutes, then a sheet of orange and white flame. The American sentry shouted and moved across the street, as Nick and Orlov ran over to the barracks. More soldiers came out, rifles at the ready. Nick pointed in the direction of the blazing car. '*Schnell, bitte! Schnell, Wasser! Wasser!*' He played the part of a demented Viennese well. The Americans grabbed water buckets standing outside the guard room and rushed past, leaving Nick and Orlov to slip through the small archway to the barracks. The centre of the courtyard was dark, and in seconds they were by the tower. The rusty metal door had a Red Cross marking on it, and was open.

Inside, the stench was foul, of bodies and stale cooking, and the floor deep in litter. In a corner, underneath the only light, an old man in ragged clothes squatted, but he took no notice of the strangers and continued searching for the lice in his coat. To one side a board, on which were pinned scraps of paper with messages in ill-formed capitals: 'Have you seen . . . ?', 'Do you know . . . ?' Bewildered, Nick and Orlov climbed to the first floor, where they were met by a small child, her hands in her mouth, before an anxious mother whisked her away to the safety of a curtain – an old blanket slung over rope which divided the space into living accommodation for four families. There were no windows, or at least none that were open, and the walls were damp. Haggard faces with hungry, expectant eyes peeped from behind blankets. Someone spoke. He was Hungarian. On the next floor it was similar, only this time Czech was heard. The tower was packed with Displaced Persons, refugees from the Eastern territories. Fifteen floors, sixty families, perhaps two hundred people, all waiting their processing by the authorities. And somewhere among them Nick and Orlov would have to find a space for the night.

Beria's face was triumphant, his attitude arrogant. He had won a victory, and had no wish to hide it.

'You should have seen the swine's expression,' he exulted, as much to himself as to Abakhumov. 'It was superb!' He started to laugh silently, though his face grimaced. 'A drink, my dear Viktor. We've reason to celebrate.'

And they had. Beria had just returned from a meeting at the Kremlin late that Sunday morning, at which Malenkov had revealed Orlov's defection.

'You should have heard our Great Leader. What he did to you was nothing by comparison. Nothing!' Beria slapped his thigh. 'And how that swine Malenkov trembled. He trembled like the baby he is. It was glorious. He's been relieved of all supervision over us, and Military Intelligence is no longer dealing with the blackmail. Control is back with me.'

Abakhumov smiled. Relief flooded over him. The pain of the dictator's displeasure, however, was too acute for him to find much enjoyment in another's humiliation. He stood silently, while Beria poured two large brandies from a well-stocked cabinet. 'To the Revolution!' the Marshal mocked, and drained his glass. Abakhumov followed greedily.

'Not so fast, my dear Minister.' Beria cautioned. 'You have work to do.'

Abakhumov fiddled sheepishly with his empty glass. 'And it may just save your neck. So do it well.' Beria might be out of danger, but Abakhumov was not.

Pouring himself another large brandy, the Marshal sat down by the side of the fire, put his feet up on the hip of one of the half-clad stone gods that held up the mantelpiece, and began to talk.

First, Orlov and Pelham had to be hunted down. For that, the MGB's Baden Centre, twenty miles from Vienna, would be brought into action. It was used by agents on their way to South-East Europe and North Africa, as well as a centre for VKR activities.

'How many agents are you holding at Baden at the moment?' Beria asked.

'Twenty at least, I should say. And three VKR assassination squads we use for dealing with counter-revolutionaries.'

'Right, so we send them into Vienna. Now what about that city?'

'Closed down completely. No one can get in or out

without passing under our eyes, and a man like Orlov is instantly recognizable. We've got the stations watched. The same with the Allied airfields and we've even got our men on that American light aircraft field at Heiligenstädter. The roads have got security checks in any case, but we're strengthening those.'

'So the VKR will have the certainty of Orlov still being in the city?'

'Unless the British catch him again, yes,' replied Abakhumov. Soviet Intelligence was reading the codes between SIS's Vienna Centre and London, and knew all that had gone on over the previous twenty-four hours.

'And what about the police?'

'We can only rely on our informers, but they are good.'

Beria smiled momentarily. 'We must catch them, Viktor Semyonovich. That is imperative. Comrade Stalin is worried the British will get them first, and if they do, then that's our deal with the Americans exposed – the Generalissimo doesn't want to risk that. This time, your Ministry mustn't fail. Your head is on it.'

Abakhumov nodded. He knew that, and shifted on his feet, waiting for further instructions. None came. 'Should I go now?'

'Go?' Beria fixed him with a glassy stare. 'Why are you still here?'

Chapter Seventeen

For twenty-four hours Nick and Orlov remained in their anti-aircraft tower surrounded by American military police, entombed in bare, windowless concrete, with nothing to eat and only sacking for warmth. There was no friendship from the Displaced Persons, no help, just suspicion and hostility, but at least the fugitives could lose themselves among them. No questions were asked, not by people whose own lives were uprooted and broken. And so on Saturday night the two men lay undisturbed in the pitch black of the fifth floor; on Sunday in the dim light of the ninth, for some reason deserted, occasionally descending to the second for a drink of rusty water which trickled from a tap let into the wall. It was a grim existence, made acute by gnawing pangs of hunger. Orlov had the added discomfort of dissecting his own excrement, and swallowing again the capsule of secrets.

But as the storm clouds scudded across Vienna's sky, at least they remained dry and safe, and they could talk. Orlov told Nick all he knew about the eleven traitors, SIS's blackmail, Lubienski's death, and the double-cross with the Americans. He described the discussion with Vivien in the Whale Room and the more recent trading with Dulles in a Soviet 'safe house' in Vienna.

And Katyn? Orlov smiled, finding Nick naïve. Throughout history, he explained, Poland had been a pawn, its people expendable. God's playground, they called it. The truth? He laughed. Since when had truth been told in war? Principle? The Russian held up his hands to heaven. The British would rob on a principle, he said. But he answered Nick's questions as well as he could, confirming that

Philby was responsible for Sikorski's death – but not through his work for SIS. The blame given to the British for the murder of the Polish leader had been a source of much amusement to those few in Soviet Security who knew the facts.

Then Orlov talked of his own defection. It upset him. 'The Revolution gave me everything,' he explained. When Nick replied that it had also destroyed him, he reacted violently.

'Not the Revolution. Never. It was those swines in State Security.' He spat. 'And that Beria. He's the one. He's the reason I'm here.'

It had begun the day after his appointment to conduct negotiations with the Americans as well as the British. Malenkov had thought it sensible that one man should handle the whole business so as to avoid any confusion which might reveal the double-cross, and who better than Major-General Gregor Orlov, a fluent English speaker, whose career in the First Division (Foreign Intelligence) of the GRU since the war had been a spectacular success?

But then came the enquiries. First, an MGB agent from the Internal Affairs Directorate stationed at the London Embassy started taking an interest in Orlov's movements. Another called on Orlov's mother, living in the Baltic seaport of Arkhangelsk. Then an old school teacher was visited, as well as former comrades in the Red Army. 'They didn't like my nose,' he explained. 'I'm half Jewish, you see.' The questions centred on the strength of his Zionist connections (he had none), and the bourgeois background of his father (a sailor who had served all his life with the whale fleets). That alone, Orlov might have survived, but the investigators had found something far more serious. 'If you sniff the streets long enough you're bound to find some shit,' he explained. 'And they found a pile.'

It was during the war when, as a Major, Orlov had first been tempted by the rich pickings there for the asking by security officers. As he moved up behind the advancing Red Army he, along with countless others, used his position to put pressure on quartermasters. In return for favours, he received stores of all descriptions, from food to clothing, which he then sold on the black market. It was a mistake. Plundering the enemy was one thing; theft of Soviet property quite another, though many did it. In 1944 he was caught and threatened with the death penalty, but because of his outstanding ability a blind eye was turned, and remained so until 1951. Then, when it wished to, the MGB restored its sight. Orlov was finished. Article 10 of the Criminal Code would do for him.

'So that's why I got in contact,' he told Nick. 'When Vivien mentioned you, I knew you were safe, and the bastards had only just begun to sniff. I also knew you were snooping around Lubienski. I enquired into your background, and you seemed ideal. I needed someone like you to take me in, to negotiate for me. At that point my weaknesses hadn't been uncovered, but I knew they were coming. They had to. You can't keep that sort of thing from State Security.'

'Why wait until now, though?' asked Nick. 'Why Vienna? Wasn't that dangerous?'

'Perhaps. But they weren't moving fast. It was almost as if . . . well, anyway, I needed to get the evidence to make me valuable. The names – they weren't sufficient, not now they're blown in any case. I had to wait to compromise the Americans – that's big fish – and now it's all here!' Orlov patted his stomach. 'London was too soon. Defection from the Motherland is dangerous enough for an ordinary Soviet citizen, but it's deadly for anyone in Security. They do all they can to get you. Too many have been buried, and I don't intend to go that way. So I have to be worth your people spending a lot of time and effort to protect me. That's why I had to get the Americans over here to Vienna. I had to take the risk.'

A pause. Orlov got up and turned away, his round face now etched with lines of suffering. He wiped his eyes.

'I love my country. It has been good to me, and now I have to betray it.'

Nick didn't reply. He had no time for the Russian's agony. The man interested him only so far as he knew about Katyn and the traitors, and no more.

'My friends, family, wife, home – they're all over there, gone . . . gone as if they'd never been.'

Orlov choked. Nick thought he was going to break down. But instead, his mood turned to hatred. 'And it's all due to those pigs in State Security,' he growled. His eyes seemed to smoulder. 'They've always lorded it over us. They go around so high and mighty – shit like Beria and Abakhumov. But we'll settle them. Military Intelligence will settle them. We've . . .' Orlov's voice trailed away as he looked at Nick.

'You've what?'

'Nothing. We've done our bit, that's all. And, I tell you, I haven't stopped yet.' Orlov put his back to the wall and slid slowly to the floor. His eyes clouded over, became distant, and his manner uncaring of the reality that had closed around him. Then he began to cry, and covered his face with his hands – strange hands for a killer, Nick thought, with thick fingers like caterpillars and dimples where knuckles should have been.

He had seen similar hands before, he remembered, smaller, but just as incongruous – Sir William's hands, more fitted to a labourer than a diplomat. A picture flashed across his mind of Strang sitting there smugly at his desk, at the centre of a cover-up, with Menzies and Vivien and God knew who else, and for a moment Nick felt very small and very ridiculous. Farting against thunder – that's how they would have put it in the Army. What could he hope to achieve? Even in the Foreign Office, among intelligent men, it had been difficult enough to get anyone to understand, when their own position depended on their not understanding. And now? Katyn, a crime ten years old, just fifteen thousand men in a war where millions had been done to death? Perhaps Orlov was right – what *was* that to the public? If Christ made his Second Coming, the British would just ask Him to tea, listen respectfully, and not smile till He had gone, to save His feelings. So what chance Poland?

The traitors, however, those eleven men, they were a different matter. The public would become moral about them.

Nick and Orlov left their tower that Sunday evening under cover of darkness. Getting out of the *Stiftskaserne* was easier than their entry, and they just walked past the guard with a cheery 'goodnight' in an American accent, leaving him to watch enviously as they crossed the Mariahilfer Strasse and disappeared into the French zone. Off-duty in Vienna could be fun, even on Sundays.

In contrast to the previous night, Nick and Orlov had a plan. First, they stopped at a block of flats. Just inside the entrance were the letter boxes, and they began poking their fingers through the gaps. All were empty, except one, number five.

Going to the second floor they found flat five and knocked. No answer. They tried again. Still, silence. Orlov put his weight against the door. 'Only one lock,' he said. 'Easy.' He took a step back, then lurched forward, striking the door sideways with the full force of his body. It burst open, the skirting board torn from the wall, and in a moment they were inside, leaning against the door, listening for sounds of alarm. None came, and an hour later they emerged, fed and washed, clad in new clothes. Orlov had a torch, while Nick carried an old canvas satchel with enough food for two days, and some washing gear.

Going down to the deserted street, the fugitives turned

back towards the Mariahilfer Strasse. At the first junction they stopped. Looking around, and seeing nothing but a few passers-by, they went to a kiosk standing on the corner plastered with posters for the Presidential election. Finding the door, Orlov gave a sharp pull. It opened, and without hesitation they slipped inside.

From the shadows a policeman emerged and walked over to the kiosk. It was bare, except for an iron staircase which curled down into the ground. Gone were the men, one tall and slim, the other ox-like, who had attracted his attention. He looked at his watch – ten forty-five – then went to the nearest telephone. Within an hour the British were informed of the presence beneath the streets of two men resembling Pelham and Orlov – a fact which, unofficially, the Russians also learned.

But relieved though the authorities were to know the two fugitives had not escaped the city, their problem in locating them underground was almost as great as it had been above. For Vienna's sewer system was vast, cavernous, running the length and breadth of the capital, a network of inter-connecting mains and branches in which a man could live for years. During the war deserters from the German Army had done so, emerging like rats at night to scavenge the streets. In such a world Pelham and Orlov had disappeared. The police could only rely on special teams to flush them out on to the surface at specially selected points. Elsewhere, the kiosk doors, normally left open at the request of the Soviet authorities, were locked. And at midnight, when preparations were complete, police units descended below.

Beneath the streets Nick and Orlov had their problems. Their destination was the Westbahnhof (one on the list of fifteen probables the police had drawn up), an hour's walk down the Mariahilfer Strasse. Below, however, it was a different matter. Gone were the lit streets, the buildings, shops, cars, people, sky . . . Instead, there were sewers, some as tall as houses, others so small that a man had to crawl on all fours, combined sewers, lateral sewers, sub-main, main trunk and outfall sewers, interceptor and relief sewers, and storm water overflows. The sound of water was everywhere, the trickle of streams, the splash of waterfalls, the loud rush of mains, all echoing from the blackness. Then the water, ebbing and flowing, carrying all forms of human waste and microscopic life, the air heavy with damp, the walls dripping. And the smells, the putrid reek of decay, the tang of ozone, the dark odour of slime all distinct, all revolting. To both men, however, Vienna's sewers were a refuge, a guarantee of life at least until the following morning.

At the bottom of the staircase, Nick and Orlov found themselves in a dry passage leading downwards to a sewer where water trickled, lapping over their shoes. Orlov flashed the torch, and found what he wanted: a metal sign, '*Königskl.* NW-SE'. Nick looked at a map they had taken from the flat. Turning left they walked a few yards and came across the entrance to a larger sewer, an arched hall, cavernous, with deep, fast-flowing effluent. On the wall opposite was a marker: '*Mariahilfstr. W-E*'.

On the surface, the Mariahilfer Strasse went straight from the Ring to the Westbahnhof, and if the main sewer followed that route, all would be well. Taking the westerly direction and getting on to a raised platform along the side, the two men began their walk.

It was only eight in the evening, but General Bedell Smith was already in his dressing gown, preparing to spend the rest of Sunday as he most enjoyed: watching television with his wife, eating steak and fries from a plate balanced on his lap. But then Dulles arrived, unannounced. He was unwelcome, but even more so the information he brought with him. Half an hour previously, Ambassador Panyushkin had telephoned. Over an unsafe line, which Dulles hoped wasn't tapped by the FBI, the Ambassador had told him of Orlov's defection with an Englishman, a Foreign Office official named Pelham.

Dulles was shocked, and made no pretence otherwise. Bedell Smith was stunned. His worst fears were confirmed. The possibility that Orlov would get to the British was horrific. He, alone, had the power to shatter the CIA's plans. That the names of the British traitors would become unusable was a minor problem. Orlov's revelations, properly used by a vengeful British, could prove the final nail in the Company's coffin, the last and most spectacular in its long line of failures. No American President, surrounded by men such as Hoover and McCarthy and leading a country resisting Communist aggression, could for one moment condone his intelligence service bargaining with the Russians, especially against the United States's allies. Bedell Smith and Dulles would not survive the resulting storm; nor, in all probability would the Company.

The CIA chiefs were confronted with a dilemma. Clearly, the Soviets would do all they could to eliminate Orlov and Pelham, but they might, after all, fail. They might, even, have planned the defection. However, to pursue Orlov with CIA operatives would be to risk British detection.

It took an hour for Bedell Smith and Dulles to arrive at a solution: the Gehlen Organization would be brought into operation. And at midnight Washington time, a signal was sent to Pullach, West Germany, though neither man was happy with the decision. The Gehlen Organization, though invaluable to the CIA, was an embarrassment. Composed of former German military and Nazi Security officers under General Gehlen, their role in the fight against Communism was highly sensitive. No one was to know of American Intelligence's connection with its former enemy against its still nominal ally. The strictest secrecy was imposed, so that even the children of the Organization's headquarters personnel were not allowed to leave their Pullach compound. To call on the skills of the Germans to eliminate a Soviet defector and a British citizen hunted by their respective intelligence services was a sign of the CIA chiefs' desperation. By Monday morning, however, Gehlen's operatives would be on the trail, supported by an extensive network of informers in the Austrian underworld.

While Dulles and Bedell Smith arrived at their decision, Nick and Orlov continued underground towards the Westbahnhof. There, they planned to get Orlov's suitcase from the left-luggage lockers and, with the money it contained, purchase their freedom through one of the various black market organizations that operated in and out of the Soviet sector of Vienna, whose smuggling routes were often used by criminals and former Nazis. The occupying authority had done its best to clamp down, but, as always, money proved of greater attraction to the petty officials on whom Soviet administration depended. From such human weakness, Nick and Orlov hoped to benefit.

After an hour and a half walking along the main sewer under the Mariahilfer Strasse the two men were weary. The journey was made in pitch black to conserve the torch batteries, and they had been forced to inch their way along, hands feeling the slimy walls, feet stumbling against debris. The older man called a halt, and they rested on the platform. Two minutes were all they allowed themselves before their muscles began to stiffen, but just as they were getting ready to continue, they caught sight of strong lights moving from side to side, no more than eighty yards away.

Nick grabbed Orlov. 'To the turn-off,' he shouted, his voice raised above the noise of rushing water. Fifty yards back they had come across an opening to a smaller sewer branching off to the right. In minutes they reached it, but the lights, moving faster, were catching up. Once inside, Orlov turned on the torch. In front was a small waterfall, with steps by its side. They clambered up and along, coming to another sewer. It was quieter now, and they could hear their own footsteps. They turned the corner.

'*Halt! Wer ist das?*' came a shout from the blackness.

Orlov switched off the torch and jumped back. Nick pulled out his gun.

'*Wer ist das?*' echoed again down the sewer.

'Police,' hissed Orlov. 'Must be another patrol.'

Three beams stabbed the blackness, searching the entrance to Nick and Orlov's hiding place, as the two men retreated to the waterfall.

'No good. We'll be caught,' said Nick. 'Let's take this lot on. There are more the other way.'

Orlov grunted. 'Take the right, then. I'll cover.'

Nick slipped the safety catch off his pistol and, crouching low, his left arm cradling the satchel, moved to the right of the entrance. Orlov took the left. Nick heard the sound of splashing feet as rings of light searched the walls. The men were near.

'Now!' Nick shouted. A shot rang out, the noise reverberating off the walls, magnifying before echoing away. Nick jumped out and ran to the right as Orlov continued firing, then turned. The torches had gone out, but he saw the flash of a gun. He fired and threw himself to one side just as a man cannoned into him, nearly knocking him over.

'It's me,' yelled Orlov, and the two fugitives, gripping each other by the arms, stumbled and bumped their way up the dark sewer as bullets ricocheted off walls, hitting and boiling the water around them.

More shots, and a torch went on. Orlov turned and raised his gun, leaning against the wall to steady his aim. He fired. The light went out, only to go on again almost immediately.

A turning to the left, and Nick fell into it, pulling Orlov behind. The Russian lost his balance and landed in the water. Picking himself up and cursing, he switched on the torch. The new sewer extended back twenty yards, and came to an end. Halfway along was another turn-off. The two men took it, then the next. And so they continued. Some of the sewers were large, others small, and none seemed to go for long in any particular direction, but with every turning Nick and Orlov felt safer.

After twenty minutes they stopped, bending low to control their breathing. Nick felt sick. His limbs were aching. He longed to sit down, to get rid of the satchel, but he couldn't. Everywhere there was water.

Orlov's voice coming from the darkness sounded hollow. 'They were Russians. I heard them shouting. They called my name.'

Nick put his hand to his head. His hair was dripping. He felt his jacket. It was soaking, wet through with sewer water. He shifted his feet, and felt something hard bobbing around his ankles. The stench was rotten. He felt like death.

Unknown to Nick and Orlov, their assailants had been positioned near an exit from the sewers. After the shooting, in which neither had been hit, one climbed the iron staircase and emerged into the fresh air. Police closed in immediately, but after inspecting his credentials they let him go. Straight away he went to a telephone booth to call MGB Centre. Orlov and Pelham were in the area of 6th and 7th Districts, heading towards the 14th and, presumably, the Westbahnhof. Within minutes, three VKR squads were on their way.

Chapter Eighteen

Their escape had lost the way for Nick and Orlov. By means of a few rusty wall plaques they managed to locate their position on the street map, but that was all. Although they had travelled only several hundred yards, the connecting sewers, most without name or direction, proved a nearly insoluble maze. Dark tunnels stretched away to what seemed infinity, others came to dead ends, directions ceased at Y-junctions, and it took three hours to return to the Mariahilfer Strasse main, making their way through water sometimes up to their thighs, underneath trickles of waste that went down their necks, brushing against slime that covered the walls. Occasionally, the squeaking of rats would rise above the sound of water, and furry bodies crashed into their legs in a desperate scurry to escape.

But at last, at about four o'clock that Monday morning, Nick and Orlov came to the spot they had been searching for – the staircase which led up to the Mariahilfer Strasse, at a point just a few minutes' walk from the Westbahnhof.

Gingerly, they mounted the metal steps, trying to stifle their echo, expecting at any moment to hear shots. But none came. Nick tried the door. The handle moved down, but the heavy iron didn't budge. He called Orlov. The Russian leaned his weight against it, but to no use: it was locked fast. There was nothing for it but to descend again to the watery hell. The next exit, they reckoned, would be in the square facing the Westbahnhof, too near the station for comfort, an area well-lit and heavily policed, but there was no alternative.

After half an hour, the sign indicating the way to the steps was found: '*Ausgang, Westbnhf*'.

They turned up the side sewer. There was little water there, and the noise was hushed. Orlov switched off his torch and both men stood still, listening, peering into the darkness for any sign of life.

Nick began to move forward, but Orlov caught him by the arm. 'Steady,' he whispered. 'If they are here, let them move first.'

They squatted, guns at the ready. The darkness gave them an advantage, if only they could wait long enough.

After a minute, Orlov began groping around the water. 'A brick – anything,' he hissed.

Nick joined the search and found a brick, one of the many that had come away from walls laid the previous century. They flattened themselves against the side. Orlov weighed the brick in his hand, then flung it back down the sewer. It clattered against the wall, and splashed into the water. The sound echoed.

Ten yards in front, lights pierced the darkness, and Orlov fired. Nick was close after him. The lights went out. Shots came in reply. Four flashes. Four men. Too many for Nick and Orlov. They turned and ran.

Through a connecting sewer they dived, and then Orlov turned on the torch. In front of them the ground fell away – a small waterfall, barely a trickle. They jumped down, and ran on. There were no signs of pursuit. The deep rumbling gush of a main sewer grew louder, obscuring all other sounds. Turning a corner Nick and Orlov nearly bumped into a group of five or six men in overalls standing smoking, their presence illuminated by the torches which hung from their belts. Police.

Nick and Orlov pulled back, but too late. A shout, then a whistle. The two men clambered up the waterfall as shots hit the wall around them and sent brick dust flying. Nick loosed off two rounds. He had only one left. They ran along the sewer to the end. To the left, there were stairs. Nick grabbed Orlov.

'Shoot behind us. I'll fire to the left.'

They waited until the torches came over the top of the waterfall, then Nick slapped Orlov on the shoulder. 'Now!'

Three shots rang out, and Nick pulled Orlov to the right. Their fire was returned, in front and behind, as the sewers dissolved in a cacophony of sound. Lights went out, orders were yelled, and both sides deployed for battle. Hunter shot at hunter, while hunted got clean away.

When they were beyond the sound of echoing gunfire, Nick and Orlov halted.

'There's no way out,' panted the Russian, bending low to relieve the pains stabbing his side. 'The doors that aren't locked will have guards on them, and I'm out of bullets.'

So was Nick. He felt weak from hunger, and opened the satchel for some bread. Its contents were soaking wet. 'Shit!' he exploded, and threw it to the ground. Until then excitement and movement had kept him warm, but now fear and tiredness were taking their toll. He was beginning to feel the cold too, and by the indirect light of the torch the pain of the older man was clear to see.

They stood in silence.

'We could double back,' suggested Orlov, half-heartedly.

'It'll be the same there – if we get back, that is. They're probably closing in now from all sides.'

Then Nick remembered the gratings he had seen when walking on the surface, appearing to cover inspection and ventilation shafts, large enough for a man to squeeze through, even one the size of Orlov.

'Look up,' said Nick. 'Just look up. Find a shaft, and we're out.'

Orlov trained his torch on the roof. Nothing. They moved down. Still nothing.

'They'll probably be on a higher level,' suggested Nick.

They turned up a slope, climbed a waterfall and moved

on up a steadily narrowing sewer, the roof becoming so low they had to crouch. But after ten minutes they found what they were looking for: an opening, four foot by three. Orlov shone the torch up, but there was nothing but blackness.

'It's worth a try,' said Nick. Orlov locked his hands together, Nick placed a foot on them, and the Russian heaved, shifting the weight to his shoulder. Nick was up, his back against one wall, a knee on the other. Slowly and painfully he brought both legs together and jammed himself into the shaft, his bottom the level of Orlov's head, then inched himself up further. The knife hanging down his back bit agonizingly between his shoulder-blades; his legs, squashed up almost to his belly, began to quiver.

Nick stopped and steeled himself, legs and arms wedged against the walls. Orlov reached up with his hands and pulled down hard on Nick's ankles, then rose into the shaft, back against the wall under Nick's feet. Orlov struggled to get a grip, and finally the pressure eased.

'Move!' hissed the Russian. Nick looked up, but still saw nothing but blackness.

It took ten minutes for the two men to reach the top of the shaft, inching their way for at least thirty feet, the only sounds the scrape on the brick and their heavy breathing, but gradually Nick could make out the black pattern of the grill against the slightly lighter deep blue of the night sky. Stars were twinkling, the air was fresher. They were returning to the world they knew.

The grill was heavy, and opened upwards on hinges. Nick edged himself as near to the metal as possible, his body shaking so violently with the effort of the climb that he felt at any moment he would lose his grip and fall, pushing Orlov down with him. Slowly, he brought one foot away from the wall, putting even more pressure on the other to maintain his position. He pushed his free knee against the grill. The metal gave slightly, then stuck. He tried again. The same happened.

Nick rested, summoning his strength for one final effort. Checking that the few feet he could see into the street were clear, and listening for the slightest sound, he moved his leg. First, his knee pushed the metal up a couple of inches, then the pressure shifted to his calfbone, and finally, when the grating was halfway vertical, to his foot. At an angle of ninety degrees the grating wavered and then fell backwards with a crash.

Within seconds, Nick had eased himself out and had rolled over the pavement into the gutter, followed by Orlov. Both lay still, trying to control their panting, searching the street, hoping their noise hadn't been heard.

The road was long and wide, lined by shops and fairly well lit, but deserted. It was the Mariahilfer Strasse. One end receded into darkness, the other into light, where lay the Westbahnhof.

Getting up and crouching low, Nick shut the grating and motioned to Orlov to follow, then darted down a side street and into the first darkened doorway, shivering in the cold night air that came down from the Alps. Again they paused until they were sure the way was clear, then stealthily moved out from the safety of the shadow, walking away from the Mariahilfer Strasse. The housing was poor, large blocks of flats with grimy walls, each with their interior courtyards from which doors and stairs led off, but at least they provided the shelter of gloom.

Halfway down the street they heard a sound, like a man stumbling. They looked back and saw nothing except deep shadow, but still they flung themselves into the nearest doorway, arched and cavernous, leading to a courtyard. Nick waited and listened, while Orlov searched for an exit. There was none. He knocked over an empty dustbin, which clattered loudly on the cobbles. Silence. Neither man moved. Then a ground floor window opened, one of the many overlooking the yard.

'*Wer ist das?*' a shrill voice shouted. '*Was wollen Sie?*'

It was the caretaker, typically Viennese, an eagle-eyed old crone eager to raise hell at the slightest provocation.

Nick edged out of the doorway, conscious that he was illuminated against the black of the entrance. He looked to the left. The street was deserted: nothing but shadow up to the corner, thirty yards away. A dozen gunmen could be hidden there, and he involuntarily flinched at the thought of a bullet's impact. He looked to the right, now pressing against the doorway for cover. There the street was better illuminated, the buildings were lower, and a hosiery shop kept its window lit. All was quiet, unmoving, but the deep doorways still held their mysteries. At the end, Nick could see the Mariahilfer Strasse, by contrast brilliantly lit, a place of danger.

Nick went back inside. The woman's voice was shriller now, and other windows had opened. A man's voice took up the chorus. Orlov was waiting patiently, propping himself up by the curl of a bannister. 'Well?'

'Nothing,' whispered Nick. 'But that's no guarantee. We'll have to take the left. If they're there, they could have an army concealed, but I doubt it.' Nick relied on the darkness being as much their ally as the enemy's.

'To the left then,' confirmed Orlov, bracing himself for a final effort. There could be no more, he knew. Then the two men went back to the doorway, and crouched down, just inside the shadow.

'When I get to three, move. If we part, see you at eight o'clock back here.' Nick's hand folded over his empty revolver as if it were a club. 'One, two . . . three.'

The two men leaped into the street, the light catching them briefly, before they disappeared into shadow. A shout went up in Russian.

Ducking and weaving, Nick and Orlov made their way up the street, slipping on the wet cobbles. Heavy footsteps followed. Nick estimated four or five men. The fugitives turned the corner, and ran into brilliant light. A man stepped from a doorway, with pistol levelled. Orlov was nearest, and made straight for him. A shot rang out, a second, then the man was flung to one side, the bear-like Orlov making short work of him. But their pursuers had reached the corner. More shots and curses as Orlov disappeared into darkness.

They continued running, at a junction turning right, down a small alley ending in a cul-de-sac. It was too late to turn back. The Russians could be heard close behind as Nick and Orlov darted into an archway. 'Look for the back entrance,' shouted Orlov, and the two men ran through a hallway into a courtyard. A flight of steps, dimly lit, led down to a small door. Orlov turned the handle. It was locked. He took a step backwards and hurled his bulk against it. The door shuddered but did not give. Shouts echoed from behind as Orlov thudded into the wood, and there was a sound of splintering. A third attempt was successful. The two men rushed through the broken door and found themselves in another yard, smaller than the previous one, with an exit to the street. They took it.

More turns, left, right, and right again. They were both winded, but Orlov in particular was showing signs of extreme fatigue, and began to stumble. They found a large doorway, and went inside, climbing the stairs to the third floor, falling up them in the dark. There on the landing in front was an open door. They entered, squeezing together. The room was small, the smell unpleasant. Nick felt something hard against his knees. He bent down to feel it. It was a lavatory.

A minute passed, and no sound. Five. Nick relaxed. They seemed to have shaken off their pursuers, but more time was needed to be sure. The streets were too dangerous. Orlov groaned and leaned an arm on Nick, who moved round to allow him to rest on the lavatory bowl. And then Nick felt it: blood. Orlov had been hit.

Nick opened the small window, covered by the muck of

years, and the faint light of a new moon shone through. He helped the older man off with his jacket, and Orlov let out a hiss of pain as his left shoulder was moved back. His shirt was soaking with blood. A bullet had gone clean through, passing just an inch from his neck.

The blood was difficult to stem. Nick ripped off a handful of square-cut newspaper hanging from a string by the lavatory and held it next to the wound, letting it soak up the flow. Then he took off his shirt, tore it, and made a bandage which he wound tightly round the shoulder. There was nothing more he could do. Exhaustion overcame pain. The Russian put his head against the wall, his body slumped and he shut his eyes.

So the two men waited in a dirty lavatory, Nick squatting, Orlov sitting, both shivering and exhausted, one wounded, urgently needing medical attention, whilst outside, patrolling the streets, were the Viennese police, the Russians and the British – soon to be joined by men of Gehlen's Organization.

It was a grey dawn of a Monday morning, bitterly cold, and, seen through the grime of the window, desolate. But three hours had gone by and it was time to leave, to find some other hiding place nearby, where Orlov could recover. But just as Nick was summoning up strength, he heard footsteps, and the door-handle turned. Silence. A minute went by. There was a cough, followed by banging on the door, waking Orlov from a fitful sleep. Nick kept his hand on the Russian's mouth until he was fully conscious. '*Wer ist das?*' came from outside, and more banging.

'*Komm! Schnell bitte!*' It was a man's voice, sounding angry. Nick peeped through a crack in the door, and saw a workman's grey overalls.

'*Ich bleibe hier.*' The man was going to stay.

The stalemate continued, the man occasionally hitting

the door, while Nick and Orlov stayed quite still, hoping he would tire and go to a lavatory on another floor.

But then the Russian, cautiously readjusting his position on the hard rim, slipped. The noise redoubled the fury of the Austrian, who began to kick the wooden door. Soon he would wake half the occupants of the block.

Nick took out his revolver. Motioning to Orlov to remain seated, he slid back the catch and pushed open the door, hitting the Austrian with such force that he was sent reeling back. Nick followed, grabbed the man's neck, and poked the gun in his face.

'*Ein Wort, und ich schiesse*,' he growled, at the same time bringing up his knee, hard.

The man sank to the ground in an attitude of prayer, looking up, his eyes wide, his mouth open, unable even to whimper. Nick had time to inspect him. He was a typical Austrian: small, with close-cropped black hair, a rugged face with pointed features and a prominent nose.

'*Wo wohnen sie?*' Nick pulled the man's hair and thrust the barrel up his nose. A shaky hand pointed to a door at the end of the landing.

'*Komm. Wir gehen.*' Nick pulled the man up and pushed him backwards, the gun at his temples as Orlov emerged, bloodstained, hardly able to stand. The Austrian stared. What type of men were they? Both soaked to the skin, smelling, one half-covered in blood. It was like a nightmare, and all because he had wanted a pee before going to work.

'They've disappeared again.' The words fell like lead.

Sir William Strang recrossed his legs, but showed no other reaction. He had known there was trouble when he had received the summons an hour earlier.

'Completely vanished,' continued Sir Stewart, standing with one arm casually draped over the mantelpiece. The grate was cold. 'The last time they were seen was at about one this morning in the sewers. That's nine hours ago.'

'The Soviets might have seen them a little later,' Vivien added from his favourite position on his chief's desk. 'The police have had a report of a disturbance in the 14th District. Shots were heard, apparently.'

'Have the Soviets got them, then?' Sir William asked hopefully, knowing it was in vain.

'If they have, they're showing no sign of it. Their men are still very much in evidence on the streets. Anyway, I think they would have told us.' The monocle was readjusted.

'Then what do we do? It's less than forty-eight hours before we pull in the traitors.'

The others shrugged.

'If Pelham and Orlov are not dead, we don't dare risk it,' replied Sir Stewart, keeping his eyes on the Permanent Under-Secretary. 'If they were to get to the Snoopers, or whoever they're making for, we would be done for. Criminal charges could be brought. Conspiracy to cover up treason. We wouldn't stand a chance.'

'So postpone the operation until we're sure of those two men? Is that what you're suggesting?' said Sir William incredulously.

'Afraid so, old man. Nothing else for it. We'll have to keep it on a daily review until they're safely out of the way.'

'And what the hell do I do about Maclean?' Sir William bristled as only a small man can, seeming to puff out. He raised his voice. 'I can't hold MI5 off much longer, you know. My Minister is going to give his consent to pulling in Maclean for questioning any day now. And if they get him before we do . . .' He struck the arm of his chair. 'Maclean's in a state. You know that, do you? He's cracking up. We've already had him under a head-shrink after his break-down. He won't last under pressure, not if he thinks he's alone. He'll spill everything he knows. He can implicate God knows how many of them – certainly Philby and Calder, probably Stoddart and Gould too. The whole lot will be blown if MI5 gets him before we do.'

Sir William was correct. Maclean was a special case, one that would not wait.

'We could pull him in before the others, I suppose,' suggested Vivien, his voice betraying his uncertainty. 'Reassure him, and then let MI5 do their worst.'

'No.' Sir Stewart was emphatic. 'I can't allow it. We must do nothing until Pelham and Orlov are out of the way. It's simply too risky, even with one man. Maclean is hardly small fry. No, it's all or nothing, and at the moment it's nothing.'

'But for heaven's sake!' Sir William's fear showed in his anger. He sat forward. 'We can't just do nothing. Maclean will ruin us.'

Sir Stewart looked pained. He hated scenes. 'Well, what do you suggest?' he asked, sharply.

'Get rid of Maclean.'

'What would you prefer? A bullet or poison? We do a very nice line in cliff falls as well, if you wish.'

'That doesn't help, Stewart.'

'For God's sake, William, nor do you. It's just a crisis we've got to weather. Nothing we can do about it. And it may never happen. We shall probably get Pelham and Orlov in time, so it's no use panicking.'

At such times, the surface politeness was easily broken. The relationship between the men had as much depth as between animals who huddle together on a cold night for warmth.

'And so we just sit back, eh? Do nothing?' Sir William got up. 'Nothing at all?'

'Batten down hatches as far as possible. That's all we can do, except for your lunatic suggestion of killing Maclean. Imagine the Snoopers' reaction. The Russians wouldn't be too happy about it, either. They take a pride in looking after their men. It's good for recruitment.'

'Who said anything about killing? He could disappear, couldn't he?'

'Kidnap? God, what fairytale stuff, William. Where do we put him? The Tower of London?'

Sir William didn't reply.

Sir Stewart continued, knowing he was winning. 'And you think the Snoopers wouldn't find out? You can't keep a man like Maclean under wraps for long, you know.'

The Permanent Under-Secretary brushed imaginary fluff from his sleeve, and avoided looking at the SIS chief. There was an awkward silence. From the desk came a still voice of calm.

'He could defect, of course.'

Both men looked at Vivien with amazement.

'Defect?' Strang blustered. 'Defect?'

'Yes, defect. It would be a blow, but far less than if he stayed and MI5 pumped him of everything he's got. The Snoopers would be made to look a bit foolish, too.'

'So would the Foreign Office,' interrupted Sir William irritable. 'Damned silly. We've been holding out on him for as long as we could, after all.'

'But it's better than being blown wide open,' Vivien continued, unruffled. 'If Maclean goes, nothing will be left except doubt. If he stays, there'll be hard facts – and too many of them. Just think about it.'

They did.

Chapter Nineteen

The past forty-eight hours had not been easy for Egon Olbrich. First there had been his surprise at the lavatory, followed by a beating, with his wife looking on, gagged and helpless, after which came threats and then the promises. Six thousand schillings – almost four months' wages; a street cleaner couldn't afford to be choosy, and all he had to do was to shelter two men for two days, purchase some medical supplies, fetch a bag from a locker in the Westbahnhof, deliver a message to an address on the other side of Vienna, and keep his mouth shut. It had been difficult in the small, two-roomed apartment, but they had managed. He was forced to miss work too, but it was worth it.

Olbrich never discovered the identity of the two men, although they were obviously criminals – deserters, perhaps. The wounded one he guessed was Russian, the other British or American, and both were desperate. He was allowed out twice, his wife as hostage, and the only time he opened the front door was to an Austrian. The man had arrived, promptly, at midday on Tuesday, and remained alone with the Russian for over an hour. The other had kept guard over Egon and his wife. They continually watched, those men, even at night when they took it in turns to sleep.

Abakhumov always enjoyed going to Beria's residence. The palace had once belonged to a nobleman, who had swung high for it, and it still retained much of its Imperial splendour. As the Minister entered the study, dominated by its vast fireplace, he thought of the last occasion he had been there, almost a month previously, in the depths of depression. How different things were now. He felt uneasy when he remembered that Orlov had still to be caught, but then, he reassured himself, it was only a matter of time.

'Well, Comrade Abakhumov, and what is it that's so startling you had to see me so urgently. You interrupted some fun, you know.' Beria was dressed in silk gown and slippers, his hair slightly dishevelled.

'My apologies, Comrade Marshal, but we've had a new proposal from London.'

Beria sat at his desk while Abakhumov stood and explained the British decision to delay pulling in the traitors until Orlov and Pelham were caught, ending by outlining Menzies's proposal: if the fugitives were not eliminated in time, Maclean was to defect to Moscow.

Beria made no reply at first, but sat staring at a bronze figurine of a wild boar on the desk before him. He reached out to touch its arched back as, finally, he spoke.

'Maclean? How appropriate.' The irony in Beria's voice was not lost on Abakhumov. In 1940, before the fall of France, when Hitler's victory seemed far from certain, Maclean had been stationed in the Paris Embassy, keeping Moscow informed of Anglo-French war plans. Clearly, at a time when the Soviet Union was Germany's ally, and the two dictatorships had just divided Poland between them, accurate information on Allied intentions was vital. That March and April Maclean had passed on news of highly secret discussions concerning pre-emptive attacks on Norway and southern Russia to cut off important raw materials for the Reich – in particular, iron ore and oil. A spectre rose to haunt Stalin: northern Russia attacked by a Finland supported by the democracies, who would also be advancing in the south and enticing the Moslem nationalities there to rise against their Communist masters. And at the same time the Poles would revolt, inspired by an Allied victory over Germany and international pressure for a restoration of all Polish territory. To the dictator's paranoia, the Polish officers in Soviet captivity became a danger. And in Stalin's Russia dangers were laid to rest.

'We have Maclean to thank for everything, in a way,' said Beria, smiling wryly. 'But what were you telling me about the spy "Hicks" the other day?'

Abakhumov was taken by surprise. 'Hicks' was the codename of the British traitor Guy Burgess, a Foreign Office official who, inexplicably, had not been one of the eleven named by SIS. A few days previously, the Minister had mentioned in passing that Burgess had just returned to London from Washington. The story had amused him, which was why he had told Beria. The man, a middle-ranking diplomat in the Washington Embassy and an intimate of Philby's, had so outraged his masters by his wilful behaviour and open homosexuality, that he had been sent back to London for almost certain dismissal.

The Minister repeated his story.

'So,' said Beria when Abakhumov had finished, 'this man Burgess is back in London, and the British are ignorant of his true allegiance. He's not much use to us now though, is he?'

'Not much, Comrade Beria. Never has been. Always in and out of jobs. He's trying to get on to a newspaper, but even if he does, it won't be fruitful. "Hicks" is washed up.'

'So he's expendable?'

'Yes.'

'Who runs him in London?'

'Yuri Modin. He also runs Maclean.'

'Modin's a good man, isn't he?'

'One of our best.' Abakhumov frowned, and Beria sensed the Minister's bewilderment. The man really was not very quick-witted: rather dull, in fact. Beria had to agree with Stalin – his removal was overdue. But the Marshal smiled, for man is the only animal who can remain friendly with the victim he intends to kill.

'You see, my dear Abakhumov, the Generalissimo was

more than a little upset that there now exists the possibility the Americans won't use the names we've so obligingly given them. Bedell Smith is running scared at the moment, and unless we make sure of Orlov, that's the end of our little deal. So we've got to think of other ways of embarrassing the British – it is what our Great Leader wants, after all. Now, if this man Burgess were to come home to us with Maclean, it would cause a bigger stink than if only Maclean came, important though he is. Two British Foreign Office officials – just think of it, with all their connections with the Americans and goodness knows what else. And there's more than just that. This man Burgess will cause suspicion to be cast on Philby. We can sink SIS, too, in a big way. And Philby knows Blunt, doesn't he? He's bound to get involved. That's MI5 implicated. So we can have three or four for the price of one – perhaps more – and all with the agreement of Menzies.' Beria laughed, a wheeze of a laugh, and finished by coughing.

'But Menzies said nothing about Burgess, Comrade Marshal. It was only Maclean.' Abakhumov was a man who took orders, and, it seemed to Beria, no matter who from.

'Have you so little imagination, Comrade? They don't know about Burgess, do they? So they can't object if we pull him out. Our little deal is not about those they haven't named, is it? And anyway, if they begin to waggle Katyn in front of us, we can always tell them that Burgess was the only person who could get Maclean away. All very understandable, don't you agree?'

Abakhumov did.

'So there you are. Agree to Menzies's proposal. Instruct Modin to prepare for the defection of Maclean on Friday, as the British want, but throw in Burgess too.'

'It's all conditional on Orlov not being caught, though,' Abakhumov reminded Beria, tentatively. 'Isn't it?'

'Still no trace?'

'None.'

'Well, we'll just have to ensure we get to them first. That's more important than ever now. And when we catch them, we simply keep up the act until it's too late for Menzies. I want those defections to take place.'

'And if the British get Orlov? What then?'

'Then, my dear Abakhumov, we do what is necessary. But make sure none of them live to remember.'

'It's a gamble.'

'Yes, but worth playing.' Beria rose. The interview was at an end. 'Bring Burgess and Maclean back here, and, believe me, we'll see the British dance a merry tune on the tip of a needle for a very long time to come.'

In 1951, the black market in Soviet-occupied Austria was one of the most highly organized rackets in post-war Europe, dealing in everything from food to cars, medical supplies to currency. Hardly an item could not be acquired on request, and for cash. Many gangs were involved, each with their slice of the market. Violence was a risk of the business, corruption standard practice. 'Bought' officials and informers abounded. Many members of the Allied Control Commission were mixed up in one way or another, and of the four nations involved, the Russians were in the deepest. To the Soviet administrators the rich pickings that came from breaking the rules were highly prized. They saw the years away from their motherland as the means to feather their nest. The poverty of the Soviet Union was the black marketeers' guarantee of success.

Orlov, as Nick now recognized, was a man of many parts. A spell of duty in Austria not long after the war had apparently brought him into contact with a gang that operated between Vienna and Salzburg, tapping the lucrative German market over the border. One of its specialities had been smuggling, and for that it needed the correct papers. Orlov had provided them, and received benefits in return. Now, he was involved again, only this time with the transport of Nick and himself to Freilassing, just over the German border, a few miles from Salzburg. The contact was a man called Johannes Bahr, and his price: 200,000 schillings, 250 pounds sterling, payable in any currency.

At five on Wednesday morning Nick and Orlov emerged from hiding, both armed with the automatics from Orlov's luggage stuffed behind their trouser-bands, their empty pistols in their pockets. They went down with Bahr to the street, still dark, where a lorry was waiting, a pre-war Mercedes one-tonner, and clambered into the canvas-covered back, squatting on the floor. Bahr knocked on the cab, and the journey began.

'Right. Your guns.' The Austrian clicked his fingers as he held out his hand. 'I'm not risking any nonsense.'

The man was typical of his kind, Nick thought, skinny, with a sallow complexion, greasy black hair that hung in strands, and eyes that never rested. But they needed him, so without a word they gave over their pistols.

'They're empty anyway,' said Orlov. 'Keep them if you want.'

Bahr pocketed them. 'Right. You go under here,' and he hit the floorboards with his heel. 'A false bottom. Room for two – just. Breathing will be difficult, but that's tough.'

Nick and Orlov nodded. They were prepared. Bahr mistook their acquiescence, and tried his luck.

'And the price has gone up. Another fifty thousand schillings.'

Pushing aside Orlov's restraining arm, Nick lunged forward and grabbed Bahr by the throat, pushing him against the taut canvas. 'You bastard. We made a bargain, and you're not going to break it.'

Bahr struggled, but realized it was worthless, as Nick's thumbs pressed harder on his windpipe. The black marketeer's tongue flickered over his lips. He was thinking fast.

'Things have changed,' he gasped, avoiding Nick's eyes. 'Security is tough. Has been the last few days. Expenses have increased.'

'How?'

'Palms require more greasing in times of trouble. There's something up. They're windy. Only more money can help.'

Nick loosened his grip. The man was probably telling the truth, but in any case there was little alternative. It was him or nothing.

Bahr shook himself free, and took the offensive. 'It wouldn't be anything to do with you two, would it?' He patted the revolvers in his pockets.

'No questions,' interrupted Orlov. 'That was agreed.'

'All right.' The Austrian stroked his neck. 'But I want the money.'

'French and German do?' asked Nick.

'Anything.'

Orlov turned sideways, his shoulder shielding the wad of paper he took from his inner pocket, and counted. Bahr took the notes without a word, and checked, moistening his thumb as he flicked through the money. 'Ten marks more,' he demanded, and snapped his fingers. Orlov handed them over without question, and the three men lapsed into uneasy silence.

After ten minutes or so, the truck stopped and its engine cut.

'Under here,' ordered Bahr, holding up a small cover concealed in the truck's floor, his eyes revealing his enjoyment in the fugitives' discomfort. Nick slithered in and lay on his back, nose almost touching the boards above, arms pinned to his side. Orlov followed. For him it was more difficult. His shoulder was painful, but he made the effort without complaint, and squeezed in next to Nick, rigid within the confined space.

Bahr replaced the cover and pitch blackness enveloped them. Above, they heard the thud of boxes thrown in at random. A bad smell of cabbages seeped through the boards, mingling uneasily with petrol. There was silence for five minutes, with not even the sound of men's voices, followed by the banging of doors and the deep roar of the engine as the truck lurched forward. No thought was spared for the passengers. Orlov cursed. Nick remained silent.

After what must have been only quarter of an hour, the truck made its first halt. The engine cut, and voices became audible. German, French and Russian. Orlov stiffened. The cab doors slammed. Silence. Then the voices returned. A man clambered into the back and began poking around. '*Alles in Ordnung*,' he said with a strong Russian accent. The cab doors slammed, the engine started up, and they were off. The first checkpoint was over. They were out of Vienna, and in Soviet-occupied Austria.

But something made Nick uneasy, not at all sure that everything was for the best. He felt like a bird being transferred from a trap to a pie, in the most uncomfortable way.

Relieved though Nick and Orlov were to be away from the city, any hope for an easy escape was ill-founded. For, in the past twenty-four hours, the manhunt had changed its nature. The second disappearance of the fugitives had raised the possibility that they might have left the city.

The police and occupying powers spread their nets wide, circulating descriptions throughout Austria. The Soviet Army, covering north-east Austria, put units on the search, while MGB Border Troops strengthened security along Austria's borders with Czechoslovakia and Hungary. Similar precautions were taken in the British zone. Spot checks were made on traffic, especially goods vehicles and public transport, trains were searched, hotels and boarding houses visited. Even the Americans, in their desperation, widened their operation, and although the CIA chiefs still refrained from using their own personnel, US military police and border guards were instructed to keep a look out for two men, unnamed and undescribed, but who would be acting suspiciously.

It took half a day for the lorry to cross the hundred miles from Vienna to the border of the Soviet zone at Emms. Nick and Orlov were allowed out of their hiding place only twice, to breathe fresh air and stretch their limbs for five minutes among dark clumps of trees, but for the rest of the time they remained cramped and in darkness, heads aching from exhaust fumes, stomachs churning over, every bump in the road jarring through their bodies.

The route taken lay across the plain of Austria, and normally would have been made without interruption, but this time checks were made by Soviet military personnel twice, once at Prinzersdorf just outside St Pölten, the other at Strengberg, ten miles from Emms, and on both occasions the soldiers, unbribable under the eyes of their officers, made thorough searches. But they left Nick and Orlov undisturbed. At the border crossing at Emms, too, the guards were strict, but Bahr's documents were in order, and an annoying delay was the only result.

Once out of the Soviet zone, American accents became audible, but just as the fugitives were feeling some relief, they heard the words 'special precautions'. The sixty miles to Salzburg would not be easy.

Twenty miles or so out of Emms the truck stopped, and Bahr's face appeared at the hatch. 'Food,' he said gruffly, and the fugitives clambered out, backs aching, limbs stiff, to share sausages, bread and beer with the two black marketeers. The meal was eaten in silence. Afterwards, Nick and Orlov took a short walk in the surrounding forest. They spoke little. It was a grey, windy day, with the fir trees in constant motion, and they returned despondently to their hiding place. It was almost half past three.

It must have been after six when successive stopping and starting indicated they had reached a large built-up area. 'Salzburg,' muttered Orlov. 'The fools could have gone round it to the border.'

A couple of minutes more, and the truck stopped and reversed sharply to the right, sending Nick squeezing up heavily against the Russian. A moment of silence, then a cab door slammed.

'All's well?' said a voice in German. Nick didn't recognize the speaker.

'We've got them,' replied Bahr, gruffly. 'Lying there as happy as pigs in shit.'

Footsteps crunched on gravel as men went round to open the tailgate. Then another voice, louder than the others.

'Any trouble?' The words were English, the accent American.

Nick nudged Orlov. 'A Yank,' he whispered.

Orlov stiffened. 'What the hell are they playing at? We were to go straight across the border,' he hissed.

'No problem,' Bahr called out, this time in English. 'The bastards were thick on the ground, though. Must be anxious to get these two.'

Somebody laughed.

'So aren't we the lucky ones?' joked the American.

The tailgate came down, and a man clambered into the back. Boxes were shifted.

'Armed?' The American's voice sounded much nearer.

'No,' answered Bahr from above the fugitives' heads. 'Took their guns off them in Vienna. They were empty, anyway.'

'Yes, they've been using them quite a bit.'

Whoever the American was, he meant trouble. Nick turned his head so that his mouth was in Orlov's ear.

'Once we're both out, we move,' he whispered, feeling for the automatic under his trouser-band.

Orlov understood. 'Right, Let me go first. Wait till I fall.'

Footsteps thudded, the hatch opened, and Bahr's face appeared. He was grinning. 'Out,' he said, jerking his thumb.

Orlov was first. He was hauled out by the Austrian, then, pretending to be stiff, he bent down in the back of the truck and waited for Nick who had been left to get out on his own.

'*Heraus, schnell,*' came the command. Nick, moving towards the tailgate, caught a glimpse of a tall, blond-haired man in his mid-thirties, dressed in a black leather coat and holding a Schmeisser machine pistol. Standing next to him was Bahr, still grinning.

'*Schnell,*' the man repeated, gesturing arrogantly with his gun. Orlov hesitated, then jumped, landing awkwardly, falling hands first as Nick whipped out his automatic and sent two shots into the blond. He was dead before he hit the ground. Orlov rolled to one side and fired at Bahr. He missed. The black marketeer turned and ran. Another shot, and he fell, a patch reddening between his shoulder-blades.

Nick, meanwhile, was on the ground, running around the side of the lorry. Catching the driver getting down from the cab, he fired, and the man fell slowly, clutching at his guts. He wasn't dead, but two bullets were all Nick was prepared to give him. Another, presumably the American, was escaping into the house. Nick fired, but missed, dust coming off the wall inches from his target's head. The door slammed.

'Back,' yelled Orlov.

Nick looked around. They were in a small courtyard, surrounded on three sides by a house and outbuildings, and on the fourth by a high wall and large sheet-metal gates, closed.

Orlov ran to the gates and shook them. They rattled, but wouldn't open. A shot rang out from the house, and the two men dived for cover behind the lorry, then a burst of machine-gun fire churned up the yard underneath the vehicle, sending dirt and gravel into their faces.

'If they get round us,' warned Orlov, 'we're dead.'

Nick looked round. Ducking low, he moved back to the outhouse door. It was locked. There was only one alternative – the truck.

'Cover me,' he yelled to Orlov, as another burst of fire ripped through the side of the lorry, tearing the tyres to shreds. The petrol tank was leaking badly.

Praying the engine was intact, Nick stepped over the groaning Austrian, and looked through the open door into the cab. The keys were in the ignition. He leaned up, and turned them. The engine spluttered into life. Shots shattered the cab's windscreen as Nick clambered in, keeping his head well down, thankful that the truck was facing away from the house, giving him maximum protection. He pushed his foot down on the clutch and put the gear into first. Orlov fired a burst of shots. Nick released the handbrake and slammed his foot on the accelerator as the Russian jumped on to the footplate. The lorry lurched forward, its back wheel flattening the driver, still writhing, as it ploughed straight into the sheet metal.

The truck burst through the gates, slewed on to the road, and stalled as Nick and Orlov jumped off. The firing from the house increased. They turned and ran, but before covering five yards, the lorry exploded, bowling them over.

Orlov, momentarily stunned by the blast, came round as Nick was heaving him to his feet. He yelled in pain. His shoulder wound had opened. Shaking his head in an effort to clear his own dizziness, Nick looked around.

They were in a suburban street, lined by small shops and houses, with people standing gaping, brought out by the noise of gunfire and the explosion. A short distance off, a car had drawn up, its engine still running.

Nick pulled at Orlov, and they both staggered towards

the black Opel, its driver standing by the door, transfixed, unable to move for fear. Nick pushed him aside and got in behind the wheel. Orlov, keeping his gun trained on the spectators, joined him, and they accelerated away.

Chapter Twenty

'Escort to the Colour – shoulder arms – remainder, stand at ease!' A crash of booted feet as five hundred men moved as one. Then a Lieutenant, slim and tight-trousered, gave his first order in a voice high-pitched with nerves. 'Escort to the Colour, close order – march. By the left – quick march!' The massed bands of the Brigade of Guards struck up. 'The British Grenadiers'.

Sir William Strang viewed the manoeuvre with bored indifference. He had seen it too many times to be impressed and would have infinitely preferred to be at his desk, working. But his master had requested his presence, so there he was, in the Secretary of State's office, standing alone, sipping sherry warm from being in his hands too long, shunning the eyes of politicians and their wives around him. Fortunately, they were safely ensconced at other windows, no doubt happy to be avoiding the Permanent Under-Secretary. He was a man of 'bottom' they agreed, but too stiff for their liking – and probably not much of a socialist either.

'Forward by the centre,' and the Escort began marching towards the Colour.

'Morning, William.' It was Sir Stewart, just arrived. Rehearsals for Trooping the Colour had always been a social occasion, a time for gathering the good and the great. 'News from Vienna,' he murmured, smiling graciously at his Minister's wife.

'Oh?' Strang was short: he had not forgotten their argument. The head of SIS, by contrast, was affable. His feathers never remained ruffled for long.

'That's my old regiment, you know, William,' and Menzies looked with pride at the Grenadiers around their Colour.

The band stopped playing, and the massed ranks of red and blue shouldered arms.

'Well?' hissed Sir William, glancing sideways.

'They're, er, they've disappeared,' said Sir Stewart, his attention seemingly absorbed by events on Horse Guards Parade below.

'Damn!'

'So we've had to postpone today's little round-up.'

'Hell!' Sir William stared fixedly at the Grenadiers, but didn't see as the Ensign saluted with his sword, then received the Colour from the Sergeant-Major. The Escort presented arms, and the band played.

'And the other little operation?' he whispered under cover of the National Anthem. Sir Stewart stood to attention, replying through gritted teeth. 'Unless we make sure of those two, Maclean is defecting. Moscow has agreed.'

The Anthem ended. Sir Stewart relaxed, as down below the Lieutenant bawled 'Shoulder arms!' at the Escort. But Sir William had left, sick in the stomach. He wanted peace, somewhere to think, alone. He wanted to be prepared. He sensed catastrophe.

Orlov had shown a surprisingly good knowledge of Salzburg, guiding Nick with hardly a false turning, and in just twenty minutes they were clear of the city and on the road to Hallein, heading south, away from the German border. Plans had changed.

The CIA had joined the manhunt, that was clear. Salzburg was the headquarters of US occupation. Southern Germany was in American hands too.

'Never trust a German,' the Russian snarled.

'Bahr was Austrian,' said Nick, swerving to avoid an oncoming car.

'They're all the same. The war taught us that. They're all swine.' Orlov wound down the window and spat.

The car screeched round a corner, its brakes full on, then accelerated.

'So Germany's no good, now?' asked Nick.

'Worse than here. The south is stiff with Americans and Gehlen's men. SS filth! And anyway, how do we get over the border?' Orlov thought for a moment. 'That one with the Schmeisser – he even looked an SS type. I've seen enough of those swine to know.' He spat again. 'I wish I had killed him. You were lucky.'

Nick didn't reply. Orlov's hate was probably a reaction. Pain, fear, loneliness . . . it couldn't be easy for the man.

They drove on, up into the mountains, following the old Roman route across the Alps, but intending to turn off eastwards well before they came to Italy, and make for the Tyrol. There, in the French zone, the way should be easier. Once they reached Switzerland, Orlov would hide while Nick went to London and the head of MI5. That was the plan.

At Hallein, an unattractive town by the standards of the region, which they reached just after seven o'clock, they stopped and filled the car's tank. The pressure on them had eased. Twelve miles from Salzburg and with no sign of pursuit, they relaxed. Outside Hallein, in a lay-by close to the trees, Orlov, who had been losing blood steadily, took off his jacket, letting Nick inspect the wound. It was bleeding badly. Using warm water from the car's radiator he bathed it and made a bandage from the clean parts of the Russian's shirt, tying them tightly, and immobilizing the arm. Crude, but at least the bleeding stopped.

At eight, cold fell from the Alps as they set off again. Nick's driving was noticeably calmer, and he had time to admire the fine views of the mountains, jagged crops of yellow-grey stone, winter's snow still capping their peaks. The sun, now it was setting, had come out of hiding, and its gold touched the greens of the Alpine meadows and forests, the white of the houses and the blue of the river running by the road. But Orlov was oblivious to the beauty, and busied himself working out their route on a map found in the car. The journey would, he reckoned, take eight hours. Early on Thursday morning, under cover of darkness, they could walk over the Swiss border, undetected – if, that is, their luck held.

It didn't. Just as they were leaving Werfen, a village twenty-eight miles from Salzburg, Nick noticed in his mirror a green Volkswagen police car. It made no attempt to overtake, but instead followed, maintaining a distance of about twenty yards. Nick accelerated. So did the police car. He decelerated. So, too, did the Volkswagen.

'They're on to us. They've been bloody quick.'

Orlov didn't answer. In silence, he checked their automatics.

And so it continued. Two miles, three, four. The road, climbing all the time, was not suited to losing the tail, and had no turn-offs except dirt tracks that led nowhere. After five-and-a-half miles they reached the town of Bischofshofen, the police car still behind. By then it was almost dark. They passed through the streets slowly, their follower keeping back, perhaps afraid to get too near. That was a mistake. Nick waited for his opportunity, and it came. A car turned out of a side road and came between the Opel and the Volkswagen. He accelerated immediately, turned right down a side street, then first left and right again, followed by two more right turns until he came back to the main road. The police car was lost in the backstreets.

Nick sped out of Bischofshofen, south, and took the first turning off the main road, the signpost indicating a place called Mühlbach. Thick, woods lined the side of the narrow road, and at the first opportunity he pulled off, stopped and deadened the lights. For an hour, the two men sat in darkness on a woodcutter's track, before moving on to Mühlbach.

Nick and Orlov had lost their tail, but not for long. The lone patrol car was not all the Austrian police had put on their track.

At six twenty-five that evening the Salzburg police had received reports of gunfire, an explosion, and the theft of an Opel saloon by two armed men in the suburb of Itzling. By six fifty, descriptions indicated they were the murderers wanted by the Viennese police. A telephone call to Vienna confirmed the identities of Orlov and Pelham, and by five past seven police stations throughout the Salzburg province had been alerted.

At the same time, senior police officers in Salzburg worked on a plan of operations. From the beginning it was made clear that the police were only to act as tracker dogs, running their prey to ground. Others would do the killing. No reasons were given. Once a patrol car had picked up the Opel, it was to alert its controlling station and maintain observation, while the emergency operations room co-ordinated other cars to take over the tail when necessary. In addition, the five provinces adjoining Salzburg were brought into the operation.

While the Salzburg police were making their preparations, the British were informed of the sighting. A short time later, the news also reached Moscow.

By eight, police preparations were complete. At eight seventeen, a patrol car at Werfen picked up the Opel travelling south, on road No 159, but after only fifteen minutes it was shaken off in Bischofshofen. Reaction was immediate. Patrol cars moved in to points on all roads no less than twenty minutes fast travelling from the town. By eight forty-seven, the cordon was complete. All the Austrian police had to do was wait.

An hour went by, and there was no sign of the fugitives.

Salzburg police headquarters began to get worried. Two hours. Then at ten thirty-six the theft of a car, a grey Volkswagen, was reported at the village of Mühlbach. It lay within the cordon. By ten-forty, all patrol cars were alerted.

Then, at eleven twenty-five, when the police had almost given up hope, the stolen Volkswagen passed the checkpoint at Saalfelden on its way westwards. It contained two men. Salzburg informed the Tyrol police at Innsbruck.

Again, a long wait. It was estimated that the Volkswagen would be sighted somewhere around twelve-forty, but in the event it was not until five fifty-eight that it emerged from the mountains at the resort of St Johann. In the grey light of dawn, the passengers were identified. From there, the car took Route 1, the main road to the west, and Switzerland.

Nick and Orlov had never intended to keep the Volkswagen long after dawn had broken that Thursday morning. They knew its loss would be reported, and all they could expect was to put sufficient distance between them and Mühlbach to elude the police. By daybreak they hoped to have left the car at the Swiss border. Tiredness, however, had caused yet another change of plan. Orlov, wounded, was unable to drive, and so left Nick to negotiate the winding roads running along sheer cliffs in the pitch black of a moonless night, the stabbing headlights blunted by drifting mists. Twice he nearly went over the side. Fatigue enveloped him. By two o'clock, they had decided to go no further without rest, and so it was not until five-thirty, after a fitful sleep, that they awoke, worked warmth into their bodies, and continued.

Half-an-hour later, an event occurred which, though minor in itself, caused the hunted men yet again to change their plans. Just out of the town of Wörgl they caught sight of a patrol car in a lay-by. It drew out into the road, drove for a distance of twenty or thirty yards, then pulled back into the side. The time taken to check their registration was not long, but it was enough for Nick and Orlov.

The next checkpoint, they reckoned from the map, would be the junction at Strass, sixteen miles distant. They drove as near the village as they dared, then left the Volkswagen, pushing it down a bank. Taking to the country they skirted the houses and walked along the railway line for two miles until, at a quarter past eight, they came to the small town of Jenbach. There, they went to the station. Two lines ran through it, one from Salzburg to the western border with Switzerland, the other, the much shorter Zillertal railway, extending twenty-five miles south to the town of Mayerhofen.

After buying tickets with their last remaining schillings, the fugitives waited, obtaining coffee and rolls with German marks, until, at nine, their train left for the ninety-minute journey along the quiet Ziller valley. Orlov dozed, head back against the wooden seat, while Nick watched the other passengers, all locals. They affected disinterest in the strangers, but Nick knew they would not forget.

Mayerhofen, when they reached it, was a large, bustling village whose position near the glacier region of the Zillertal Alps, rising to over eleven thousand feet, made it a popular resort. But they didn't linger, and by eleven had left the white, high-roofed houses that huddled round the spired church and were on their way up the Stillupptal, one of the four valleys that led into the heart of the mountains. The road, rough and narrow, climbed steadily upwards, past a solitary Christ hanging from a simple cross. The air, usually so crisp, was heavy, dampening the fragrance of the pines. A storm was brooding. Orlov especially, lacking proper sleep and still exhausted from loss of blood, found the going tiring. After only a mile they were forced to rest, the Russian, his shoulder throbbing, lying full out on the grass by the side of a stream as brown cows grazed, and even their wooden clappers were unable to wake him. After fifteen minutes, they began again, and with further stops at last managed to reach a small inn, just three miles from Mayerhofen. It had taken them over two hours to get that far.

After a meal of sausages and sauerkraut they continued, but by the time they came to Dorndlaste, a hamlet less than a mile further on, Orlov was suffering from a stitch. On the bridge they rested, the Russian pressing his side with the agony. Black storm clouds gathered. A roll of thunder was heard, gentle but ominous. The air was stifling. A goatherd's horn sounded, calling in the flock. Yet still they pushed on, past another hamlet, deserted except for a little girl in plaits, then on up until they were forced to stop again. Orlov was sweating profusely. It had been a long time since he had spoken. He required all his concentration just to continue walking.

The thunder was louder now. Down the valley, a silvery curtain of rain could be seen. Shelter was essential, even without Orlov's difficulties. Nick looked around. A night in a hamlet was to be avoided. The Tyrolese were a suspicious people, and there was always the chance the police would extend their search. Leading off was a footpath through the pine trees up the side of the mountain. They took it and climbed wearily. After twenty minutes, just as the first drops were beginning to fall, they came to a clearing and saw a Tyrolese hut, the sort that belonged to a woodcutter or goatherd. Simple, wooden, with one storey, decorative gables and a gently-sloping roof held down by lumps of stone, a wisp of black smoke curling from its chimney, it had to be home for the night. Orlov could go no further.

The man leaned against a tree, lit a cigarette and watched the two fugitives walk slowly up the path to the house. He saw them knock at the door, which was opened by an elderly Tyroler, and stand for a couple of minutes, talking. By their gestures, they were bargaining. Finally, they went inside.

The watcher remained until he had finished his cigarette, threw the stub away, and went back down the path to the hamlet below. There, he gave a message to a policeman in a waiting car, and returned up the mountainside, coat-collar up, to continue the watch through the wind and the rain.

The Tyrol police had been prepared for any disappearance. When the Volkswagen failed to pass the checkpoint at Strass, road blocks were immediately set up and a thorough search made of the area. The abandoned Volkswagen was found without difficulty, and just after nine a check at Jenbach station revealed that two foreigners, neither carrying luggage, had bought tickets to Mayerhofen. The ticket clerk was able to give a good description of the younger man. By nine-twenty, the police at Mayerhofen, a sergeant and four men, had been alerted, and when Nick and Orlov stepped off the train at ten-thirty, they were waiting. By three that afternoon the sergeant reported to Innsbruck that the two men were under observation in a woodcutter's house on a spur of the Popberg peak above the hamlet of Freihausaste, only seven-and-a-half miles from the Italian border.

Burgess moved his right arm. It had gone to sleep under his lover's weight. He adjusted the bedclothes and stretched down to lift his glass from the floor. He sipped the champagne, and grimaced. It was flat, sour. He put the glass down and turned to look at his companion, slim and in his early twenties, with fair hair and boyish features. Burgess stifled a burp, and reached out with his left hand to stroke the forehead he loved to kiss. It was all over now. He would never see his lover again.

But it had seemed so different once. The answer was

clear then, with capitalism failing, Fascism on the rise and democracy an illusion. Only Communism held hope for the future, the Soviet experiment . . . It was all so long ago, Burgess remembered, so long ago when his privileged position in the class-ridden society he despised had forced him to act. Only by supporting international Marxism could he be of use to his fellow countrymen. And to create, he first had to destroy . . .

But treason? Only if it has failed is treason called by its name; otherwise, success transforms it into patriotism, courageous, principled love of country. His hand paused in mid-air above his lover's face.

And now it was all over. Why? It had gone so well. His birth and education had been qualifications above question. He had been condemned for being a homosexual, but never a spy. Why, then, must he leave? No answer had been given by his Russian control. None, really, was expected. Some men, Burgess knew, carry their coffins from birth.

He stroked the smooth skin. His lover opened his eyes.

'Jackie, I've got to tell you. I'm going away.' Burgess withdrew his hand. The young man puckered his nose, and pouted. 'But it won't be for long. I have to go tomorrow. But not for long.'

'Where?'

'Across the sea. Paris.'

'Why?'

'Oh, work. The Embassy needs me.'

'Well, be good then.'

Burgess arched an eyebrow, but said nothing. He couldn't even smile.

Outside the storm raged, but inside it was warm and cosy. The rough-hewn cabin was lit by two oil lamps standing on the large pine table in the middle of its single room, while in the grate a log fire gave off a sweet smell of burning pine.

By it, strapped tightly to a chair, was the owner, an old woodcutter, in the lederhosen he had worn for work that morning, his mouth gagged, his eyes still fearful. At the table sat Nick and Orlov, the remains of their dinner pushed to one side, a few half-eaten dumplings. Before them were two automatics, a pile of ammunition, and an old double-barrelled shotgun the Tyroler used for hunting.

The two men were silent, absorbed by their work. The Russian, refreshed by sleep, was cutting a deep cross on the noses of the bullets, twenty-five in all, so that they would explode on impact, fragments spreading outwards, shattering and tearing. Dum-dums. They were illegal, banned by international law, but one shot was enough to kill, and that was all that mattered.

The Englishman's eyes drooped from tiredness. Sitting with his back to the fire, there were ten shotgun cartridges before him, opened and with their lead shot and some cordite removed. He was pouring the grease of a melted candle into each, replacing the shot and re-sealing the crimped tops, leaving them to stand until the wax hardened. It was an old trick he had learned during the war. Instead of spreading wide when fired, the shot would cling together in a mass, sufficient to blow a man in half at twenty yards.

Chapter Twenty-One

Nick stepped outside and stretched. It was a beautiful morning. The night's storm had done its work, and a weak sun, just over the snow-covered peaks to the east, hung in a cloudless sky. Nick breathed deep and thought of the day's walk to Italy. Nothing could stop them now. For lunch, if they pushed themselves, they would be eating zabaglione.

There was a stillness, though, as if time were waiting to begin, a feeling that he found unsettling, and for the first time in many days Nick thought of Lubienski, of Anna and little Stulpnagel. With an effort, he forced them from his mind, as he had done everything since Vienna; then he turned back to the hut, where their murderer lay, snoring.

Inside, Nick began to prepare breakfast. It would be a simple meal – a hunk of bread with coffee, all the woodcutter had left. But as he bent down to get coffee from a cupboard, a shot rang out. He dived to the floor. There was another. He crawled over to the table, and pulled down the shotgun. Orlov was by his side, automatic at the ready.

'Where?' he hissed.

'No idea,' replied Nick. 'There's too much echo with the mountains.'

They crawled to the window, and Nick peered out. He could see nothing. But there were more shots, their sound rolling down the mountainside like mini claps of thunder.

'A hunting party?' said Orlov. 'They're not shooting our way.'

'Could be. But they're not shotguns. The reports are too sharp.'

'Some sound like pistols,' added Nick. 'I think they come from the wood to our left.'

'Shall we make a run for it?'

Nick looked at Orlov. The man might be able to walk over the mountains, but he couldn't run. If it was the enemy, they would have to stand and fight. The hunt couldn't go any further.

'No. Let's wait.'

They did, each taking separate windows to cover as wide a field of vision as possible. After a couple of minutes, the firing ceased. Still no movement could be seen. Nothing, except trees and mountainside.

Five minutes passed. Ten. Neither man spoke. They watched. Fifteen. The old Austrian, petrified, began to whimper. Orlov went over to him, tightened his gag with a jerk, then returned to the window.

Gradually, the two fugitives relaxed. Twenty minutes had passed, with not a sound, and they decided it must have been a hunting party. The mountains had played tricks with the sound. Nick left his window for breakfast, but Orlov kept guard.

With steaming coffee in a jug on the table, and a hunk of black bread for each man, Nick took one last look around and sat down. Orlov, at first reluctant, was finally persuaded to join him, and he raised a cup to his lips.

'*Orlov!*' A shout came from outside, echoing away down into the valley.

The cup fell, hot coffee scalding Orlov. Nick ran to a window.

'Orlov!' The shout came again. It was from trees on the mountainside, forty yards above the hut.

'We know you're there, Orlov.' It was Russian. Orlov backed away. 'Come out, or we go in.' There was a pause as the echo died away. 'Orlov. Do you hear?'

Orlov spat in reply, went up to the old woodcutter, and untied him.

'Come out, Orlov. We won't wait.'

Orlov put his jacket over the Austrian, and removed the

gag. Pointing his gun at the man's head, he motioned to the door. '*Raus! Schnell!*'

The old man was unwilling. His eyes were sullen. Orlov kicked him savagely and sent him sprawling.

'*Raus, oder ich schiesse.*' He slipped off the safety catch. The sound unnerved the Austrian. '*Ich gehe. Ich gehe,*' he stammered, and picked himself off the floor.

Orlov went to the window. 'Will you shoot if I come out?'

'No. Come out.'

The woodcutter was at the door. Orlov opened it, and pushed him out with his boot. The man fell down the steps and staggered on to the grass, trying to regain his balance. But before he could do so, shots rang out, and his body turned violently as the bullets hit him. One, two, three. He fell to the ground and Nick watched horrified as the old man rolled over in silence, blood spurting from his wounds, mouth open, eyes bulging. It all seemed to be in slow motion. Another shot. The woodcutter twitched, then lay still.

Orlov looked at Nick. 'That's how State Security keep their word,' he grunted.

'Orlov,' the shout came again, but the Russian kept silent.

'Orlov. No more tricks. That's your last.' A hysterical laugh echoed, was caught in the fir trees, and died.

Then there were more shots. The windows of the hut shattered, and Nick was cut on the cheek by flying glass.

'Here they come,' Orlov muttered, but made no other reaction. The expression on his face was immobile, resigned.

The enemy had the advantage of greater numbers and higher ground. They seemed to be all around, six or seven of them, firing continuously from hidden positions. Bullets thudded into the hut making any return of fire dangerous, and Nick and Orlov were forced to keep moving on all fours, peeping out of empty window frames as they passed. It was risky, but the only way to see what was happening.

Suddenly, Nick caught a glimpse of a man break cover and dash down the hill towards the pile of wood standing by the side of the hut. He levelled his automatic, and, at ten yards, fired. The man's body contorted as if he had been slashed by a whip, froze for a moment in a dancing posture, then slumped to the ground.

Nick ducked away as bullets flew in at the window. Two more men emerged from behind the trees and ran down the slope, each covering the other, moving from side to side as they did so. Nick fired again, but missed. As the men reached the safety of the wood pile he picked up the shotgun. At close quarters it would be more effective.

Orlov, meanwhile, was engaged on the other side of the hut. Three man had moved into the open and were running up the slope, supporting each other with continuous fire. Orlov managed to hit one, but only at the cost of making himself the target. His right arm was grazed by a bullet, and in agony he cursed his would-be killers, Russia and all in her.

The two men remaining on their feet on Orlov's side reached the walls. Orlov shouted to Nick, and they took cover.

A head moved past the shattered glass. Orlov fired, and Nick saw the skull split open. A Russian burst in at the door. Nick pulled the trigger. An explosion, and the man was thrown out, his stomach blown away. Intestines splattered the wall. More shots from the window, and Orlov doubled up. Nick moved to the open door, saw another Russian coming in, and raised his shotgun, but too late. There was a heavy blow on the back of his head and he colllapsed to the floor.

Nick regained consciousness seconds later. A Russian was straddling him, gun aimed at his chest. He groaned, rolled over, and through the table legs saw Orlov by the fireplace, lying on his front, one man by his head, another by his feet. A third stood astride him, heel poised over his back, just above the buttocks. One kick, and his central nerve cord would snap.

The Russian said something to Orlov, which Nick couldn't understand. Orlov swore back. The heel was raised. In a second, Orlov would be dead.

The Russian spoke again. Orlov just shook his head. The Russian laughed, the same hysterical laugh that had come down the mountain. His heel rose higher.

There was a sudden crash as the door burst open, and Nick turned to see another man, MI carbine in his hands, jump in, fall to his knees and fire.

'Bastards!' he yelled in English as he sprayed high velocity bullets around the hut. The MI was lethal: before the Russians had time to react, they were dead.

Nick rolled away as the Russian over him slumped to the floor. He grabbed his shotgun, which lay by the table, swung it up, and fired. The Englishmen opened his mouth as he saw the gun, but too late, and the blast slammed him against the wall. His body, torn to reveal the shattered ribcage, fell slowly to the floor.

A ringing silence followed. Nick scrambled up, felt in his pocket for more shot, reloaded, and waited.

In London, at about the same time as the woods of the Stillupptal echoed to the sound of gunfire, Sir William Strang was sound asleep in bed. The telephone rang. Snores rose, and ended abruptly. An old, puckered mouth, like the opening of a miser's purse with its strings drawn tight, gaped open, then shut. Sir William fumbled in a glass for his dentures, put them in and picked up the receiver.

'William, good morning,' came the voice the other end. 'Sorry to disturb you so early, but I thought you'd like to know as soon as possible.' It was Menzies. He sounded cheerful.

'Pelham?' asked Sir William, shaking the sleep from his mind.

'Yes, and Orlov. We've got them holed up in the Austrian Tyrol. Lovely spot, I should think. Our men are going in for the kill sometime now.'

'And the Austrians?' The head was clearing now.

'They're holding off. The police don't want to get involved. Cold War, and all that. Those two are all ours.'

'You're sure?'

'Absolutely, William. The minute confirmation comes through, we bring in the traitors. Vivien's got everybody standing by. It will all be over by this evening at the latest. So no need for Maclean to defect now, thank God.'

The Permanent Under-Secretary breathed a sigh of relief, replaced the receiver and laid his head on his pillow. It had been a near run thing.

Four men lay outside, five within, riddled bundles of death. Nick made his count and sat down by the table, shotgun across his lap. Orlov, his arm bloody and a bullet in his left thigh, tightened the tourniquet, wincing as the pain burned through his body. Nick put his hand on the coffee jug. It was still warm.

'Are you fit to walk?' he asked, fearing the answer.

Orlov shook his head. He was vacant, like a man lost, washed up on a deserted shore, alone with nowhere to go.

'We can make a splint and some crutches.' Nick tried to sound hopeful.

'Nicholas, there's nothing you can do for me now. It's all over. I'm finished.'

'People have done more with worse. We've got ten miles to cover, half of it downhill. In Italy it will be different.' Nick lied, and knew it. They had to keep going.

'No, Nicholas. Nothing will be different in Italy. We'll have a rest, maybe. But not for long. They'll be after us again.' He pointed to the men, shattered by bullet and shot, who lay around them, dead in pools of their own blood. 'There's no escape from their type.'

'We've managed so far.' Nick was aggressive. After so much, he had no intention of giving up. 'We can continue. We've just got to hide you, and then I can get to London. Once there, our troubles are over.'

'You dream,' the Russian said roughly, flinching with pain as he tried to move his leg. 'We're *shavki* and always will be, just homeless mongrels. We'll be shot on sight.'

'Some live a long time.'

'Not in our world. Not when you've got three security services after you.' Orlov raised his hands in a gesture of despair. 'No, Nicholas, you dream.'

'So what do we do? Give up?'

'You can. But not me.'

'So what the hell do you suggest?' Nick flared up.

'Death.'

'Death?'

'Suicide.'

'*Kill* yourself?'

'In my condition?' Orlov pointed to his wounds. His right arm was bleeding badly, his leg hung limp. 'That's impossible. You must do it.'

Nick jerked forward. That was the last thing he had expected.

'I want to die,' continued the Russian. 'I don't want to be a *shavka* for the rest of my life. And that's what I'll be, I know that now.' He shifted his position, painfully. 'I've known it ever since Vienna. I want it over quickly. But suicide isn't easy. I've seen a man with half his face blown away and still alive. Even a bullet in the mouth isn't certain, Nicholas. That's why you have to do it. I want it done well.'

Nick looked down at the gun in his hands, then at the bodies around him, and he remembered the others who had gone. Would one more make any difference?

'But what about your information? Katyn? The traitors – they'll go free if I kill you.'

'The traitors, Nicholas? You worry about those "traitors" as you call them? Now? After all you've seen and heard?' Orlov struggled to get up, but couldn't, and sat back, breathing heavily. 'Those men – I sometimes feel they are the only true men in the whole business. They have lived by their consciences. The others – they found other rules. You've seen that. History will tell lies about the traitors, Nicholas. History always does. But the "patriots" – what do they do? They just hold opinions as they're told. If it's to be war, they fight. If it's peace, they cheer. And who tells them? Their leaders, the men who sit safely at home and sell their country's principles in the name of principle. They're the real traitors, Nicholas. When fish begin to smell, they start at the head – just remember that.'

Nick was silent.

'And if you went these secrets so much, you can always cut me open. They're all down here.' Orlov patted his gut, and laughed for the first time Nick remembered since they had left Vienna. Nick made no reply. He felt empty, dazed. There was nothing left.

'But bury me well, Nicholas. They mustn't find me. And you too. Disappear. That will ruin their plans. All of them.'

They walked for five minutes, Orlov limping, leaning on Nick's shoulder, Nick with one arm round Orlov's waist, the other carrying a shovel, making their way through the forest, moving straight down the side of the mountain. They came upon the spot by chance, a clearing, green with meadow grass, on which were clumps of forget-me-nots, vivid blue. Grasshoppers filled the air with their shrill chirping, but not so much as to drown the sound of a hidden stream. And beyond, over the tops of the pines soared the eagle-like ridges of the mountains that marked Italy.

Nick helped Orlov to a stone, where he sat in silence, watching the Englishman dig. It was warm, and Nick took off his shirt. Orlov looked jealously at his firm body, the muscles on his back glistening with sweat, and swore softly.

The grave was finished in an hour, the black Alpine earth dug to a depth of five feet, enough for any man. Nick put his shirt back on, and walked over to Orlov, sitting stock still, staring at the ground. Memories were crowding in on him, and his face was white and fixed, like some totemic image. Aware of the Englishman, he struggled up, refusing help, and for a moment the two men stood looking at one another, before the Russian slowly turned towards his grave, pushing Nick's hands away. His last walk was going to be his own, and he shuffled painfully towards the black earth. Halfway he turned, a smile spreading across his face. It was his last joke. 'If you should ever meet Menzies or any of the others,' he said, 'just tell them that Gregor Orlov was once Gregor Khopliakin, back in '48.'

'Khopliakin?' Nick was puzzled.

'Yes. Khopliakin. Don't worry. They'll understand. It might even amuse them. Tell them it didn't turn out as we had hoped – Military Intelligence, that is – but it's been some use. State Security aren't so proud now.'

Nick shrugged his shoulders, knowing only he would never fully understand of what he had become a part.

'Just remember,' repeated Orlov, 'Khopliakin.'

By the side of his grave, Orlov knelt, his legs burying themselves in the fresh earth. Head erect, hands clasped behind his back, he waited.

Nick took the automatic from his waist band, cocked it, and looked down at the Russian. He hesitated, feeling cold sweat break out on his forehead.

Orlov sensed his reluctance. 'In the nape of my neck,' he said. 'Upwards. It destroys the medulla.'

Still Nick delayed. His guts were rising and turning within him.

'We killed the Poles this way,' said the Russian.

Nick pressed the barrel against the man's thick flesh, and fired.

It was raining in London that Friday, 25 May as, throughout the day, Menzies, Strang and Vivien waited for news from Austria. It didn't come. Other events, however, would not wait. Late in the morning, MI5 at last received authorization from the Secretary of State for Foreign Affairs to interrogate the head of the American Department the following Monday, the 28th. A weekend arrest was likely.

At lunchtime, the object of MI5's attentions, Donald Maclean, celebrated his thirty-eighth birthday over oysters and champagne in a Soho restaurant. In the afternoon, work at the Foreign Office continued until about four, when the diplomats left for the weekend. Maclean walked to Charing Cross station to catch his train to Tatsfield and home, and, as usual, was shadowed as far as the ticket barrier by a man from Special Branch.

Early in the evening, Guy Burgess arrived at Tatsfield, introducing himself to Maclean's pregnant wife as Roger Stiles from the Foreign Office. After dinner, Maclean packed an overnight bag, explaining he had a pressing engagement which might keep him late, and drove with Burgess to Southampton, where they caught the midnight ferry to Saint Malo, just three minutes before it left. The journey to Moscow had begun.

Postscript

Orlov had predicted well. None of those involved in the events which led to his own death and Nicholas Pelham's disappearance achieved their aims. As Soviet Military Intelligence had planned as early as 1948, their rivals in State Security suffered a severe blow. Not only did they lose prestige with their spies, but Abakhumov was removed from office and replaced by Ignatyev, a Party *apparatchik* and disciple of Malenkov. Beria, however, survived, and his enemies had to stay their vengeance until after Stalin's death in 1953, when, along with Abakhumov, he was shot.

In the United States, the CIA managed to weather the crisis of confidence without using the eleven names locked in Bedell Smith's safe. The support of the President proved too great for its enemies. Never, though, was the Company to be free of criticism.

In Britain, the storm broke in early June, when news leaked of the defection of Burgess and Maclean. As Beria expected, it was the beginning of a story which has never died. Menzies, Strang and Vivien, however, survived into honoured retirements.

In Poland, repression continued. In the summer of 1951, show trials of senior officers took place, all accused of being British spies. They received life imprisonment; others were secretly executed. But that solved nothing. Poland remained an unhappy country, its troubles reaching crisis in 1956, 1970, 1976 and again in 1981. And so it continue.

And Katyn? In September 1951, the US House of Representatives set up a select committee to enquire into the massacre, and a year later it reported with a strong indictment of the Soviet Union. The United States' Government, however, did nothing, and the matter was taken no further. In Britain, too, despite repeated requests, the Government has failed to acknowledge the truth. To this day, Katyn remains an official lie. It, unlike its victims, will not die.